SAVING SOPHIA

THE DADDIES OF WOODLAND RIDGE
BOOK 1

PIXIE PARKER

Saving Sophia

The Daddies of Woodland Ridge Series, Book One

Written by: Pixie Parker

Editing by: Karen Washo/Utterly Unashamed

Proofreading by: Secret Words

For my beloved husband, who has always made me feel like I am enough.

And for my writing tribe - this book would not exist without your amazing support. Thank you for helping me make this dream a reality.
Love you guys!

A WORD FROM PIXIE

Welcome Beautiful Reader!

I really hope you love this story as much as I do. However, I have to let you know - it's a kissing book. Actually, a lot more than just kissing.

This is romance with no closed doors. No fade-to-black teasers. In fact, this book explores some slightly taboo topics, including elements of ageplay, with spankings and discipline that happen between consenting adults.

There are a few dark moments, but also a lot of fun, a lot of play, and a lot of swoony-sweet bits too.

Intrigued? Ready to feel that big-sappy-grin, happily-ever-after feeling?

Then what are you waiting for? Let's go!

1

SOPHIA

*A*ccording to Cinderella, the right pair of shoes can change your life. So what can the wrong pair do? In my case, they almost ended it.

I was halfway through my shift at Renaissance, a strip club that looked like an Italian-themed casino and a futuristic dance rave had a baby. Blue neon hummed beneath the music while armless sculptures hid in alcoves, staring blankly at the dancers and their patrons.

I was just a cocktail waitress, so I wore a toga-like, white tube top and a tight, white pleather micro mini skirt, but the shoes were the worst. Gaudy, gold platform gladiator sandals with buckles and straps halfway up my calves. I never made it through a shift without a blister.

I didn't envy the dancers' shoes either—six-inch acrylic Pleasers that I would have broken both ankles on immediately. It never ceased to amaze me how gracefully Callie, my roommate and best friend, could dance in them, spinning on the pole, one long, glitter-covered leg extended out to a group of rapt college guys as they frantically waved bills toward her neon garter. She danced like she was born in those shoes, biting her lip, shaking her beach blond hair then dropping into a split as if she were barefoot.

"Umm, so … did any of you want another round?"

I tried to project my voice over the blaring club music and capture the attention of the nearest guy at my table. His eyes were glued on Callie's arched body and perfect breasts, bouncing to the beat of the music.

He let out a whoop as she crawled toward him, a seductive smile plastered across her face.

"Hey … you guys … need more drinks?"

I tried again, resting my server's tray on my hip. Brad was going to be pissed if I didn't get another order out of them. I leaned in toward the table and collected empties. Maybe then they would see me and realize they were still thirsty.

One guy pushed forward as Callie approached, bumping my tray.

"Oh, sorry," I muttered, somehow avoiding dumping the empty beer bottles onto the floor.

"What?" The first guy finally noticed me for a half-second before returning his gaze to Callie. She was perched on the edge of the stage, gyrating her hips and resting her hand on one guy's shoulder. She tossed me a tiny wink and a grin they didn't notice. She'd chosen her mark.

"I was asking if I could … get you another round? Of drinks?"

"Aww yeah, get it, Pete," the first guy yelled as Callie wrapped her arms around her mark's shoulders, bringing her impressive chest exactly three inches from his astonished eyes.

They weren't going to order, and I was looking more and more pathetic, hovering around the table and being ignored.

Callie paused and raised a sharply arched eyebrow, watching me. She swung into Pete's lap, wiggled then leaned toward the group. "What do you say, boys? Does Petey need a lap dance?" They answered with enthusiastic cheers. She casually caught Pete's hand as it wandered onto her thigh, then tossed another seductive smile to the group. "You boys look thirsty." She looked around to make sure all eyes were on her and gave another wiggle on Pete's lap. "Have Amber Jade bring another round, and we can have some fun."

They all turned to me at once and called out their orders.

Just like Callie to see me struggling and throw me a lifeline. Even if she used the silly fake name she'd invented. Amber Jade—my *stage* name, she'd insisted. As if it mattered. She could have called me Briney Blue McThundersplash, Lost Princess of Atlantis. These guys wouldn't have cared.

When I got back to the bar and set my tray down to punch in the order, Brad, the bartender, smirked. "You're lucky your roommate is the best dancer in this place." He pulled out two glasses from the shelf and started filling them. "Without her, you wouldn't make shit for drink sales."

I tried to think of a response, but he had already walked away. And he was right. Callie got me this job, and this wasn't the first time she'd helped me.

It's easy, Sophia. Use your stage name and be an actress. Make Amber Jade a whole different persona. She's exotic, mysterious. Men are dying for her attention. Bat your eyelashes. Smile like you have a secret. Make them beg.

Easy for *her*. Not so much for me, but I needed to figure it out. I already owed her two months' rent. I needed money if I wanted to keep living on my own, away from my parents' disappointment.

One of the faux marble statues next to the bar, a naked woman clutching at her breast in a sixteenth century inspired pose, stared at me, silently watching, her gaze empty and serene. No help there.

Brad slammed the drinks on my tray with a hard clink and waved his hand in my face. My flinch was involuntary, and I hated him for making me do it.

"Hello? Earth to space mouse? Drinks aren't gonna serve themselves."

"Sorry," I mumbled, picking up the tray. The apology was involuntary too, and I hated it worse than the flinch.

When I got back to the table, Callie was still in Pete's lap, but her eyes had moved to the buddy to his left.

Be an actress. Be Amber Jade. Bat your eyelashes and smile like you have a secret. You can do this.

"I have your ... the round of drinks you wanted," I said, hoping my face was more secret smile and less nervous grimace. "Fellas," I added after a beat. My insides cringed. I tried to bat my eyelashes, but I'm pretty sure it looked more like I was blinking a hair out of my eye.

They ignored me.

Callie shimmied over to Pete's buddy, and all eyes were on her.

"So ... here you go," I continued, setting the drinks on the table. I was no Amber Jade. I was invisible.

One guy, handsome and clean-cut, who looked slightly embarrassed to be there, grabbed his beer and made eye contact.

A flush of nerves ripped through me. I stared at him, wondering what he was thinking. Maybe he was the kind, considerate frat brother, the one who made all his pals do philanthropy and adopted their mascot from an animal shelter and was only there to be the designated driver and make sure they all got home safely. Maybe he was a big tipper who could—

"Daddy's Little Cutie, huh?"

"What?" I jumped at his words, my hand instinctively going up to the golden, heart-shaped locket around my neck, my finger tracing the inscription.

"Who gave that to you?" He took a drink and grinned at me with perfect, straight, white teeth. Maybe his father was a cosmetic dentist to the stars.

"No one," I snapped. I didn't mean to; it just came out that way. His grin dropped, his immaculate teeth retreating behind lips full and slightly damp with beer.

The guy next to him looked over and rested his hand on my hip, his fingers digging in through the pleather skirt. "Daddy's Little Cutie?" He winked at his friend. "Think she needs a daddy, Craig?" Craig, the celebrity dentist's son, snickered.

My face froze, and my cheeks burned at their laughter. The fingers

4

on my hip squeezed harder. Anxiety and humiliation shot through my veins. "Let me go," I croaked out, trying to pull away. He let go, which I wasn't expecting. I lost my balance and stepped back again to compensate, slamming into the tray of another server hustling by.

Good news, the tray only had a few bottles on it.

Bad news, two toppled and spilled, soaking me with warm beer and the spit of strangers.

The frat guys burst into laughter as beer ran down my costume and dripped into those gold platform gladiator sandals. Any hopes I'd had for tips faded into a puddle between my toes.

"Hey!" Callie climbed out of Pete's lap and stepped between me and the laughing frat guys.

"Is there a problem here?" John, the new bouncer, materialized next to me. His massive arms were crossed over a tight, black T-shirt that read *Renaissance Staff* across the chest, and he had an earpiece tucked in his right ear.

"No problem," Craig said, his cosmetic dentistry smile reappearing. "Just an accident."

John looked at Callie.

"It's fine, John," she said, but anger snapped in her eyes. If we weren't at work, she would have leveled these guys.

"Alright then." John shot one more glare at the guys then took a step back.

Callie gave me a quick squeeze and whispered, "Go get cleaned up. Don't worry about these fuckers. I'll make sure they go home broke for being such dicks." She snapped her fingers and stalked over to the dentist's son, propping her spiked heel on his knee, dragging her hands up her thighs and leaning toward him. "You have been a naughty boy," she said in her patented, seductive purr.

The guys all turned back to Callie, bills waving again, my beer bath and locket forgotten.

I took a step toward the employee dressing room, tugging at the toga top clinging to my skin. Perfect. Three more hours in a damp, smelly costume before I could go home, pull on some fuzzy pajamas, shove my nose into my Kindle, and forget this embarrassing night ever happened.

"Hold up." John blocked my path like a wall. I raised my eyes as far as his chest before dropping them to the floor. He was a hawk, and I was a field mouse, praying I might fade away beneath his notice, but no such luck.

"I'm sorry ... I—"

He held a finger up with one hand and touched his earpiece with the other, freezing me in my tracks. He tipped his head toward the stairwell that led up to the VIP rooms. A wall of mirrored windows looked down onto the main floor. Shadows moved behind it, mostly hidden in the neon glow.

John nodded and looked back at me. "Sorry kiddo, you're out."

"What?"

"Boss says get your shit and go."

"But that wasn't my fault. He grabbed me," I said, panic tightening my throat. I looked up at the windows. The club owner, Tommy Roscoe, was a man known for wild parties and even wilder fits of temper. He must have seen my little incident and decided I was bad for business.

John stared down at me impassively then walked off toward a customer getting grabby with a dancer at table four. He wasn't worried about me not going. I was obviously a girl who did what she was told.

So much for the mysterious Amber Jade. Callie would say she understood. She'd cover the rent, again. But who was I kidding? I had to face facts. Go home. Swallow my pride along with my father's I-told-you-so's and my mother's embarrassment at having *me* for a daughter.

An unfamiliar flash of anger hit me, turning my skin hot. He already fired me. I had nothing to lose. This was my chance to be something besides a mouse, incapable of handling a drink order for frat boys. My beer-slippery shoes stomped themselves up the stairs to the VIP rooms before I could stop them. Amber Jade hadn't helped me be mysterious and seductive, but maybe she could help me fight for my job.

I paused when I reached the gold lacquered VIP door, clutching my tray like a shield, my cheeks already burning, my bravado fading. What was I going to say? Was this me, urged on by Amber Jade to be brave and speak up for myself? Or had I gone completely insane?

Most likely guess was insanity.

I took a deep, shaky breath. That flash of anger drove me up those steps, but it cooled once I saw that imposing door. Maybe I could get a job at a second-hand toy shop. I could work in the back repairing broken dolls, hidden away, never having to talk to anyone who might talk back.

I was about to turn around when the door opened. A man looked down at me, clearly surprised to find someone standing there. He filled the doorway, big and shadowy and scary looking, with a sharp, protruding chin that made me picture the man in the moon for some reason. "Well, what do we have here?"

"Nothing ... I ... was just ... never mind," I stammered out, turning to leave.

"Hold on." A beefy hand darted out to catch my shoulder in a pincer grip. "It's not polite to lurk in doorways." His voice reminded me of a villain who captured stray cats to torture. "Come in."

"Who is it?" an annoyed voice called out.

I stumbled in, propelled by the moon-faced man's fingers digging into my shoulder.

Electric blue light filled the space, and a wall of windows over-looked the main floor below. Anyone in here would have a perfect view of table eight, where I so recently embarrassed myself. Several more Renaissance-themed statues stood in alcoves around the room, staring emptily at the blue velvet couches and round chairs. The glass and chrome tables looked jarring against the wall frescoes of Italian countrysides, and the blue light reflected in a glass chandelier turned everything lurid and strange.

A small stage with flashing lights in the center of the room threw a disco element into the confusing mix of themes. Two dancers were grinding around on it, twisting their bodies to the music.

Two men lounged on couches near the stage. One was the owner, Tommy Roscoe, relaxed in an expensive Armani suit, his eyes locked on the man seated across from him. His arms stretched out along the back of the couch, and a cold smile played across his lips.

I didn't recognize the other man. He was thin and wiry with slicked back, dark hair. His suit looked expensive too, but ill-fitting, as if it were wearing him and not the other way around.

Mr. Roscoe slowly panned a predatory gaze from his guest to the doorway where I was standing. I was a mouse again, only this time I wasn't hiding from a hawk. I was staring into the eyes of a cobra.

"Well?" His body shifted slightly, balancing his attention between me and the other man.

I had no idea what to say. Amber Jade brought me here only to abandon me. My mouth opened, but I was helpless to control what words might fall out. "I ... Mr. Roscoe ... Sir ... I ... my ... rent's due ... please ... they grabbed me." I snapped my mouth closed. That was worse than I'd expected.

"Oh. The clumsy one." His insult sat in the air between us like a boulder.

I shifted on my feet. My default words popped out before I could stop them. "I'm so sorry, Mr. Roscoe, I didn't—"

"Come here."

I stepped forward automatically, compelled by those two words. My sandals made embarrassing squelching noises.

He curled his lip in disgust. "Stop." He glared at my feet. "Take those off. I can smell them from here."

"It's beer," I said, my face burning. I bent down to unbuckle the clasps and stepped out of the shoes, leaving them in a heap by the door.

"You look like a maid." His eyes raked over me, noting every flaw. "Take your hair down."

My hand twitched at my side, then reached up to obey, the mouse in me eager to appease. "I'm sorry," I muttered, my cheeks flaming.

As I pulled out the hair tie, one of the dancers snickered. I turned my eyes toward the noise. They were watching me, still dancing. One bent over, holding onto the pole in the middle of the stage with legs spread while the other gyrated with the music. My already raging blush intensified.

"Like what you see?" Mr. Roscoe sneered. His friend laughed.

"What? Oh. No. I just ... I'm sorry. I ... I need this job and I—"

"Join them." He pointed toward the dancers.

"Oh. I ... I just serve drinks. I'm not a dancer."

The girls paused, waiting. Everyone in the room watched me, even the silent statues.

"If you want this job, you do what I tell you."

My fingers clung to my serving tray in a white-knuckled grip. "I ... can't." The last word dried up in my throat and came out cracked and small, a strangled, squeaking whisper.

The other man let out another nasty laugh.

Mr. Roscoe's attention pivoted from me to him like a whip. "Something to say, Nikki?"

The man with the ill-worn suit shifted uncomfortably under Mr. Roscoe's aggressive gaze, his face souring. "I thought we were here to talk business," he snarled.

"The only business we have to discuss," Mr. Roscoe said in a cool voice, "is what you and your bitch wife owe me."

I tugged at my clammy tube top and shifted from foot to foot, unsure what to do.

"Go home, maid," Mr. Roscoe said to me without taking his eyes from the man. "If you can't entertain our guests, you're useless here."

I hesitated, grasping for something to say.

Mr. Roscoe jerked his chin toward the door. The moon-faced man turned me around forcibly and gave me a shove. He snapped his fingers at the dancers. "You two. Get back out on the floor."

The dancers brushed past me on the way out. As we retreated, I heard Mr. Roscoe say, "I thought I made myself very clear before, Nikki. Or should I be talking to your wife directly?"

9

Nikki let out a snort. "Valerie doesn't call the shots. She just thinks she does."

"Does she?, Mr. Roscoe said. "Perhaps you can help me solve that problem once and for all."

The moon-faced man shoved me through the door and slammed it closed.

So, still fired.

I walked past the bar on my way to the dressing rooms. "Tough luck, space mouse," Brad said. "Mr. Roscoe just did you a favor." I dropped my tray on the counter and tried to glare at him. He ignored it and kept going, his smug mustache twitching.

"Callie should never have brought you here." He wiped a cloth over the bar and watched Callie, who was now dancing for a group of businessmen, his eyes glowering. "You got no sense of self-worth. It's bad for business." Then he looked at my feet. "Where the fuck are your shoes?"

Shoot.

I'd catch hell from Barb, the manager, if I didn't return the uniform intact. I looked miserably up at the VIP room's shadowed windows.

"No sense at all," Brad muttered, turning away to fill another drink order.

Barefoot, I trudged back up the stairs and stood in front of that gold lacquered door for the second time. The music blared around me, making my teeth rattle. The sandals were right inside the door. I wouldn't have to say a word. Just a quick step in to grab them and back out. They might not even notice me.

I turned the knob and pushed the door open, my eyes staying low, aimed at where I left the shoes. My troublesome mouth couldn't help itself and decided to blurt out an explanation as I reached forward, grabbing the sandals by their straps. I didn't look up until the words were half-spoken. "I'm sorry to bother you again. I left my—"

Then my eyes connected with my brain, filling me in on what I was seeing.

Mr. Roscoe. Standing. A big black gun in his hand.

Nikki, slumped over one of the rounded, blue velvet chairs. A dark stain pooled beneath his body.

His *body*.

Mr. Roscoe's eyes swiveled from the dead man to lock directly onto me. Somewhere across the distance of a thousand miles, he said the command that compelled me earlier. "Come here."

But this time, I didn't obey.

I turned around and sprinted out the door, those stupid shoes still dangling from my hand.

2

SOPHIA

a gun.

In Mr. Roscoe's hand.

The dark, spreading stain on the blue velvet.

Had I seen a wisp of smoke coming from the barrel? Or was my imagination filling in awful details?

I ran blindly through the club, pushing past patrons, my bare feet making decisions for me while my brain tried to wrap itself around what just happened. I managed to get out of the building on simple luck and adrenaline, bursting out and racing along the sidewalk into the dirty haze of nighttime streetlights and smog.

Where should I go?

Was I being followed? At any moment would a hand fall hard on my shoulder? Turn me around to face the barrel of a gun?

I was panting, half-running, bumping into people and earning glares and curious looks. I needed to calm down and make a plan. Where could I hide? Where could I go?

I turned down a side street into a big outdoor shopping mall, busy with shoppers. Maybe I could lose myself in the crowd, tuck into the corner of a vendor's stall and stay out of sight. At least get my ridiculous shoes back on my feet.

I ducked behind a huge pile of Persian rugs.

"Looking for a carpet this evening?" a thin, nasal voice asked, so close it made me flinch.

"Oh, no thank you ... just looking," I babbled, tracing my finger over the pattern of the nearest rug as though I had a clue what I was looking at.

"Beautiful, isn't it?" The merchant's voice had a permanent wheedling tone as though he might have swallowed a bee. "Do you have a particular room in mind?"

Why couldn't this guy leave me alone? I didn't exactly look like someone shopping for carpets. I searched the crowd, terrified of who might be pursuing me. "I don't ... have a room."

The merchant's eyes narrowed, assessing my skimpy costume, complete with sandals still dangling in my hand where a purse should be.

A purse.

Shoot.

I'd left my bag with my money, keys, phone, and ID in my locker at the club.

"Perhaps you might care to—"

"Excuse me," I squeaked and darted away.

I ran down a few stalls toward a dress vendor, with several racks of huge, fluffy dresses for proms, quinceanera celebrations, and weddings. Maybe I could fade into the sequins and lace.

I bent over, trying to catch my breath as I strapped those miserable, beer-soaked sandals back on my feet. What should I do?

I needed my stuff. I had to go back to the club.

No way.

But they wouldn't expect me to do it? My mind grasped for every chase sequence of every movie I'd ever watched—it was a common tactic to double back to the scene of the crime.

Could I seriously walk back in there?

Callie was still in there.

A dead body was in there.

"What's your occasion, dearie?" A short woman with Kool-Aid

red hair smiled up at me. I closed my eyes in frustration. I never got customer service this attentive. Maybe I should run from a killer every time I needed to go shopping.

I needed to decide what to do, or I'd end up buying a living room rug and a prom dress.

Except I couldn't buy anything, couldn't *do* anything, without my bag.

"I'm sorry," I stammered and pushed past the red-haired woman.

Two blocks from the club, I stopped. No one seemed to be following me. Could I really go back in there? The employee locker room was near the kitchen, in the back on the first level. I wouldn't even have to walk out on the main floor at all if I used the back entrance. Scoot in, grab my stuff, scoot out. If anyone tried to talk to me, I could say I had food poisoning and needed to go home. This could work.

One more block. My heart jackhammered behind my ribcage. My mouth was dry like old paint. The plucky heroine always made it through the scary situation in my favorite romance novels, right? But what if I wasn't the heroine? What if I was some expendable side character like ... cocktail waitress number two?

I arrived at the back entrance. My knees shook, and those darn sandals felt like they weighed two hundred pounds each on my feet, but everything looked normal. I visualized the path through the dark hall to the locker room where the dancers changed costumes and did their makeup.

My locker was fourth from the last on the right. The combo was 43-18-8. I could do this.

Get in, grab my bag, get out.

Should I talk to Callie?

No, she wasn't in any danger. Killing that man seemed personal. Private. Mr. Roscoe wasn't going to shoot up his own club. If I talked to her, then she would be involved too, making her a target.

My hand rested on the tarnished doorknob of the back door.

I turned it, cracking the door open.

I walked in.

The familiar heavy bass matched my heartbeat. There was no screaming. Nothing indicating a murder recently happened here.

I snuck down the hallway.

Could I have misunderstood? Doubt began to creep in. What exactly had I seen?

The gun, smoking. The dead guy slumped over in a dark puddle. Mr. Roscoe, staring at me. A loose end.

Come here.

What could I have possibly misunderstood?

I made it to the fourth locker. Crouched down. My trembling fingers turned the combination dial. 43-18-8. The lock clicked open like a helpful little friend.

I grabbed my bag. No one was around. Two minutes and I'd be back out on the street.

I walked back down the dark hallway.

The doorknob felt cool in my grasp.

Holy cow, I'd done it.

Plucky heroine, that was me.

I opened the door, breathing in the warm, slightly smoggy L.A. air.

"Hold it right there." A man grabbed my arm.

Goodbye, plucky heroine. Hello, expendable cocktail waitress number two.

I WAS HALFWAY into the police car before I realized the man who seized my arm and dragged me away from the club was a cop. Relief mixed with confusion as we headed to the station. He escorted me into a grim interrogation room still completely clueless as to why I was there.

A uniformed officer stood guard by the door, silent, arms crossed, staring straight ahead like I wasn't even in the room. The concrete walls were dark gray, with paint chips flaking off in several places. I stared at the eyeball-shaped security cameras in the corners, wondering who was watching me.

Was this how a murder investigation went down? Was I being handled as a witness? I was in a police station. I was safe. But could I tell them what I saw without stammering and sounding like a crazy person? Would they believe me? Would Mr. Roscoe go immediately to jail, or would he get out on bail? Would I have to testify in a court, in front of a judge and jury? My mind flipped through every crime show episode I'd ever watched again, trying to imagine what any of that would look like.

A man with dark hair, shorter on the sides and a thick scruff of beard came in, holding my bag in one hand, my ID in the other. "My name is Hayden Valero. I'm a detective," he said before nodding briefly to the officer at the door.

"Hello," I said. Was I supposed to shake his hand? I had no idea. I half-lifted my right hand up, then let it drop on the table, awkwardly patting the surface a few times.

I was off to a great start.

"Sophia Butler? Twenty-four years old? Is that true?" He read my ID then looked at me skeptically.

"Yes," I said. It came out all squeaky, like a mouse. Should I start now and confess what I saw, or wait for him to question me?

Confess wasn't right though. I hadn't committed a crime. Why was I so scared and guilty? I held onto the edges of my chair, trying not to squirm with nerves.

"You work at Renaissance?" He tossed my bag down on the heavy laminated table, slightly out of my reach.

"Yes," I said. Not quite as squeaky as before. I could get through this. "I'm just a waitress though," I added, inwardly cringing at my words.

He sat down and pulled a notebook and pen from his pocket.

I squeezed my hands tighter on my chair.

"Ms. Butler, are you aware of any underage hiring going on there? Girls using fake ID's? Does your boss check that sort of thing?"

"No ... I mean, yes." I took a breath and willed myself to calm down. Was that relevant to the murder?

"So, is it yes, or no?" He tapped his pen on his notebook.

"I mean ... no, I don't think so? They checked mine when I got hired." Did my age matter as a witness? I couldn't remember that coming up on any of the shows I'd watched.

"You sure?" the detective asked. "You don't sound sure."

"I'm ... sure." He was right, I didn't sound sure.

What if he didn't believe me? What if I told him everything, and he didn't believe me, and then Mr. Roscoe didn't go to jail, and he found me ...

"—activity going on?" He stared at me, waiting on an answer.

"Umm? ... What?"

Detective Valero sighed, tapping the pen against his notebook again. "Look, Ms. Butler, there is significant illegal activity going on at Renaissance. If you have information, I need you to speak up."

Murder. Murder was illegal, for sure. Was this it? This was when I was supposed to tell him what I saw? I looked to the silent officer at the door, but he offered no help.

"Are you afraid of losing your job?" The detective's voice was weary. "Worried about getting in trouble with your boss?"

My job? I blinked, confused. "I don't ... understand? Are you going to arrest him?"

Detective Valero scratched at the edge of his beard with a thumb. "We have hard evidence of some pretty significant crimes. Underage hiring, questionable tax practices." He counted the crimes off with his fingers. "Potential money laundering, organized crime."

But not murder. He hadn't said murder and surely that was a bigger crime than any of those.

"Why would you bring me in for any of that? I'm nobody?"

"We're questioning employees brought in from the raid."

"What raid?"

"Sir," the formerly silent officer by the door said. We both looked at him. "She was caught coming out the back a few minutes before the raid went down. They brought her in early so she couldn't tip anyone off inside."

Understanding bloomed in Detective Valero's eyes.

"You really are just a waitress, and you have no idea why you're here, do you?"

Okay, his dismissal of me wasn't the bigger picture point, but it still hurt. I knew my own insignificance. He didn't have to rub it in.

"I'm sorry. Let me start over." His face was neutral and calm, as if I were a child lost in a department store. "Hi, Sophia. I'm Detective Valero."

"Hello," I mumbled. Oh man, I *was* an idiot.

"We conducted a raid on your club this evening, and now we're questioning employees about any illegal activities going on there."

It all finally fell into place. It was a big, awful coincidence. The cops were investigating the club and happened to do a raid right after Mr. Roscoe committed a murder that I stumbled into witnessing. I didn't know whether to laugh or cry.

I really was expendable cocktail waitress number two, and expendable was exactly what I would be if I blurted out what I saw. The detective was already doubting my credibility. If they raided the place, they clearly didn't find any evidence of the murder. So Mr. Roscoe must have cleaned things up somehow. I would sound like a lunatic. They weren't even ready to arrest him yet. If he was free, and I talked to the cops …

There was too much I didn't know to take any chances.

"I'm sorry, detective, but I really am just a waitress. I don't have any information about any illegal activities." I squirmed in the uncomfortable chair, flicking my eyes down to my lap. "I wish I could be of more help."

I hoped I sounded reasonable and sincere.

Detective Valero frowned then stood up, his chair scraping harshly against the gritty linoleum floor. "Thank you for your time, Ms. Butler." He pulled a card from the same pocket his pen had been in and slid it across the table. "If you think of anything else, please call me."

"I will." I took the card, looking at it and nodding so he'd believe me. I half-stood and collected my bag, tucking the card into a pocket. "Can I go?"

He sighed and glanced at the officer by the door then back to me. "I need you to sign some paperwork first." He walked to the door. A muffled buzzing sound happened and he pulled it open. "Down the hall. The officer will take you. Then you can go."

I followed them out through the interrogation room door, not at all sure if I was escaping or sealing my fate.

"Wait here, Ms. Butler." The officer pointed to a row of green vinyl chairs along the wall near an old wooden door with frosted glass.

When he walked away, I sat down in the chair closest to the door, propped my elbows on my knees, and dropped my face into my hands, letting out an undignified, gulping half-sigh, half-cry.

I glared down at the stupid platform gladiator sandals hanging unbuckled around my ankles. I hadn't done up the clasps properly in my hurry. The straps sagged, looking as hopeless as I felt.

"You okay?" a rich masculine voice rumbled from two seats away.

I almost jumped out of my skin, letting out a surprised little squeak. I hadn't noticed him when I collapsed into my seat.

"Sorry," I said, catching my breath and reaching down to buckle my traitorous shoes, as if he hadn't caught me crying into my hands. "I'm fine. Just ... loose." I bit back a groan. Why did I speak? "Gotta strap up ... these."

"They look complicated." His voice was warm and kind so I snuck a look at him as I buckled up my shoes.

Holy Toledo. He was handsome, like Kindle romance hero handsome. He watched me, his lips pulled up into a half smile, the angle of his jaw shadowed by a tidy goatee a few shades darker than his sandy hair. His eyes were a delicious cashmere gray flecked with amber and gold and framed by well-groomed brows, slightly lifted in curiosity. One hand rested on his knee as he leaned forward to hear my answer, the other hand thoughtfully scratching his chin. He wore an expensive-looking suit jacket in a sharp navy blue, with a crisp button-up shirt but no tie. He looked professional and sexy, yet still laid back.

My foot made an embarrassing squelch as it slipped against the obstinate buckles.

"There's beer in them," I tried to explain. Could this day possibly get any worse?

"Does that help?" he asked, a tease of a smile playing at the corner of his lips.

"Oh ... no ... an accident ..." I let out an embarrassed laugh. His hair was just the right amount of tousled on top, the color like wet sand with a precise side part leading to a smooth fade, and the goatee framed his tilted rockstar smile perfectly.

"Is that why you're here? An accident?" His eyes narrowed slightly from curiosity to concern.

"No, I ... nothing like that," I said, finally getting my buckles done. I tucked my feet tighter under my chair and tried to find some shred of dignity in my uniform, sitting up as straight as I could and hoping I didn't reek too badly of Budweiser.

"People rarely find themselves in police stations under happy circumstances," he offered.

I blew out a sad little puff of air at the accuracy, but before I could say anything, my stomach twisted and let out a long, slow, unrepentant growl.

"Whatever happened, it must not have involved dinner?" he chuckled, a soothing sound that somehow eased my embarrassment.

"No, I guess not." When had I last eaten? I remembered a PB&J before my shift, but that felt like weeks ago.

"Here, maybe this will help?" He reached into the inside pocket of his jacket, pulled out a bright red object, and held it out to me.

I stared at it for a minute before a burst of laughter escaped me. Apparently, this ultra-attractive and mysterious man traveled with a supply of oversized, cherry red lollipops in his pocket. This day could not get any weirder.

His amused smile turned into a full grin. "It'll give your tummy something to do till you can get some real food."

Helpless against his charm, I grinned back. "Don't they literally warn about taking candy from strangers? It's like ... a standard rule, I think?"

It was his turn to let out a laugh. "True. You should follow those rules." He put out the hand not holding candy. "I'm Ethan."

I hesitated a second, then shook it. The warmth of his grasp surprised me. He didn't hold my hand too long or squeeze too tight. When he released me, I was almost sad to let go.

"Sophia," I said, following it up with a self-conscious laugh. I dropped my eyes to my lap, unable to keep looking at him. He was so handsome, and I wasn't exactly great at casual conversations.

"Nice to meet you, Sophia." On his lips, my name sounded like silk sliding against bare skin, and I shivered, wishing he would say it again.

"You too," I mumbled. My stomach let out another growl. I clutched it with my hand, trying and failing to silence it.

"And now we aren't strangers, Sophia." He tipped the lollipop toward me.

If he kept saying my name like that, I could be persuaded to eat anything.

I took the lollipop, unwrapped it, and popped it into my mouth.

"I would have been more impressed if you had a plate of spaghetti tacos in there," I blurted out around the lollipop.

Really, Sophia?

Why was my mouth determined to humiliate me?

"Spaghetti tacos? Now that's something I haven't heard of before," he said with another warm chuckle, raising an eyebrow. His brows were thick and expressive, and his eyes were gorgeous, but his laugh was becoming my favorite part about him, that, and the fact he had candy.

I sat quietly for a moment, rolling the lollipop around in my mouth to prevent any more ridiculous comments from popping out.

The intense cherry flavor was actually helping my rogue stomach behave.

"So why are you here?" he asked again. "Want to talk about it?"

I sighed as it all came back to me. This stranger might be handsome and distracting, but I would need more than a lollipop to escape my problems. Did I want to talk about it? No. I wanted to talk to him about happy things, like books and puppies and his favorite kind of coffee.

"A big misunderstanding. There was a raid, I guess," I mumbled around the lollipop. "I ran away before the cops came, but I needed this." I kicked my bag with my foot. "They grabbed me so I couldn't warn the other girls." I heaved a sigh. "They're after the guy I work for, and I don't think they believed me when I said I wasn't doing the illegal stuff."

I shifted in the chair, suddenly aware of my skimpy uniform combined with my words. What misunderstanding would involve me getting swept up in a raid, dressed like this, with a shady employer? "I'm not a prostitute," I blurted out, my cheeks burning. "If that's what you were thinking."

"No assumptions," he shook his head and held up his hands in a stopping gesture. His face was kind. No judgment. It was nice.

"I'm the victim of the worst, most horrible coincidence in the history of coincidences," I said, blowing at a strand of stray hair that flopped down on my forehead. The memory of Mr. Roscoe commanding me to take down my ponytail made an unpleasant shiver run down my spine.

Ethan nodded but didn't press for more. "Coincidence can be a funny thing," he said.

"You have no idea," I answered.

He leaned back in his chair, completely at ease in the drab hallway. It was evening, but his suit was still crisp. A slight hint of rich, woodsy cologne lingered within his space that I could smell even through the dried beer, adrenaline, and misery scent I wore. Was this the cherry on top of the coincidence cake, to bring this too-good-to-be-true man across my path in the middle of the worst night of my life?

"What are *you* doing here?" I asked, the thought finally catching up in my mind. What if he was a criminal mastermind? Or a serial killer? Most likely a serial killer considering how my luck was going.

"I'm visiting my brother. He works here."

"Your brother's a cop?"

His lips quirked. "A detective."

So probably not a criminal mastermind or a serial killer. Maybe the universe wasn't out to get me.

"Sophia Butler?" A bored-looking female officer poked her head out from the nearby door, looked me up and down, rolled her eyes, and gave an overly dramatic sigh. "Your paperwork's ready, step inside."

I stood up, feeling like a child outside the principal's office. Ethan stood with me, reaching out a hand.

"It was nice to meet you, Sophia. I hope you have better luck with coincidences in the future."

"You too," I said before I could stop myself. "I mean meeting you ... was nice too. And ... good luck with ... visiting your brother." That was me, determined to say the most awkward thing possible.

He reached out and pulled the lollipop wrapper from my fingers. A tiny zap shivered up through my wrist. I wanted to say something else. But what?

"Well, take care then."

He let out one of his delicious chuckles. Did I really just say that? Like an elderly spinster aunt?

"We don't have all night, Ms. Butler," the bored police officer grumbled at me.

"Yes, of course, I'm sorry." I grabbed my bag and scuttled after her. Before I went through the door, I looked over my shoulder. He stood there, still gorgeous, still watching me.

"Oh!" I said, causing him to raise that eyebrow in expectation and the female officer to heave another exasperated sigh. "Thanks for the lollipop." I waved it at him like a little red flag before she shooed me through the door. Perfect. From spinster aunt to little kid.

3

ETHAN

"The cop shows we used to watch never mentioned all the paperwork," Hayden complained, coming down the hall to where I stood, staring at the door Sophia disappeared through. "It was all car chases and locking up the bad guys. If I'd have known how much paperwork was involved, I might have become a big shot investor like you instead."

I pulled my attention away from the door to my brother. His hazel eyes looked tired, almost yellow in the harsh fluorescent lights.

"Rough night?" I asked.

Hayden grunted and rubbed at his temples. "Almost done. Thanks for waiting."

He led the way back down the hallway toward his desk. "Were you talking to that little waitress from the Renaissance raid?"

"Sophia," I said, liking the way it felt on my tongue. "Does she have anything to do with the guys you're trying to take down?"

"Nah," Hayden answered. "I'm pretty sure she doesn't know anything. She's just a waitress."

I'd never put the word 'just' before any description of her. She was gorgeous in a tender, innocent way, with dark smoldering eyes even when she blushed and a sweetness that pushed all my Daddy protector buttons.

Hayden jabbed a finger on the enter key and snapped his laptop closed, grabbing his keys. "I don't think she was entirely truthful with me." He locked his desk drawers and headed toward the back. "Something in her eyes made it seem like she was in some kind of trouble."

I remembered the forlorn little cry she let out when she thought no one was around, her growling stomach, and the slight tremble in her handshake.

"Can you help her?" I asked.

"Nothing I can do. I gave her my card, but I doubt she'll call." Hayden shrugged. "Come on, if we hurry, we can grab Thai food before they close."

I followed him out, trying to let go of the image of her pink, heart-shaped lips, sucking on the lollipop, pretending she was fine.

I was still trying a half-hour later when we got to Hayden's apartment with several white plastic takeout bags in hand. She'd mentioned coincidence. I wondered if that's what meeting her was. Part of the worst, most horrible coincidence in the history of coincidences, according to her.

I wasn't so sure. The way her eyes lit up when I offered her the lollipop didn't seem horrible to me at all.

"So, you're going back to Seattle?" Hayden asked as he went into the small, galley kitchen and pulled two beers from the fridge. "I figured when the Hotel Hedon renovation was done, you were officially part of the rich and famous, and we'd only get postcards from the Eiffel Tower and shit."

I laughed and sat down on a shapeless tan recliner in the tiny living room. "Remember Woodland Ridge?"

"That old resort we used to go to? Sure." He handed me a bottle before collapsing onto his well-worn couch and rooting through the bags. "Remember the time we wanted to sleep in a tent outside the cabin, but Uncle Joe had to stay with us all night because Rook was afraid of Big Foot?" His smile faltered, and his eyes went wistful. "Why? Is it even still open?"

"It's closed, temporarily. New management. Undergoing a major renovation."

He looked confused for a second before realization dawned in his eyes. "No shit? You bought it? For real?"

"For Aunt Carol," I replied. "And all of us."

"You big sentimental sap," he said with a grin.

"I'm not a sap. It's a great investment opportunity." I pulled out a Styrofoam bowl from one of the bags.

"Sure, sure." Hayden rolled his eyes and grabbed the remote. "She's gonna love it, bro. Rook said she's been sorta lost since ... Uncle Joe ..." He trailed off, then pushed a button, making the giant T.V. roar to life.

He clicked through the sports channels, neither of us wanting that thought to finish.

His phone rang once, then stopped. He looked at it, puzzled, a frown forming before he turned his attention back to the T.V.

Less than a minute later, his phone rang again. This time it kept ringing, and he answered it, his frown intensifying. He listened to the caller for a moment then leaped off the couch, barely landing his curry on the table before grabbing for my phone. "Give me your phone. Now."

He threw his phone at me. "Stay with her, Ethan. Don't hang up." He punched at numbers on my phone, then barked orders into it.

I barely caught the phone, fumbling it up to my ear, dreading what was on the other end.

"Hello?"

"Ethan? From the police station?" the voice whispered, thick with terror and confusion, but I still recognized it.

The worst, most horrible coincidence in the history of coincidences wasn't done yet.

"Sophia? Where are you?"

"In my closet," her breath hitched. "Someone's here."

Fuck.

Hayden grabbed his keys and charged toward the front door. "Her place is only a few minutes from here," he called over his shoulder. "We'll get there before the uni's."

"We're on our way. Hayden, uh, Detective Valero's calling it in." I tried to sound calm, for her sake, as I ran after Hayden toward his car.

"Please hurry," she squeaked, her voice high and terrified.

"Stay quiet." I hurled myself into the car. Hayden pulled off before I even had the door fully closed. "I'm right here with you. We're coming."

Hayden sped toward her apartment building, sirens blaring. My mind played the image of her waving the lollipop at me before walking through the battered police station door on an infinite loop.

Her breath caught and she let out a tiny moan.

"Shh. I'm still here."

"He's coming ..." she whispered.

I had an insane urge to get out and run toward the sound of her frantic breaths. I had no idea where she lived and the car was faster, even with traffic, but the urge to *do* something was overwhelming.

"Which apartment are you?" I kept my voice low when we pulled up in front of a white stucco four-story building.

"T-two-thirty-eight."

We blasted through the open entry gate, Hayden pointing toward a stairway past the dusty courtyard. I barely knew this girl, but she was in trouble. And she called out to every protective instinct I had. We charged up the steps, two at a time.

"Oh no, no, n—" she screamed. The hollow thump of the phone falling to the ground echoed in my ear. Muffled sounds of struggle and her high-pitched shrieks for help filled my head.

We sprinted down the covered hallway till we got to the door with the numbers 238.

"Police," Hayden shouted, kicking the flimsy door in with two tries and running into the living room, gun drawn.

"Sophia?" I roared, running right behind him, probably breaking a million protocols, but I didn't care. I needed to see her, alive and unharmed. I couldn't get her terrified voice out of my head.

A small figure lay crumpled on the floor just inside a bedroom at the end of a short hall. My heart lurched to a stop until I saw her moving. Alive. She was alive.

"Sophia?" I yelled again as I got to the spot where she lay. I was vaguely aware of Hayden running through the apartment.

"The balcony," she gasped and pointed to a sliding glass door standing wide open. Hayden cursed and ran to the tiny patio, but I could only see her, curled into a ball by the edge of her bed.

"Hey there," I crooned, easing down next to her. She didn't move away. I opened my arms to her, and she slumped against me. "Are you hurt?"

"N-no. I don't think so," she whispered, burrowing her face into my chest and wrapping her arms around me like a vice.

"Shh, baby, you're safe now." I didn't mean for the endearment to slip out. She wasn't mine. I had no right. But relief shoved that thought aside as I held her.

"He was gonna ... he almost ..." She gulped in a ragged breath.

"But he didn't." I ran a hand over her plush dark hair.

Hayden was moving through the room, on the phone giving orders, all business. "The team's here," he said brusquely, flipping on the lights. "You stay with her." Murmured voices and heavy footsteps echoed back from the living room.

Sophia shuddered against me. "Who are all those people?" She sounded dazed.

"More cops," I said. "They'll want to talk to you."

"Are you a cop?"

"No. Detective Valero's my brother."

Her brow furrowed as she put it together. "The one you were visiting?"

"Yes. We were eating Thai food when you called."

"I'm sorry," she mumbled.

I shifted my arms carefully around her, trying to make her more comfortable. "I'm not."

She shuddered and pressed tighter against me. "Do I have to talk to them?"

"They'll want to know what happened," I said. "And they'll want to make sure you're okay. Make sure you're not hurt. I'll feel better knowing that too."

She sniffled and shook her head into my chest. "But … I'm not …"

"They won't hurt you," I said, trying to ease her fear. She might not have the most trusting feelings toward cops after being hauled into the police station earlier.

"I'm not dressed," she whispered. "I'm in my pajamas."

And she was. Baby blue, terry cloth short shorts and a cropped T-shirt with Eeyore on it. Not revealing, but thin enough to see she wasn't wearing a bra. She must have been getting ready for bed when she was attacked. I forced myself not to notice the sweet curves of her body so close against me, or the cuteness of her pajamas compared to the costume she'd been wearing in the police station.

"Can you stand? We can get you decent before they come in." Keeping my arm around her, I pulled her gently to her feet.

4

SOPHIA

The paramedic gave me a skeptical look before her eyes swept around my bedroom, taking in the numerous fashion dolls on my dresser, my desk cluttered with paints and supplies, and my smiling unicorn face comforter dangling from my unmade bed. "Are you sure you don't want to go to the hospital? You've had a traumatic experience and it might be—"

"No. Thank you." I didn't have insurance since my father removed me from his plan, so a hospital visit was out of the question. "I'm fine." I was about a million miles from fine, but a trip to the hospital wouldn't do anything to fix that. It would only make things worse.

"Well, don't hesitate to go in if you start feeling not fine." The paramedic packed up her medical kit and left.

"You sure you're okay?" Ethan leaned against the door frame of my room, his deep gray eyes scanning over me before pausing on my legs. "You're bleeding."

I looked down at a small cut on my thigh that the paramedic missed. It wasn't major enough for concern, just another embarrassment.

"Let's get something for that." He moved quickly down the hall. The hinge of the medicine cabinet in the bathroom let out its signature squeak, and I hoped he wouldn't notice my bubble gum toothpaste.

This was the worst night of my life, and somehow the universe decided the most attractive man I'd ever met needed to witness it all. He was being so nice, even when I crawled in his lap, cried like a baby, and wiped my nose on his once-crisp shirt.

When he returned with cotton balls, Bactine, and a box of Princess Band-Aids, my cheeks burned. The universe wasn't done embarrassing me yet.

"This should fix you up." He opened the box. "Belle? Or Ariel?"

I pointed to Belle, speechless as he cleaned the cut, peeled back the paper and applied the cheerful bandage on my leg. My tummy fluttered when his fingers touched my thigh.

Detective Valero, coincidentally Ethan's *brother*, was talking to a uniformed police officer in the hallway. The universe might be determined to humiliate me, but apparently it wanted me alive. Thanks to Ethan and his brother showing up so fast, Mr. Roscoe's henchman hadn't had time to finish me.

And I knew for sure that's who it was. I recognized his voice. The moon-faced security guy from the VIP room, with the cat-torturer voice, growled all the awful things he was going to do in my ear, his jutting chin digging into my neck before the door kicked in.

I shuddered, and Ethan scanned my face, a frown of concern tugging his lip down. He opened his mouth to say something, but before he could, Detective Valero came back into my bedroom with his notebook and pen in hand. "Okay Sophia, walk me through it." Ethan stood up but stayed by my side, his hand barely touching my shoulder. The detective glanced at his brother's hand before looking at me. "Don't leave anything out. No detail is too small."

What could I say? I lied about not knowing anything before—did that make me an accomplice? "I'm sorry, detective," I said, resigned to my fate. "There's not much to tell. I was brushing my teeth, and I heard a noise ..."

"What kind of noise?" he prompted.

The sound had been soft. If the water had still been running from the faucet, I would have missed it. A tiny, metallic *snick*, followed by the barest hint of a creak. I knew it wasn't Callie. She never made a quiet entrance. When I heard that sound, I simply knew. He was coming for me.

"Just ... the door," I said. "It creaks." I shivered. Ethan brushed the edge of my shoulder with his thumb. My skin raised up into tiny, pebbled goosebumps at his touch.

Detective Valero sighed and tapped his pen on the notebook.

"So, the intruder came in. What did you do?"

"I—I grabbed my bag and hid in the closet. Called you."

So stupid. I should have called 9-1-1. I'd be talking to a random cop who might not make the connection between me and the club ... and Tommy Roscoe.

But adrenaline drove my brain and coincidence put the detective's card in my hand. Maybe it was a good thing after all, though. If I called 9-1-1, they might be here dealing with a murder scene.

I shuddered again.

"Does anyone else live here?" Detective Valero looked through the hall at Callie's open bedroom and the messy explosion of clothes and shopping bags inside.

"My roommate, Callie."

"Callie Greene? From the club?" He jotted something on the paper when I nodded. His eyes settled on my necklace, reading its inscription. "Do you have a boyfriend?"

My hand reached up to clutch the locket. "N-no." I glanced at Ethan. He was listening to my every word.

He doesn't care if you have a boyfriend, don't be a weirdo.

Detective Valero looked at me impassively. "Anyone who *thinks* he's your boyfriend?"

I pulled my eyes from Ethan, guilty and embarrassed. He didn't think I thought Ethan was my boyfriend, did he? "No ... I ... what ... what do you mean?"

"Stalker types? Guys from the club? Anyone who might want to hurt you?" As he said it, my brain untangled his words, and my mistake became clear.

"I d-don't think so?" My cheeks burned and I wondered if a blush could become permanent if used too much.

"Did they catch this guy, Hayden, or is he still out there?" Ethan's question came out in a low growl.

"He hasn't been apprehended yet," Detective Valero said stiffly, giving his brother a careful glance and running a thumb along his beard.

I put a hand up to my mouth. The moon-faced man was still out there. He knew where I lived. And I couldn't tell the cops anything about him.

"Do you have somewhere to stay?" Ethan asked.

I blinked. Where was I going to go? What could I do?

"Get the fuck out of my way! I live here." Callie's loud voice boomed out at the front door.

Detective Valero turned toward the commotion. "Ahh, sounds like Miss Greene has arrived. I'm going to go talk to her."

Ethan gave my shoulder a gentle squeeze. "You doing okay?" His voice was warm and soothing.

"I don't know what to do." It was the truth, and I was too overwhelmed to hide it.

"You can't stay here. Not with that guy still on the loose."

I looked at my closet door, still hanging open from when the moon-faced man found me. My nightstand lay half tipped over against my bed. I'd smacked into it when he pulled me out by my hair. My little glass unicorn, a gift from Mrs. Helmsley, the one teacher who encouraged me and inspired my love of reading, lay broken on the floor. Maybe that was how I'd cut my thigh.

"Are your parents close by?" He asked.

"No." My parents were ... not an option.

He frowned, then looked toward Callie's room.

"What about your roommate? Do you guys have a friend's place you could—"

"Soap? Where are you?" Callie's voice bellowed down the hallway, using the nickname she gave me years ago. "Jesus, Soap. You okay?"

She blasted into the room and swooped me into a glittery, perfumed hug. "I can't believe this. I've been saying security in this place is shit forever. Did he hurt you?" She jerked back and held me at arm's length, her emerald eyes scanning me. "He didn't rape you, did he?"

"What? No." My cheeks flamed hot while my eyes darted to Ethan before I could stop them.

Callie caught it and turned her attention to him. Her gaze was suspicious at first, till she registered his supportive stance and then how handsome he was. She turned on a sly grin. "Who is this? Are you the hero who busted down our door and rescued my best friend?"

"I just happened to be in the right place at the right time." He stuck his hand out to shake hers. "Ethan Abbott. Nice to meet you."

"Nice to meet *you*, Mr. Right-Time-Ethan," Callie said, shaking his hand but looking at me. I couldn't help smiling, just a little. We could be under attack from zombies, but if a man was in the room, her matchmaking instincts went into overdrive. She couldn't help herself. "So, you're not a cop?"

"No, my brother is the hero who broke your door." He flashed a crooked smile. "Sorry about that."

"Valero's your brother? I thought you said your last name was Abbott?" Callie tipped her head, narrowed her eyes, and puckered her lips like she'd detected a hole in his alibi.

"Half-brother." He tried to straighten my broken closet door. "We were talking about where you guys might stay tonight. It's not safe here."

"Hmm," Callie hummed thoughtfully. "We can crash at TJ and Crystal's place. A bunch of people from the club are there anyway, talking about the raid. They won't even notice us."

I froze. I didn't want to see anyone from the club, and Crystal was a huge gossip. If Mr. Roscoe was looking for me, and she knew where

I was, he would know before I could say 'dead waitress.' "You go ahead, Callie, I'm gonna ... get some stuff and ... I'll call you later."

She frowned, about to argue, then looked at Ethan and back at me. Her face lit up. "Sure thing, Soap. That's just what Amber Jade would do." Her red lips parted into a dazzling smile. "Be safe and call me with the details." As she turned and headed to her messy room, she winked and called out, "See ya 'round, Right-Time-Ethan."

My cheeks were hot enough to start a fire at her assumption, but at least she wouldn't expect me to show up at TJ and Crystal's place.

"Who is Amber Jade?" Ethan asked, kneeling down to inspect the wreckage of my nightstand.

Just when I thought my cheeks might cool down, they flamed right back up again. "Oh, nobody. It's stupid. It's just ... Amber Jade is my stage name. Which I don't even need because I'm just a waitress, but Callie insisted, and she's always telling me to make a persona ... like Amber Jade is exotic and mysterious ... she says I'd get better tips, and ... I ... don't know why I'm telling you this."

"Makes sense." He rubbed his chin like the idea had merit. "An alter ego can help. As long as she doesn't get you into trouble."

"Like taking candy from strangers," I blurted out, then cringed.

His smile lit up. "We aren't strangers anymore, remember?"

"Oh yeah." I relaxed slightly.

He stood up, his face serious. "I am concerned about where you're going to stay tonight."

He was concerned? About me?

"I don't want to scare you, but that guy's still out there."

And he wanted me dead. My tummy turned queasy. "He was probably just ... a burglar or something ..." Somehow, it felt bad to lie to him.

"Probably," he looked skeptical. "You should still be someplace safe. You've been through a lot tonight."

He didn't know the half of it, and I couldn't tell him. I was running out of options. I reached my hand up to twist my necklace till it tightened like a tiny gold noose around my throat. Maybe I *should* call my parents, accept defeat, and resign myself to my fate. My jaw clenched to the point of pain at the not so silent I-told-you-so that waited for me in my parents' cold, sterile house.

"Tell you what?" He reached out his hand and gently tipped my chin up. My jaw relaxed at his touch. "I can give you a lift to my hotel. You can get a room there and sort things out in the morning? If you need anything, I'll be close by. And if you don't, well then at least I'll know you're safe?" His eyes were so kind, deep gray with gold flecks like a cozy blanket by a warm fire in winter. And he literally saved my life.

But hotels cost money, and I was probably going to have to go on the run like in the movies. I didn't even know how to do that. I only had forty-eight dollars in my wallet, and a little more than three hundred dollars in the bank. That wouldn't last long.

I needed to think.

He gazed down at me, eyes warm, waiting for an answer.

Well, he was right, I had to go somewhere. I could make a plan and figure out how to break the news to Callie. She'd be hurt, but honestly, she'd be safer if I wasn't around. This could work. How much could one night in a hotel possibly cost anyway?

ETHAN'S CAR was really nice. Nicer than my father's pre-owned, A-class Mercedes. The hotel looked really nice too, making me regret my casual assumption that it couldn't cost that much.

"Umm ..." I said when he pulled up to the valet. "This place looks ... really nice."

"Recently renovated," he said. The twinkle in his eye said there was a joke I wasn't getting, but I was too worried about the cost to sort it out.

"I'm more of a Motel Six kind of girl," I said with a lame little laugh.

He studied me for a moment before the valet came to the window.

"Good evening, Mr. Abbott."

"Hey Zach, could you give us a moment, please?"

"Yes sir, Mr. Abbott," Zach the valet said, fading into the background.

"Are you worried about the cost?" Ethan asked me.

"I just … I don't usually stay at places with valet parking."

"Don't worry about this." He got out and handed the keys to the valet then came over and opened my door, holding my hand as I climbed out. The valet set my small duffel bag on the curb and whisked the car away.

Ethan picked up my bag and turned to me. "You've had a rough night, and you need a break. I can cover your room, no problem, and it will give me peace of mind to know you're safe."

"Oh, I can't, I—"

He held up his hands. "No strings attached. Your own room. You owe me nothing but the knowledge that you'll sleep safely tonight."

I should argue. I should not let him pay for my room. I could only imagine what my parents would say about this. But I was at my limit, and I had no fight left. "Thanks."

"Good girl." His words made that flutter in my tummy happen again, but before I could say another word, he ushered me through the huge sliding door into the hotel lobby.

5

ETHAN

"Good evening, Mr. Abbott." The man at reception snapped to attention as we entered the spacious lobby and approached the front desk.

"Hello, Tobias," I said. "I'll need the room next to mine for my friend, Ms. Butler."

"Right away, sir." Tobias tapped on his keyboard.

Sophia stepped away, her curious brown eyes flicking from the chandeliers to the quietly tinkling water feature separating one of the two bars from the front seating area. She reached a small, tentative hand out to touch a textured wall, her head tilted in thought. When she didn't think anyone was looking at her, her features relaxed, her eyes brightened, and her mouth tilted into a curve like a rosebud. There was no reason the softness of that expression should affect me. She was a girl in a bad situation. I was helping her out, like I would anyone else. Still, I liked seeing her at ease.

"Here you are, sir." Tobias slid the cards across the black marble counter.

I collected the keycards and walked over to where she was contemplating a large, abstract sculpture.

"This place is beautiful," she murmured when I reached her.

"I like it," I said and led her inside the rounded glass elevator.

At the top, the elevator doors slid open, and we walked out into the hall. I stopped at the first door, unlocked it, then handed her the keycard.

"I'm right there if you need anything." I pointed to black double doors at the end of the hall, the double H's of Hotel Hedon's rebrand embossed in thick gold script in their center. "Or call down to the reception desk. They can help you too."

"Thank you, Ethan."

"My pleasure. I didn't want Amber Jade to have to put on her dark and mysterious glasses to find a place for you to stay."

She laughed, a cute, hiccuppy sound that filled me with warmth.

"Sweet dreams, then." I handed over the small duffel bag. Her fingers brushed against mine when she took it, and I had to fight the urge to ... to what? Kiss her forehead? Cuddle her and promise Daddy would take care of everything? I blinked hard and turned away. She was a stranger with a problem I could solve. That's all. So why was walking away from her so hard?

I opened the door to my suite and walked inside. What a fucking day. My laptop waited quietly on the polished oak desk. I should check emails and confirm details for tomorrow's travel. Instead, I headed over to the window and looked out over the glittering lights of the city below. I couldn't get Sophia out of my mind. How coincidence had crossed our paths twice in one day. How much it had gutted me to find her crumpled on her bedroom floor. How much trouble she seemed to be in, and how alone. Even though I'd just met her, I felt compelled to protect her.

That's your Daddy instincts reacting to a damsel in distress. You don't need any more complications in your life right now.

I sighed and rubbed my temples. I needed to concentrate on Woodland Ridge. For my family. It was our best shot at staying together after losing Uncle Joe. I needed to keep my thoughts on that.

No matter how much a pair of espresso brown eyes kept trying to sneak in.

I took a shower, changed into a pair of black flannel pants and a white T-shirt, and settled in to skim emails. I considered calling the kitchen for something to eat. I hadn't gotten more than a few bites of the Thai food at Hayden's.

She might be hungry too. I remembered her stomach growling and wondered if she ate anything other than the lollipop before the attack. What had she said she liked to eat?

I walked halfway to my door to go check on her, then paused, my hand resting on the back of my neck. I'd barely reached for the door handle when a tentative knock on the other side brought a half smile to my lips.

I opened the door.

"I'm sorry," she said. She was in her Eeyore pajamas again, her glossy brown hair thrown up on top of her head in a messy bun. She looked so different from the self-conscious club waitress I'd met at the police station. I liked this version better.

She winced and looked down the hall toward her room like she was measuring the distance for retreat. "I mean ..." She stood before me, her sock-clad feet overlapping each other as if they weren't sure what to do with themselves. "Oh. You're in your pajamas. It's late. I ... never mind." She turned to go back to her room.

"Wait." I reached out and gently caught her elbow to stop her. "Would you like to come in?"

After a moment's hesitation, she nodded but didn't move. I stepped aside and guided her in, barely tugging at her arm for encouragement. The morning was hours away, and every instinct in my head demanded I spend at least a few of them with her.

"Wow." She looked around the main room. "Is this the penthouse? I thought my room was gorgeous, but ... holy crickets."

I laughed out loud at that. She was truly adorable. She covered her mouth and looked at me with suspicion, so I forced my grin away. "Would you like something to drink?" I asked, heading toward the kitchen.

"Water?" She shuffled over to the sunken entertainment area and sat down on the edge of one of the white sofas.

"Can't sleep?" I handed her a water bottle and sat down across from her.

"It's stupid but ... I was ... I didn't want to be alone. Or in the dark."

"That's not stupid. Someone threatened your life only a few hours ago. If you fell asleep without a care in the world, I might have to have a talk with Amber Jade about how seriously she takes your safety."

She let out her little hiccuppy laugh, then bit it back. "I don't want to bother you ... if you were going to bed."

"No bother. I want to know you're safe, remember?" I picked up a remote and adjusted the lighting until there wasn't a shadow anywhere. "Are you hungry? I was thinking of ordering something."

"Maybe something small?" It was a question, seeking permission, and it hit me hard. She was a girl someone should be doting on, protecting, cherishing.

"Perfect. I'll order something small." I stood up to make the call. She flinched and looked over her shoulder like she expected a monster behind her.

"Why don't you stay here tonight? There's a separate bedroom over there." I pointed at a closed door across from the main bedroom. "Or you can stay right there on the couch with all the lights on. Whatever you prefer."

She clenched her small hands into fists, indecision putting a little furrow between her brows. "But you paid for the other room. I don't want to be wasteful."

"It won't be a problem," I assured her.

The relief on her face broke my heart a little. "Okay. If you're sure."

She left to grab her things from the other room, and I picked up the phone for room service, surprised at just how sure I felt.

SOPHIA

WHEN I CAME BACK, Ethan was in his bedroom, speaking to someone on the phone in a low voice. His sectional looked bigger than the entire living room of our apartment. I set my bag down and sat on the edge of the huge white expanse wondering what the heck I was doing.

When the lock had turned in my hotel room, a wave of panic washed over me. Monsters lurked in dark corners. I saw Mr. Roscoe glaring at me, smoking gun still in his hand, and I stifled a scream, but it was just my reflection in a wall mirror.

Going to Ethan's door was stupid. I'd already asked too much. But my feet made the decision before my mind could protest. Then he opened the door with a smile, his pajama pants hanging on his hips like he was carved from stone, his sandy hair slightly tousled. He was so perfect I almost ran back to my room without speaking at all.

I could hear Callie lecturing me in my mind.

Relax. Be Amber Jade. You can sit and eat a room service salad and have a conversation with this man.

I could do this. I scooched back on the couch, forcing out a breath and making my body relax. My thigh responded with a needle-sharp stinging. I looked down.

Oh no.

The Band-Aid peeled back from my thigh, reopening the cut and leaving a bright red smear on the pristine white couch.

I jumped up in a panic to get the offending blood off the couch before he could come in and discover what I'd done. I clutched my leg with one hand and grabbed for the water bottle with the other, while muttering, "Oh no, no, no!"

And at that exact moment, Ethan walked out of his room.

"Sophia?" Alarm rang in his voice as he crossed over to me. "Are you okay?"

"I'm sorry." I spun around hopelessly. What if I ruined the couch?

Would I have to be on the run from both Mr. Roscoe and this fancy hotel for destruction of property?

His eyes fell on the Band-Aid dangling from my leg. He rested his strong hands on my shoulders to stop me from my hopping and spinning. "Come with me."

He pulled me into the kitchen. I followed, wondering how much dry cleaning a couch would cost. Could a couch even be dry cleaned? Was Ethan going to throw me out for racking up his bill?

He faced me, his hands resting on my shoulders for a moment, grounding me, before sliding down my arms and finding my waist. I shivered, staring at him. His grip tightened, then he lifted me onto a thickly padded cream barstool. I held my leg up awkwardly to avoid getting blood on that too. Why was every piece of furniture in this place white?

He grabbed something from the pocket of his suit jacket, which was casually slung over another barstool. "I brought Ariel along too, just in case." He fluttered the second Band-Aid in the air at me, and my mouth fell open. Who was this man?

My skin burst into goosebumps as he cleaned and bandaged my thigh for the second time in one night. I searched for something to say.

"It was Mrs. Helmsley's unicorn."

"What?" His lips twitched upward, and he paused in applying the Band-Aid, his hand still resting on my thigh as he looked up at me.

"She was my teacher ...the horn is ... sharp." I slumped my shoulders in frustration with my babbling. "It's glass. It's broken now."

He let out a little ahh of understanding. "Can it be fixed?"

I sighed, picturing the things I left behind in my room, broken, disheveled and picked over by investigators, and my nose began to sting. Sadness and loss swept over me, and I shook my head so hard my hair almost came undone. I bit the inside of my cheek, determined not to cry.

"Well, good thing *you* can be."

My nose stung again, and tears hovered behind my eyes. Why was he being so sweet? "I'm so sorry," I said, wincing.

"What could you possibly be sorry for?" He looked genuinely perplexed.

Everything.

"I ... the trouble ... the room ... the couch ... it's—"

"Just a couch?" He stroked a finger gently along my chin then stood up, grabbing a towel and wetting it at the sink's arched silver faucet.

I trailed behind him, back to the scene of the crime, then stared as he crouched down by the couch and wiped at the smear with the wet towel. The stain vanished, and I gasped, realizing I'd been holding my breath. "Problem solved." He winked, the gold flecks in his eyes dancing.

I stared at him, then at the couch, then back at him. He wasn't mad. He fixed the couch. He fixed me. My hand drifted up to my locket and I traced the engraved letters with the ball of my thumb. His gaze dropped to the little gold heart, and I wrapped my fingers tight around it, hiding it from his view.

A rapid knocking at the door made me flinch. He stood up and tossed the towel aside with a flourish. "Food's here."

A hotel employee in a neat, black uniform with two golden capital H's embroidered on the lapels wheeled a cart over to the coffee table in the living room, directly next to the recently fixed couch. At Ethan's direction, he set out several platters with silver covers. The smells coming from them were yummy ... and familiar somehow?

The server carefully lifted the one nearest me.

"Spaghetti tacos!" I didn't even bother to hide the happy squeal.

Ethan's face lit up with a mischievous grin. "Took some research, but apparently, it's a thing." The server finished setting out the spread and quietly left us to our meal.

I sat down on my knees by the coffee table.

Ethan sat across from me, eyeing his dinner dubiously.

"You're going to love it," I said, grabbing mine and a bunch of napkins before sinking my teeth into the crunchy, saucy goodness.

"Well, I'm enjoying the company," he said with that tilted, half smile. I was glad my mouth was too full to answer. I didn't trust what I might say to that.

"Want to watch some T.V.? Take your mind off recent events?" He picked up a remote.

I nodded, crunching into another bite.

He took a small bite then hit the power button.

"Do you like it?" I asked.

"It's honestly not bad." He took another bite and clicked through the channels. The cheerful notes of a cartoon theme song chirped into the room. A yellow sea sponge and his pink sea star friend frolicked across the screen, and I bopped my head along before I could stop myself.

"I used to love this show," I said sheepishly.

He looked at me for a moment, his expression almost pensive. Then he grinned. "Who wouldn't? SpongeBob is hilarious."

My mouth dropped open, then I giggled. "And Squidward is such a grump."

By the end of the first episode, I had scarfed three tacos. By the second episode, my eyelids were drooping, heavy and thick. The last thing I remembered before drifting to sleep on the big white couch was Ethan, tucking an impossibly fluffy blanket around me and folding back a wild strand of my hair. As sleep overtook me, I almost thought I heard him say, "Sweet dreams, baby girl."

6

SOPHIA

"*S*uch a disappointment."

Even in my dreams, my father's words pulsed and ached like an old wound.

"You were never gonna cut it, space mouse," Brad the bartender added, wiping down a glass. His teeth glowed in the blue light of the club.

A circle of people surrounded me, arms all crossed in judgment.

"Think she needs a Daddy, Craig?" The celebrity dentist's son and his friend laughed and dumped beer bottles into my shoes.

"You look like a maid." Mr. Roscoe glared at me. "Come here." He pointed his still-smoking gun at my face.

"No!" I tried to scream, but it came out a whisper. "I didn't see anything. I didn't say anything."

The moon-faced man gripped my ponytail, dragging me out of my closet. I clawed at him, crying out as I smashed into my nightstand. The sharp tinkling sound of breaking glass mixed with his creepy laughter ringing in my ears.

"Shh. I'm here with you." A rich, deep voice that sounded like safety echoed around me.

The moon-faced man frowned, and his grip loosened in my hair.

"I'll be back," he whispered in a bad Terminator impression before letting me go and running away.

"Baby, you're safe." The deep voice swirled somewhere in the darkness. I threw my hands out, reaching for him and feeling only air between my fingers.

"Sophia, wake up."

My eyes flew open, and I gasped for air, slapping at the hands that gripped my shoulder.

"It's me. It's Ethan. You're safe."

"Ethan?" Saying his name broke the nightmare's grip. I sucked in a shaky breath as the hotel room took shape around me, bright with morning sunshine. "I'm sorry."

"Shh, stop that." He leaned back, giving me space.

"Did I wake you?" I sat up and pulled the blanket to my chin, blinking away the last confusing tendrils of the awful dream still clinging to me.

"I'm an early riser." He stretched, the muscles of his arms flexing under the tight cotton of his T-shirt. "Are you a coffee girl?"

Coffee. Yes. Coffee sounded like an oasis of calm in the chaos that was now my life. I nodded.

"Excellent." He patted my shoulder and walked into the kitchen.

I wrapped the blanket around my body like a protective cape and followed him, pulling out one of the elegant cream stools and seating myself at the bar, careful to make sure my Band-Aid was firmly in place this time. I kept my eyes pinned on him. The nightmare was fading, but I still felt safer with him nearby.

He moved efficiently, pulling mugs from a cabinet and filling the Keurig with water. I tried not to stare at his firm chest when it flexed from opening the fridge and hefting out the milk. The machine made its signature groan as it dispensed fragrant black coffee.

"Milk and sugar?" he asked, then loaded my cup when I nodded enthusiastically. "Do you have any plans for the day?" He handed me the steaming cup and watched me inhale.

"Umm." I busied myself by grabbing a spoon and stirring vigor-

48

ously. "Find a new job and start a new life." I tried to laugh as if I were making a joke, but it came out strained.

"A new life?" He frowned, his head tilting. I squirmed on the stool and stared into my mug. "You're quitting the nightclub?"

I shuddered before I could stop myself. "I can't go back there."

He sat down next to me and took a sip from his own mug, his eyes steady on me over the rim. "Was the guy who attacked you from the club?"

I shook my head and chewed on a thumbnail, hoping that would keep my mouth busy. It didn't matter how safe he made me feel, or how handsome he looked, I should not be having this conversation. I'd told the detective, his brother, that I didn't have any stalker-types and I didn't know who might want to hurt me.

He leaned forward on his elbows, his mouth opened slightly as he considered his words. The movement drew my attention to his lips. I wondered how it would feel to kiss them. I blinked and forced my eyes onto the veined marble countertop. I needed to make a getaway plan, not fantasize about kissing a handsome good Samaritan who could get me in trouble with the police.

"You were talking in your sleep."

Shoot.

"I was?" I blew out a dismissive breath and clutched my mug like it was a life preserver. "What ... did I ... say?"

"You said you didn't see anything. Or maybe it was say anything." He rested his hands on the counter, fingers lightly folded together. "You were whispering so I'm not sure which it was."

"I'm sorry," I blurted out. "Strange ... dreams are ... I don't ... are you sure?" I took a huge gulp of my coffee, which went down the wrong way and started a coughing fit. Embarrassing, but at least I couldn't babble anything else. I needed to go.

He patted me on the back until my coughing fit subsided, keeping his hand there until I had control of myself again. I couldn't help but lean into its warmth.

"Starting a new life is a big project." He cast his gaze toward the huge windows where the sun was already brightening the morning sky over the city. Trees lining the six-lane road far below glowed greener against the gray, and the cars glinted as they inched along. "What kind of job are you looking for?"

"I'm a waitress ... so ..." I shrugged and took a cautious sip of coffee. When I didn't choke, I tried another sip, happy my throat worked again but still unsure how to answer. I wasn't much of a waitress, to be honest.

"Are you planning on staying in the area?"

I stared into my cup, wishing the answer would appear like a Magic Eight Ball in the creamy liquid. Where could I go? Could I even stay in California? Should I go someplace else ... Toronto, or ... Toledo, or ... Tallahassee?

"Where do you live?" I asked, hoping to get the conversation off myself. He was staying in a hotel and visiting his brother, so he probably wasn't local. When his lips turned up into a lopsided grin, I realized how the question sounded. "I didn't mean ... I'm not looking to ... where you live has nothing to do with where I ... I was just ... making conversation." I put my head down on the counter and pulled the blanket up over my head.

"I'm going to Washington State for a new project. I'm leaving later today." The blanket muffled his voice, so I pulled back a corner and snuck a peek at him. He was gazing at me as if it were the most normal thing in the world for me to be hiding under a blanket.

I forced myself to sit up again, curiosity giving me courage. "What do you do for work?"

"Real estate acquisitions, mostly. I purchase distressed properties and make them profitable again. I specialize in hotels and resorts."

I blinked, then looked around, remembering the valet and the front desk guy knowing his name, the kitchen staff creating spaghetti tacos at his request. "This ... hotel?"

His lips turned up in that grin that turned my tummy to melted butter. "My next project is a mountain resort, a few hours outside of Seattle."

"Wow." I let the blanket slip down further and shifted on the barstool. "That's a big job."

"Mostly it's a lot of meetings and paperwork. But Woodland Ridge is special. We used to go there as kids. My Aunt Carol and Uncle Joe ... well, technically they're our foster parents, but we call them—"

"You and Detective Valero?"

His smile widened. "Yep. Hayden and I are half-brothers, and Aunt Carol and Uncle Joe kept us together. But there were four of us altogether, plus their own son."

He rubbed a hand against the neat scruff of his goatee. "We went to Woodland Ridge every year. There were cabins and rivers and hiking trails. Snow and skiing in the winter. There's a little town nearby, with a café, coincidentally called 'Carol's'. Uncle Joe always joked that he would buy it for her someday, and they could move up there, and she could run it."

"They did it?" I asked, picturing it all in my head. "And you're helping them renovate?"

A fleeting moment of melancholy darkened his eyes before it flickered away. "My uncle passed about a year ago."

My heart fell. "I'm so sorry," I said, daring to rest my hand on his for a moment before I second-guessed myself and pulled it back.

His fingers flexed, stretching toward my withdrawn hand before tapping the handle of his mug. "She's been a little lost without him. We've all moved out. She needs something to focus on."

"Aunt Carol's Café." I ventured a smile at him. He returned it, taking my breath. He had a gorgeous smile—easy, kind, understanding. I could have sat there forever, grinning at him and admiring that smile.

Until I remembered that my life was not about cafés and cabins in the woods. I grabbed our empty mugs and took them to the sink, needing to break the spell he kept casting that made me forget my problems. "She must be so excited," I mumbled.

"She will be," he said as he checked his phone screen then tucked it back into his pocket. "My first order of business when I get there is to hire her an assistant." His mouth twitched up in that amused way I was starting to love as much as his laugh. "You know, Washington is a great place for finding a job and starting a new life."

I straightened my back and turned from the sink to look at him, biting my lip in confusion. Was he saying what I thought he was saying? "I don't ... are you ... but you aren't ..."

He stood up and pushed the barstool in. "You're looking for a fresh start? You could come out and see the place and meet Aunt Carol," he offered. "If you don't like it, you can come back to L.A. No hard feelings."

My head shook back and forth, almost involuntarily. Coming back to L.A. was not an option. I needed to go somewhere. Washington was somewhere. Maybe even far enough away for Mr. Roscoe to forget about me. And honestly, part of me wanted to keep being near this man who made me feel so safe, even though we met less than twenty-four hours ago.

This was a crazy idea, but so was moving to Toronto, Toledo, or Tallahassee. Why would he offer me a job though? A job I wasn't remotely qualified for?

"I'm not ... I mean, I'm just a waitress."

His amusement faded as he walked over to stand beside me at the sink, his thick eyebrows pulling together in a stern scowl that set butterflies off in my tummy. "You are much more than just a waitress. If you were mi—" He cut himself off and shook his head, easing his frown away. "If I had my way, you wouldn't be allowed to talk about yourself like that."

I blinked, the butterflies intensifying, his nearness threatening to overwhelm me. If he had his way? My cheeks burned. I dropped my eyes to the gray tile floor and stammered out a whispered protest. "I just ..."

"Look at me." His words were a quiet command. I tipped my head slowly up until there was nothing I could do but stare into his eyes. My hands fluttered uselessly by my sides. He caught them in his own and held them still. "I can see the weight of something big on your shoulders."

Heat rose up through my body, and I willed myself not to burst into flames under his gaze. I shook my head and tried to push away the truth he was inching toward. Before he could open me up, before he could draw out my confession, my phone pinged from the coffee table.

New text message.

I flinched and pulled my hands away. He let me go.

CALLIE

Where are you? Brad says Mr. Roscoe's looking for you.

A cold dart of fear ripped through me. This wasn't over. I had to go somewhere Mr. Roscoe couldn't find me.

Ethan moved across the suite to a big oak desk. He was tidying papers, tapping them together with long fingers before packing them into a briefcase. He was leaving L.A. in a few hours, and I could go with him. I could escape the murderer who was looking for me and stay in the presence of the only man who'd ever made me feel safe, not stupid.

Or I could take my three hundred forty-eight dollars and try my luck.

Alone.

I took a deep breath. "It's ... only an interview, right? With Aunt Carol?"

He looked up from the desk at me, head tilted, white T-shirt almost glowing against his chest in the bright morning sun. "No strings attached."

A twinge of guilt tickled my tummy. I wasn't being dishonest, I just wasn't telling him everything, right? I could be in Washington by late afternoon. Mr. Roscoe wouldn't know anything about Ethan, so he couldn't follow me. This could work. "I have to call Callie ... pack up my stuff ..."

"Great." He snapped his briefcase closed and ran those long fingers through his hair, his eyes crinkling up with his smile. "Flight leaves in three hours."

7

SOPHIA

One ring.

What was I going to say?

Two rings.

I was a terrible liar. The truth wasn't an option. The only way Callie stayed safe was if she knew nothing.

Three rings. Then the click of her answering.

"Soap! Where are you? Tell me you stayed with the detective's brother."

I blushed and looked toward Ethan's room where he was making calls to that detective brother as we spoke. "Umm, I did, but—"

"Holy shit, you did?" Callie let out a squeal of pure joy. "Look at you! Amber Jade scores at last. I knew you could do it. He's scorching hot too. How was he?"

My cheeks burned as I realized I wanted to know the answer to that question. "It wasn't like that ... I slept on the couch."

Callie groaned. "Well, you've got another chance. The cops are still tearing up our apartment. You can at least suck his dick before we go back."

She was incorrigible. I laughed, letting the sound fill the space while I mentally formed the words I didn't want to say.

"I'm not sure I'm coming back." I closed my eyes, counting the beats of silence.

"Are you serious? You're *leaving* me?" The hurt in Callie's voice made my throat tighten. "Why? Is it the club? Brad's been asking where you are. Mr. Roscoe wants to talk to you. If you're nervous, I could go—"

"No," I barked out. The more Callie talked to them about me, the more danger she faced. I dug my fingernails into my palm, using the pain to focus, willing my voice to sound calm. "Don't say anything ... to anyone at the club about me. If anybody asks, tell them you haven't heard from me since the break-in."

Callie sighed. "This is bullshit. Something's wrong. I can hear it in your voice."

The lump in my throat grew to the size of an avocado. I wanted to tell her. She would wrap me in one of her perfume-infused bear hugs, crack a joke, and make everything okay. But telling her would make her a target too. I couldn't let her get involved. I needed to protect her. "I can Venmo you the rent money. Some of it, anyway."

"Fuck that. You think I give a shit about the rent money? You're dumping me over the phone when you're obviously in some kind of trouble."

"I'm fine." The lie burned on my tongue. "Seriously."

Was I trying to convince her or myself?

Her fingernails tapped on the edge of her phone. "Fine. You've got two days. Then, I'm going to the detective and telling him there's something else going on. I know you, Soap, and this isn't you."

"Don't ..." I looked toward Ethan's bedroom and lowered my voice, "say anything to the detective."

"Two days," she repeated. "Then we're figuring this out over margaritas. You're not getting rid of me this easily."

"You're a good friend, Callie."

"Yeah," she sighed. "You're very lucky to have me." Her voice lightened. "Are you staying with Extra-Sexy Ethan?"

"Sort of." How much could I tell her? The less she knew the better.

"Well then." She dropped her voice into her breathy imitation of Amber Jade. "I want details. I want you to get on your knees, wearing nothing but cherry red lipstick, and blow his ... mmmmind." She dragged the word out in an exaggerated humming. "That's an order."

I laughed away some of the painful avocado lump. At least Callie was consistent. I was really going to miss her.

LATER THAT MORNING, we returned to the apartment to gather my things. I looked over the wreckage of my bedroom. Broken glass glittered in the miserable, brown carpet. The nightstand tipped over, everything covered in white dust—for fingerprints, I guessed. My body shook. I dropped my head, closing my eyes to combat the sudden dizziness threatening to take over. I'd almost gotten killed here. In the same room I painted my toenails and read romance books and doctored my dolls. I once read a book where ghosts stayed confined to the place they died, and if that were true, I'd almost been doomed to haunt a cheap two-bedroom L.A. apartment.

"We can have the rest of your things shipped," Ethan said, his voice like a solid oak tree in the chaos of my thoughts. He gently took some chunks of broken glass out of my hands. "Mrs. Helmsley's unicorn?"

I hadn't even realized I'd picked them up.

"It was a gift," I said sadly. "She was my reading teacher when I was a kid." I walked over to the closet, refusing to look at the door hanging from one hinge. I pulled out an old, boxy suitcase and laid it open on the bed.

"These are exquisite."

He was standing in front of my dresser, looking at the row of dolls carefully posed in stands across the top. "Were these ... Barbies?"

"Oh, they're nothing," I answered, grabbing clothes and tossing them into the suitcase. I'd already embarrassed myself in so many ways. How could I explain that I rescued old, broken fashion dolls, imagining my room to be a doll hospital, and me a magical doctor who gave them new lives as fairies and sprites and whatever else they might whisper to me?

I walked into the bathroom I shared with Callie. The police hadn't disturbed much in here. I'd been getting ready for bed when the moon-faced man came in, but he grabbed me after I left the bathroom. I packed my hairbrush, deodorant, and makeup bag. Was the sum total of my belongings really this small? The toiletries strewn across the counter all belonged to Callie. A gold faceted tube of lipstick caught my eye.

I opened it and twisted up the shocking red matte stick. I never wore anything that bold. I stared at it and at myself in the mirror. What had she said?

Get on your knees, wearing nothing but cherry red lipstick ...

"—beautiful on you."

I jumped. Ethan was standing in the bathroom doorway, holding a picture frame in his hands. His eyes found mine in the mirror and held me. My breath stopped. I tried desperately to look like I hadn't been thinking about ... wearing lipstick for him.

"It's the only thing salvageable from the nightstand." His lips twisted apologetically as he held the photo up. The picture was of me and Callie, smiling together in front of a frozen yogurt stand. "But I'm glad. You look happy. Happy looks beautiful on you."

"Oh," I said.

Say something else, say anything. Anything would be better than 'oh'.

"Banana bread Froyo."

Anything but that.

His chuckle wrapped around me like a hug. "I'm learning you have interesting tastes in food." He set the photo on the counter and turned to leave. As he did, he pointed at the extended red lipstick. "A happy color."

When he was gone, I twisted the lipstick back down and shoved it in my makeup bag, certain Callie would approve. A strange bolt of confidence shot through me. Maybe the universe was offering me a gift, a wonderful, sexy man gift, to make up for the mess it had made of my life. I could do this. I could escape Mr. Roscoe. I could wear red lipstick. I could redefine myself. This plot twist gave me an opportunity if I could only embrace my plucky heroine and take it.

8

ETHAN

"*H*oly cow!" She placed her hands on the dash of the Range Rover and craned her neck as we drove under the rusted metal arch declaring:

Woodland Ridge Resort

"It's like a fairytale," she exclaimed, her eyes widening as the three main buildings came into view, interconnected by a series of wooden stairs. "Like an enchanted forest castle."

I followed her gaze. Mt. Tahoma Lodge House, the welcome center and largest of the hotel buildings, nestled into the crook of the mountain, cloaked in evergreen. Its aged red cedar structure held both rich history and future promise. The connected buildings, Summit Lodge House and Promise Point Lodge House, extended out on either side, each stretching up four stories and boasting rounded stone towers complete with turrets. They needed a ton of work but did create kind of a forest castle vibe.

"Perfect for a princess," I said as I pulled the car into the worn asphalt lot adjacent to the front entrance and put it in park. Her hand reached up to clutch at the little gold locket she wore around her neck. I wasn't sure if she was even aware of the gesture, but when her fingers touched it, a guarded shadow crossed her face.

The locket said 'Daddy's Little Cutie'. A relic from childhood? Or something else? I wondered, not for the first time, if she might be a Little. Her sweetness, her innocence, all pointed to the possibility, but it might just be my own wishful thinking.

She also seemed so utterly alone. She needed help. She had a problem, and I sensed I could solve it, if she'd only tell me what it was. Until I could figure it out, I wanted her close to me.

"Would you like to explore before my brother Rook and Aunt Carol get here?" I asked.

She bounced up and down in the seat in answer, her eyes bright again.

I got out of the car and went to her door, helping her step down. She hopped out toward me to avoid crushing a tenacious, early dandelion poking up through a crack in the pavement. I caught her and turned her, pointing to a break in the trees where a perfect view of Mt. Rainier's peak loomed.

"It's huge," she gasped. I'd explained how big the mountain was on the plane, but she hadn't believed me till it appeared, rising majestically from the clouds. She'd been looking for it ever since, fascinated by its ability to hide in the sky.

She took a deep breath then slowly spun around, her arms half-thrown out as she took in the view. "This whole place ... it's so, so green!"

"For now," I acknowledged, watching her skirt flare out as she spun. "It's whiter in the winter."

"And the air ... it's ..." she took in a big gulping breath, "like air freshener for my lungs!"

I laughed. "It's different than L.A. smog, that's for sure."

She stopped spinning and gave me a serious look then trotted to the steps leading to a porch wrapping halfway around the main building. "Oh, a swing!" She ran up the steps and sat down gently, grabbing onto the heavy chain holding the wooden bench seat and giving a light push with one foot.

The creak of the swing took me back. Aunt Carol had sat with me there when I was a newly orphaned nine-year-old boy. We rocked while I grieved, and I had started to believe that Hayden and I might not be completely alone.

Sophia was pushing herself on that swing, her sneaker trailing along the porch planks as she swayed back and forth. Her shoulders twitched at a particularly loud creak. "Sorry it's so loud."

"Been that way as long as I can remember." I approached the swing, holding her gaze.

She dragged her foot to stop, and I sat down beside her. Her perfume smelled sweet, like summer berries. I took over pushing the swing and she tucked her feet up, letting me.

"This is more than I imagined." She pulled a faded floral cushion into her lap, her head swiveling to take it all in. Winding paths extending out from the looming stone and wood lodge houses led to stand alone cabins, and the ski pavilion was barely visible off in the distance. And all of it surrounded by endless green forest.

I wanted to show her everything, see it through her eyes. "My lawyer thinks I'm crazy."

"I don't think you're crazy." She said it low, but firm, like she'd take on anyone who said different. It made me grin to see that little hint of fierceness beneath her soft exterior.

"I'm glad you decided to come here," I said. My arm rested on the back of the swing, just an inch from her shoulder. My fingers tingled, wanting to touch her hair, to pull her into my arms and press her close to me again.

"Me too." She traced a pattern on the cushion. "I didn't ... I wanted—"

"Holy fucking goddam shit, bro ... the back cabins are a disaster. You either really respect what I can do, or you really fucking hate me. Don't tell me which it is, I'd rather not know." The familiar, booming voice of my youngest brother burst out from behind us, coming up the main path. Sophia leaped back from me in whale-eyed terror.

61

"Rook," I said, checking my watch and standing up. "I wasn't expecting you till four." I reached a hand to help her up. When she was standing next to me, I didn't let go, and to my happy surprise, she stepped in closer, keeping her hand in mine.

"Dude, there's a family of bats living in the cabin at the end. I get the nostalgia, but are you sure about this?" Rook stomped up the steps, his steel-toed boots thudding so heavily the porch boards shuddered.

He paused when he saw Sophia standing next to me. His sharp blue eyes looked her over, noticing our clasped hands before his wolfish grin widened. Her fingers tightened on mine.

"What do we have here?" He folded his arms across his chest and tipped his head back, the red and black checks of his standard flannel making him a wall of plaid. "You didn't mention bringing company?"

"Rook, this is Sophia. She's going to work with Aunt Carol." I tipped my head toward him in a mock warning. "Be nice."

"Fuck you, I'm always nice," he scoffed. "Lovely to meet you, Sophia." He took some of the boom out of his voice and reached out to capture her free hand in his, swallowing it up in a vigorous handshake.

"Nice to ... meet you," she said as if he might be about to eat her for dinner.

"Aww, she's a tiny thing." Rook beamed his toothy smile down on her. "Just a tiny little dove."

"Everyone's tiny to you," I said.

Rook was the youngest of us, and Aunt Carol and Uncle Joe's only biological child. He hit a growth spurt in middle school and kept growing, until eventually he towered over everyone, even Uncle Joe. "Rook's construction company is handling the renovation," I explained to Sophia.

"Is she staying here?" Rook released her hand and leaned against the rough stone pillar of the porch. "The hotel isn't ready for occupancy, and the cabins need a lot of work."

I frowned. "How much work?"

"I had the first crew working on one for you since you gave us the green light Monday, so it's livable, but the rest aren't fit for pissin' in." He flinched and tapped his mouth as if he could pull his constant stream of curses back. "Sorry, little dove."

She shook her head and twisted the edge of her T-shirt in her fingers. "I don't want to be a bother."

"No bother." Rook waved a hand at her. "I can have the crew start work on one of the base models in the morning, but I don't have a magic wand."

The answer was simple. She should stay with me. I didn't like the idea of her staying alone anyway. But I didn't want to push her. It wasn't like she was mine, even if that idea was starting to appeal to me.

"I could sleep on your couch, then? Again?" She blinked up at me. "I mean ... if there is a couch ... never mind." Her cheeks turned pink. It was beautiful.

"You liked sleeping on my couch?" I gave her a teasing smile. Rook said nothing, but his amusement was clear. He was going to give me so much shit later.

She blushed harder. "I didn't want to be a bother."

"I like having you close. Knowing you're safe." I squeezed her hand to ease her embarrassment.

"There's a couch." Rook decided to be helpful. "King size bed too." A little too helpful. "And there's no place safer than with my brother." He clapped a hand on my shoulder.

"It's silly," she started, her eyes darting from Rook's shoes to mine. "But I'm a ... little afraid to be alone anyway." She swallowed then added, "In the woods."

"City girl." Rook tossed her a wink. "The quiet out here can be unnerving. Don't worry, you'll be safe and sound. On his *couch*."

I rolled my eyes and shook my head.

"Well, then." Rook clapped his hands and pushed away from the wall like he suddenly had somewhere to be. "If that's settled, shall we take a tour?"

SOPHIA

WELL DONE, Amber Jade.

I'd taken some teasing from Ethan's foster brother, but I survived. I'd been worrying about where I was going to stay the entire trip from California. Ethan mentioned cabins, but the idea of staying in a cabin alone terrified me. I dreaded the moment the question would come up. But it did, and I spoke up. Said what I wanted. Maybe I stuttered a little, but the result was the same. And now I would have another night … with him.

I already felt safer. With hundreds of miles between me and the club, that whole fiasco was becoming more and more like some book I read. And now, that book might be turning into a romance. I was ready to reinvent myself. To have an adventure. To kiss a prince. That tube of cherry-red lipstick in my bag approved.

"This is one of the luxury cabins, so it's got some amenities," Rook said as he led us up from the main building toward a two-story cabin with a wraparound porch and a ton of windows. "We got the electric upgraded and the plumbing is all new. Finchie was working on stocking it with the essentials for you."

"Who's Finchie?" I asked, sticking close to Ethan along the dark gravel path. His fresh cedar scent wafted out and I followed in his wake, trying not to make my appreciative sniffing too obvious.

"My assistant, Evie Finch," he answered. "She's been out here for a week or so working with Rook and prepping for the start of the project."

My heart sped up, and my stomach churned. He had an assistant? A female assistant? Of course he did. That was a completely normal thing for a successful businessman to have. My foot caught on an oversized rock and twisted, pulling me down. "Ouch!" I cried out, falling on my knees, my skirt hiking up over my thighs. Perfect.

"Are you okay?" Ethan was at my side in an instant, helping me up.

"Path's a bit bumpy, little dove," Rook advised. Apparently, he was a fan of nicknames. And stating the obvious.

"I'm fine," I mumbled, brushing down my skirt, hoping my butt hadn't been hanging out too badly. Before I could add any more insult to my injury, a hearty woman's voice echoed up from the main parking lot. "Boys? Ethan? Rook? You up there?"

"Here, Ma," Rook called out, waving a hand as a robust woman with steel gray hair, thick and barely contained in a low ponytail, came striding up the path. She wore patched blue jeans rolled above her ankles, a light button-up denim shirt with big pockets, and bright red Converse.

"My boys!" She ran the last few steps and grabbed Ethan in a bear hug before looking him over with a motherly eye. "Ethan, honey, how are you? It's been too long since you've been home."

"Good to see you, Aunt Carol," he responded, his eyes crinkled with happiness.

"How's Hayden doing?" She released him with a parting pat to his shoulder.

"What am I? Chopped liver?" Rook grumbled and opened his arms to her.

"Oh, quit it and come here." She stepped into his arms and gave him a squeeze. She didn't even come up to his shoulder. "Don't act like you weren't at my house for supper last night."

"Hayden's doing well," Ethan replied. "Sends his love."

I tried to imagine the gruff, bearded detective being swooped into a hug from this delightful woman. The image made me almost giggle.

She turned to face me, her blue eyes twinkling with curiosity. "And who is this?"

"This is Sophia," Ethan said.

"Hi," I said, too quickly. Then I stuck out my hand.

She looked at it, hanging in the air between us. "No."

I froze, horrified. What had I done? Did she see me fall? Did she think I was trying to steal her son?

"I'm a hugger," she announced. Then she stepped up and enveloped me in her arms. It was warm and kind, and I was so surprised I could only surrender to the fresh baked cookie vanilla of her perfume. I tried to remember ever getting a hug like this from my mother. Nothing came to mind.

"Now what brings you here?" she asked as she finally released me. "In fact, what brings us all here?" She looked at Ethan expectantly.

"Woodland Ridge." He waved his hand toward the main building behind us. "I bought it. Including Carol's Café down in town."

"What?" Disbelief spread across her face. "You didn't?"

"I did," he said. "And I need you to run it."

Her mouth dropped open as she turned from Ethan to Rook to me and back. "Are you serious?" Before he could respond she asked Rook, "Is he serious?"

"Apparently." Rook waved his hands in the air like he couldn't be held responsible for his brother's crazy ideas.

She looked at me like I might be the only one who'd tell her she was dreaming. I bounced on my toes and shook my head happily up and down, swept up in the moment, as if I'd been a major player in the surprise. I couldn't help myself.

"I ..." She grabbed at her shirttail and dabbed at one eye. "I don't know what to say."

"Say yes," Rook said.

She swatted playfully at him. "I suppose you knew all about this too?"

"He couldn't possibly take on a project like this without me," Rook said, giving a not-very-humble bow of his head. "There's a lot of fuckin—I mean fricken'—work to be done." He offered a guilty grin at the slipped-in curse. "Sorry, Ma."

"Well, you boys have really managed to surprise me, so I'll let it slide." She rested her hands on her hips. "I just can't believe you did it. And you kept it so secret. Evie didn't breathe a word, and I saw her yesterday."

Evie. His assistant. Of course, Aunt Carol would know her. Why did that fact make my tummy churn even more?

"She knew I wanted to tell you myself," Ethan explained.

I let out a tiny sigh, trying not to picture Ethan and Evie, hatching this lovely plan together.

"And Sophia?" Aunt Carol was looking at me again with that bright, piercing curiosity.

"You'll need an assistant," he said. "Sophia's here to help."

I tried to give her a helpful smile, even though I still had no idea how I was going to do that.

"You mean I get my own Evie?" Aunt Carol asked, grinning.

My smile froze. "Those sound like big shoes to fill," I managed to choke out.

"Well, you're off to a great start." She pointed first at her red Converse high tops and then to my own sky blue low tops. An irrational and fierce wave of loyalty washed over me. I would be the best Evie ever for this woman, and I would do it in blue Converse.

"I knew you two would get along." Ethan dropped a hand on Aunt Carol's shoulder. "I was lucky that coincidence decided to cross our paths at the perfect moment." He rested his other hand on my shoulder. It was a slight touch, not overpowering, but it held me. A thousand butterflies hatched in my tummy, and I sucked in a surprised sip of air before I could stop myself, trying to keep my knees from trembling.

I had called coincidence a horrible meanie, but he called it lucky.

Aunt Carol tipped her head, her eyes flicking from me, then to Ethan, then back to me before a tiny smirk twitched across her lips. After another round of quick glances, she slapped her thighs. "Well, I've got book club in an hour." She breezed around to give Ethan another big hug. "But I'll be at the café bright and early in the morning and we can get started." She hugged me again and gave Rook another playful swat when he dodged her advance.

"Bye-bye," she called over her shoulder as she headed back to the parking lot, whistling a tune I recognized but couldn't quite place.

"Winds of Change," Rook called out to her retreating back. "Scorpions. Nice." She stuck a thumb up in the air but didn't look back.

"Subtle, Aunt Carol," Ethan called out to her. He ticked a shoulder up into a half shrug when he saw the question on my face. "A game we used to play. Uncle Joe started it. He was a fiend for old pop music. He'd whistle and we'd guess the tune."

I tried to imagine my father playing any kind of game with me. I could only remember his phrase from my dream ... *such a disappointment.*

"I think you got the job," Ethan said.

I looked down at my shoes and smiled. Beer-soaked gladiator sandals had gotten me into this, and then a pair of Converse helped me out. Things were looking up.

9

SOPHIA

"Welcome home," Rook said with a flourish as he opened the door. The ancient welcome mat declared 'It's always a good day in the mountains.'

"Holy Toledo, this is big." I said before I could stop myself. The space was open to the back wall, which was mostly windows, displaying a breathtaking view of the tree-dotted mountain slope and the wide-open sky above. An outdoor deck, visible through French doors, hosted a seating area and a covered hot tub.

Rook walked into the center of the living room and leaned against the open stone fireplace. I could see through it to the kitchen in one corner. A connected breakfast nook linked back to the central living room, and all of it centered around the fireplace. A short hallway to the right led off to what I guessed would be a bathroom. A spiral staircase twisted up to a loft that covered half the cabin. I could make out a four-poster bed up there in the growing darkness. The décor was dark and dated, but it was still an amazing space.

"We got a delivery of firewood yesterday, so there should be enough for now." Rook kicked a log-filled box with his steel-toed boot. "It's May, but it still gets cold up here at night." He walked toward the door. "There's more out on the porch if you need it. I'm gonna go call an exterminator about those bats, and then I've got a date. Kelly." He waggled his dark eyebrows. "Yoga instructor."

"Thanks, Rook," Ethan said, rolling his eyes. They were so easy with each other. It was nice.

"I'm doubling my rates if one of those fucking flying rats comes at me," Rook replied before winking in my direction. "See ya' round, little dove."

"Bye," I said, waving as he walked out the door.

And then, we were alone.

"You're shivering." Ethan's voice was closer than I expected. I flinched and turned, surprised at his nearness. I could reach out and touch him if I were brave. My fingers twitched by my sides at the idea, so I distracted them by clutching my elbows. "It's cold."

Smooth.

"Let's get you warmed up," he said, stepping closer.

I was helpless to the pull of his buttery smooth voice. I took a breath and held it, waiting.

His arm brushed against mine, and I shivered again. My eyes drifted closed ... and then back open. I tilted my head as he walked past me to the wood box by the fireplace.

Oh.

A nervous laugh jerked itself out of my throat. "Fire. Right. Because it's cold. Wow. Is it always this cold? I didn't know it would be this cold." I cringed at my babbling.

He crouched down by the hearth and pushed up his sleeves. He wore a thick, forest green sweater and dark jeans instead of a suit, sexy in a fresh cotton, outdoor adventure sort of way. He tossed logs into the fireplace, his forearms flexing with the effort. He pulled a long lighter from a small box on the mantel and started lighting the smaller pieces in strategic places. The wood crackling as it ignited tickled my ears and made me shiver again.

Dark shadows danced across his face as the flames brightened, his profile almost stern while he concentrated on the task. I wondered what I would do if he turned that stern concentration onto me, calling me to him like one of the heroes in my romance novels.

Come here.

His voice would be gruff, commanding. I would step closer.

Take your hair down.

Suddenly it wasn't Ethan I imagined. Gone was his rugged goatee and the woodsy suggestion of an outdoor romance. Instead, Mr. Roscoe's Armani suit and ruthless stare condemned me to a terrible fate.

I shivered again, even though the fire's warmth reached out for me. He couldn't find me here. Right?

"Better?" Ethan stood up, brushed ash from his hands then leaned on the back edge of the couch.

"It's nice," I said, forcing those bad thoughts away. His nearness charged between us like static electricity. Would Amber Jade lean into that spark? Whisper something provocative? She seemed content to watch me struggle, offering no suggestions. I stood awkwardly, my fingers tugging at my elbows. I chewed my lip and scanned the floor for something interesting to say. Nothing there but dust.

The fire released a loud pop that made me flinch. His eyes flicked to the barrier of my arms across my chest, then back to my face. "How are you holding up?" His words sounded gentle, sympathetic. They hit some target spot inside my heart I'd been avoiding.

"Fine." My voice came out small and breathy. Not sexy breathy. More trying-not-to-cry breathy.

"You've been through a lot." He tilted his head, his gaze soft. "It's okay not to be fine."

A surge of emotion suddenly roared over me with that permission. I'd witnessed a murder, been attacked, my belongings broken, and I'd had to leave my best friend behind. My life was small and not exactly what I wanted it to be, but it had still been ripped away in one confusing, horrible moment.

"Sophia?" Ethan's arms opened as my breath hitched and the first sob rose to the surface. I wasn't sure if he came to me, or I went to him. I only knew that his shoulder hid my face perfectly, his sweater soaked up my tears, and his clean, woodsy scent made me feel safe. Safe from Mr. Roscoe and safe from the pressures inside my own head.

He murmured soft words into my hair. I couldn't make them out over my gulping, tearful breaths, but the rumble of his chest against me when he spoke them soothed me just the same. He held me close, hiding me away in the comfort of his embrace until my tears ran dry. When I began to match his calm, measured breaths, I felt empty, but for once, my mind was quiet.

Too soon, his arms loosened, his body shifted, and the doubt creeped back in. I probably ruined his no-doubt-expensive sweater with my tears. I wiped the edge of my T-shirt across my face, trying to remove anything embarrassing from my nose. "I'm ... so sorry ... I shouldn't have fallen apart like that."

He frowned. "I can't believe you held it together so long." He laced his fingers into mine and led me to an overstuffed loveseat across from the fireplace. He sank down into its cushioned folds and pulled me down next to him. I curled into the crook of his arm as if I belonged there and rested my ear on his chest.

"If there was more to that attack ... something you couldn't tell Hayden about, you can tell me." His voice rumbled deeper, and his fingers stroked a strand of hair away from my tear-dampened cheek. "I'd like to help. I'm a good listener."

I squeezed my hand so tightly that my fingernails dug little crescents into my palm. Why did he have to be so nice? I wanted to tell him everything. But Mr. Roscoe killed a man with apparently no consequences. He tried to kill me too. I couldn't endanger Ethan, no matter how tempting it was to trust him. "I ... can't." I pinched my face and squeezed my eyes shut.

"Not today." He cradled my fist, gently tugging at my fingers to loosen their death grip. "When you're ready."

I took a shaky breath, letting my fingers relax. How could his touch fill me with electricity and make me feel protected at the same time?

I was drifting into one of those deep, post-cry sleeps, which would explain why I didn't register the door creaking open and light footsteps crossing the threshold.

"Ethan? You here?" a feminine voice called. "I brought enough groceries to set you up till I can make a proper list, and I've got—"

A gorgeous woman about my age stood in the doorway, her mouth hanging open mid-sentence. Her long, elegant neck arched back in a clearly shocked posture. A bunch of overflowing grocery bags dangled in each hand. Her light eyes stared at me through sleek, thin-framed glasses. One brow arched so high it threatened to join the glossy burgundy hair piled into a neat twist high on her head.

I jumped away from Ethan as if we were teenagers caught kissing in his parents' basement, my cheeks hot with guilt and embarrassment.

"Evie. As usual, you think of everything." Ethan stood, bringing me up with him and putting a gentle arm around my shoulder. "This is Sophia. She's going to be helping Aunt Carol get the café up and running." He turned to me. "This is Evie Finch, my personal assistant."

This was Evie? She wore an elegant pencil skirt, silky button up, and fitted blazer in tasteful shades of gray that made her look both professional and absolutely stunning. Exactly three tendrils of hair curled down from her updo, softening the angles of her heart-shaped face. I fiddled with the edge of the shirt I'd just wiped my nose on and looked down at my blue, half-untied sneakers, childish compared to her sleek, gray pumps.

"Oh." Evie pulled down her glasses then pushed them back up, composing her face into a mask of professionalism. "Of course, Ethan." To me she offered a clipped, "Nice to meet you."

"Hey, Evie, I've heard … about you," I stammered out, hoping my eyes weren't still red from my recent outburst and my face wasn't a streaky mess, but who was I kidding? "I'm glad to—"

My throat chose that moment to involuntarily close and gulp all at once. "Sorry. I'm glad to meet you … too."

Ugh. I wished I could open a hole in the ground and sink into it.

"We'll help you bring in the bags." Ethan put a hand against my back and guided me toward the door. Evie's brow remained in that skeptical uber-arch, but she followed us without another word.

Once we put away the groceries, she moved efficiently around the kitchen, simultaneously setting things up, asking Ethan questions, and creating additional lists of things Ethan needed on an iPad that never left her side.

"I brought a case of that Pinot you liked from your last trip to Napa," she told Ethan as she opened a drawer to put away a bottle opener. I noticed a tiny trill of an accent when she spoke. "I set up fresh linens and towels earlier, so you should be all set ... although I wasn't expecting you to have a guest." Her eyes flicked over at me, but her face remained a professional mask. "I can bring more tomorrow."

My cheeks burned just from imagining her thoughts. "I'm staying on the couch," I blurted out before I could stop myself. "So it's fine. I saw a blanket. That's all I need." I bit my tongue, willing it to stop talking.

"Thanks, Evie." Ethan stood close to me, his arm brushing against my shoulder. "I'm sure we'll be fine."

Evie adjusted her glasses and pulled out a business card from a pocket on her iPad case. "It's my job to ensure Ethan has everything he needs. If I can be of service to you, please don't hesitate to text me your request." She handed the card to me.

"Thank you." I took the card, my cheeks still burning.

"What's the schedule like tomorrow?" Ethan asked as we left the kitchen and paused by the fireplace.

She recited his schedule for the next day, which sounded packed full of meetings with investors and partners and collaborators and all kinds of people who sounded very professional and important.

Ethan listened, nodding and scrubbing at his chin. "Move the meeting with the partners to nine a.m. and reschedule the meeting with the architectural team."

"Of course, Ethan." She tapped at her iPad.

He looked at me, his mouth turned up in a crooked smile. "After you meet with Aunt Carol tomorrow, I thought we could take a field trip. I want to show you something."

Evie nodded, pushing at her glasses. "I'll free up your afternoon, then."

"Oh." I watched Evie tapping away at the schedule she just read out. "I'm sorry." The hated words popped out of my mouth before I could stop them. "I don't want to be any trouble."

"It's no trouble at all." She made a few final taps and looked up. "I'll be going then. Was there anything else, Ethan?"

"No, thanks, Evie." He gave her a wave and walked back toward the kitchen.

She snapped the iPad case closed and held out her hand. "I look forward to working with you."

I blinked at her and waved before realizing she was waiting to shake my hand. "Oh. Thanks. I ... can't wait to ... work with you at ... work." I shook my waving hand like it had misbehaved then poked it toward her. She took it, barely pressing our hands together before letting me go, turning in one slow movement and walking gracefully out the door.

"Hungry?" Ethan called from the kitchen. "How about grilled cheese and tomato soup?"

"Sounds yummy." I walked in and leaned against the island, grateful Ethan hadn't seen or heard my awkward good-bye. "Can I help?"

"Just keep me company while I cook?" His smile was wide and genuine.

I sat down at the kitchen island and drummed my fingers on the counter, trying to think of something normal to say. "How long has she worked for you?"

"Evie? I guess she's been my assistant for five or six years. But she's been around since high school. She was" —his voice muffled momentarily as he bent into the refrigerator to retrieve a block of cheese and some butter— "like a little sister to us, especially Hayden and me."

"Oh."

I tried to imagine the cool, professional woman I just met as a high school kid hanging around Ethan and his brothers. And to ignore the tiny green flame that image sparked inside me. "Did your aunt and uncle foster any girls? Do you have any sisters?" I chewed the inside of my cheek.

"No, just us boys." He pulled out two red and white soup cans from a cabinet.

"Wow."

I took a breath. I needed to come up with something better than one word answers. "But you and Detective Valero are ..."

"Half-brothers." He set the cans down on the counter. "Same mom, different dads."

"Oh."

I zipped my locket back and forth on its chain. I wondered why they had needed a foster home but didn't want to ask.

He grabbed a spatula from a drawer with one hand and waved it toward my neck. "Are you and your dad close?"

Nope. Not going there. No way.

"Mm-hmm," I muttered vaguely, casting my eyes around the kitchen and searching for anything else to ask. "Do all your brothers live here? Except for Detective Valero?"

"Vincent does." He set a pan to heat on the stove. "Griff's been out in L.A. the past few years."

He put butter in the hot pan, and it sizzled, releasing a smoky-sweet aroma.

"So ... what do ... Vincent and ... Griff do?" I stumbled over the brothers' names and tried not to worry about Ethan's full lips smiling at me while he worked.

"Well, Griff's a security expert. He works with a lot of Hollywood types. You'll meet him soon. He's coming here to upgrade the security system for the resort." He dropped a sandwich into the pan. A hint of a frown flickered across his face. "Vincent owns a club in Seattle."

"Oh," I said again.

Why couldn't I answer with more than one word? "Cool," I added. Smooth.

I sat quietly while he flipped the sandwich until it was golden brown. He deposited it on a plate and started another.

"Thank you," I said, my voice small. "For making dinner ... and for before."

"I want you to feel safe here." He paused, turning his full attention onto me. "I want you to feel safe with me."

"I want that too," I said. To my surprise, it came out a little low and breathy and maybe ... a little sexy? I was pretty sure his eyes flicked down to where I was biting my lip for a fleeting moment.

"That's good." He smiled and then turned his attention back to the pan.

"I mean, of course I want to feel safe, not that I don't ... feel safe ... why wouldn't I?" I babbled, any sexiness evaporating.

Ethan's mouth curved into a half smile. He flipped the sandwich then opened the cans of soup and poured them into a pot on a different burner. "Want to know a secret?"

I nodded vigorously, relieved at his ability to ignore my awkwardness. His smile was infectious. I loved the way it made his eyes crinkle, and was that a dimple in his left cheek?

He pointed to the refrigerator. "Pull out the heavy cream and bring it to me."

I hopped up, eager to have something to do besides flounder with small talk or embarrass myself trying to flirt. When I had the cream, he motioned for me to pour some into the bright red soup.

"This is the trick to making canned soup taste homemade," he stage-whispered, stirring with a big wooden spoon while I poured. The soup turned a luscious shade of orange-pink.

"Is that enough?" I whispered back, grinning in spite of myself.

"Perfect." He nudged me gently away. "Now, go hide the evidence." He pointed the spoon accusingly at the two cans. I giggled and scurried away to throw the cans in the trash.

When I turned back to him, he was holding up the big wooden spoon, full of soup, over the pot, urging me to taste. I stepped close to him, breathing in the warm soup and his scent just below. I took a tiny sip.

"Take a big girl slurp," he urged, gently pushing the spoon closer to my lips.

I giggled again and took a vocal sip. "Delicious," I declared. "Homemade for sure."

"Good girl."

Those words, along with his smile, his scent, and his nearness, made my heart flutter.

10

ETHAN

Sophia needed a Daddy. I was sure of it. Everything about her screamed lost little girl who needed to be cherished, guided, and protected. My need to provide that for her was becoming a physical ache, demanding to be satisfied.

The way her voice hitched and her eyes widened when she was brave enough to look squarely at me, her response to my praise, her adorable attempts at flirting, and her overarching innocence all pointed to a Little side wanting to come out.

But the necklace. I still needed answers on that. She couldn't possibly have gotten in the predicament I found her in if she was someone's 'Little Cutie.' So then why did she cling to it whenever her eyes clouded with worry?

And that wasn't the only thing I needed answers for. There were things she wasn't saying. Things she wasn't ready to trust me with. There was something more to that attack. Something that drove her to pack up and move to another state with a man she just met. I needed to maintain control, build her trust, and help her deal with whatever she was really running from.

After dinner, she headed to the bathroom to get ready for bed. When she came out, she had on a light pink cotton shirt with little sleeping stars all over it. One shoulder slipped lower than the other and the hem barely reached the top of her thighs. The Ariel Band-Aid on her thigh peeked out from the trim of her matching pajama shorts.

"How's your leg?" I laid out a pillow on the couch and fluffed one of the blankets Evie left, smoothing it along the cushions.

Her hand brushed hesitantly against that sweet bare skin. "Better."

"Good." I patted the couch. "Let's get you tucked in."

"Oh," she said in her smaller, hesitant voice, the one that made me want to scoop her up in my arms and kiss her troubles away.

"Sophia," I said as she wound her arms tightly around her body in a protective grip and looked down at the floor. I slowly reached out a hand to touch her face, tipped her chin up and tried not to wonder how soft her lips would be. "I want …"

Her eyes were kitten-wide, almost pleading as she stared up at me, her chin in my hand, her body tense.

Don't push. Give her time.

"I want you to let me know if you need anything." I let go of her chin and stepped back, picking up another blanket and holding it like a shield between us. She sighed and bent over, rummaging through her bag. She straightened, clutching a Kindle in a case emblazoned with cartoon owls wearing glasses.

When she sat down, leaning against the pillow and curling her legs up beside her, I tucked the blanket around her and crushed down the urge to kiss her forehead, or any other part of her.

"A little reading before bed?" I asked, nodding toward the Kindle.

She puffed a stray strand of hair and nodded. "Is that okay?"

An idea formed in my mind. I rubbed my chin and sat next to her on the couch, careful not to squish her feet. "Would you like me to read to you?" I reached out for the owl-encased Kindle.

She clutched it like a secret diary, sucking in her bottom lip and staring at the screen, some inner conflict playing out on her face. "You don't have to do that."

"We don't want to disrupt your bedtime routine," I said, tipping my head and giving her a mock-serious eyebrow arch.

She blew out her cheeks, but when I didn't drop my hand, she slowly handed it to me. "You wouldn't be interested in the books I like ..." A blush of pink spread across her cheeks, and I wondered if I could make her blush in other places.

"Quantum physics?" I quirked my lips and leaned back, pulling her feet casually onto my lap.

She giggled and snuggled down into the blanket, peeking up at me. A longing stirred in my chest, an ache to win her trust and make her mine.

Trust took time. I needed to be patient.

I forced myself to focus on the Kindle. "*A Ruthless Choice*? Sounds intense. Looks like you're on chapter five, want to catch me up on what's happening before we start?"

"Uh, well ..." She worried the edge of the blanket between her fingertips, embarrassment and excitement warring on her face.

Excitement won, and she rushed through the recap in one big breath. "The heroine is Ruthie Luddington. She was on a ship headed to an island in the Caribbean to meet Lord Borthwick. He's awful, but she has to marry him because of her father's spice empire. But a storm sank the boat she was on and she was lost at sea."

Her face relaxed as she described the rescue of the drowning maiden by a dashing yet dangerous pirate. It was beautiful to watch.

"This sounds exciting," I said. "Let's dive in."

I started reading, stealing glances now and then at her rapt face as she lost herself in the story. She was exquisite when the near-constant worry she wore faded into the background.

She sat up straighter and brought both fists up to her mouth when the pirate threatened to thrash Ruthie's backside for misbehavior, forcing me to suppress a grin. Her Little side hovered right there, dancing below the surface, and I would read pirate stories every night if it would coax her out to say hello.

She nodded off before the pirate made good on his threats, so I set the Kindle aside and tucked her in, allowing myself a brief stroke of her hair before I headed off to bed, alone with my thoughts.

Neither of us were in a place to jump into anything new. But if coincidence dropped the perfect woman right in front of me, a woman who hit all my protective buttons and called to all my Daddy instincts, then who was I to argue? I needed to confirm my suspicions about her, and make sure she wanted what I could offer her.

The next morning, I woke up early and eager to see her before I headed into the office. I found her still asleep, curled against the couch pillows, her breathing steady and her face relaxed. I quietly set out a plate with a banana and a mix of strawberries and blueberries next to a bowl of instant oatmeal. All she had to do was add water. I left her a note and signed it with a pirate smiley face, complete with eye patch.

I HEADED up the path to the Mt. Tahoma Lodge House, pausing to savor the early sun peeking through the pines and the fresh scent of glacier water and deep forest earth that permeated the air. It was going to be a perfect day to be outdoors, and I couldn't wait to show Sophia one of my favorite spots on the mountain. The scenery might help her relax and maybe even open up to me about why she needed a whole new life.

Our offices were on the third floor, down a long hallway with burgundy carpet and wood paneling on the walls. Evie had been working on set-up for a week. We had furniture, wi-fi, and interviews for key hires scheduled. She knew how special this place was to me, and she believed in this renovation as much as I did.

I arrived to find her standing next to an industrial-sized printer, deep in discussion with a repairman. I waved, not wanting to interrupt her on the way into my office, but she excused herself, grabbed her tablet, and followed me in.

"Good morning, Ethan. I put the notes for your meeting with the partners on your desk and rescheduled the meeting with the architectural team to two on Friday. The printer tech says he should be able to have the printer up and running before noon." She consulted her tablet, pushing her glasses absently up the bridge of her nose. "Is there anything else you need?"

"Could you arrange for a car to take Sophia down to meet Aunt Carol at the cafe?" I asked as I flipped through the folder of notes she prepared. "And pull together a nice picnic lunch for us?"

"Of course, Ethan." Her fingers tapped sharply on the tablet.

"You okay?" I asked. Evie could be intense sometimes, it made her good at her job, but something else simmered in the tone of her voice and the way she was pursing her lips.

"I'm a little surprised, that's all," she said. "This girl came out of nowhere. You don't usually hire anyone without having me do a proper vetting process."

I smiled. "Hayden ran a background check on her. No need for vetting."

"Hayden?" Her voice faltered and her eyes narrowed. "Well then, I guess that's that."

I sat down at my desk and rummaged through the drawer for a pen.

She opened a different drawer, pulled out a black-ink Montblanc PIX Ballpoint—my favorite—and handed it to me. I clicked it gratefully at her. "What would I do without you?"

"Good question." Her mouth turned up into a little smirk. "Keep it in mind when it's time for raises." We both laughed, but Evie's faded quickly, and her face turned serious again. "You like this girl?"

I smiled at her concern, always the protective little sister. "I do."

She blinked back her worry and scooped her tablet up, consulting the schedule. "Five minutes till your call with the partners." She turned to go, but hesitated, looking back at me. "I just want you to be happy."

I tapped the pen on the folder and smiled at her. "I'm working on it."

SOPHIA

AUNT CAROL WAS a human ray of sunshine, and I still couldn't believe she was my new boss. I spent the morning going over an inventory of the equipment and documenting what needed repairs with her, while frequently slipping my hand into my pocket to touch the note Ethan left for me. The note he signed with a pirate smiley face. The note that gave me butterflies every time I felt its edges with my fingers.

He was picking me up at one o'clock. I waited in an old, oversized rocking chair on the wide porch surrounding the café. When he pulled up in a big black SUV, climbed out, and opened the passenger door for me, Aunt Carol poked her head out the door and waved.

"Have fun, you two," she called before puckering her lips and letting out a happy whistling tune.

"The Bangles. Walk Like an Egyptian," he called out over his shoulder as he settled me into the front passenger seat. "That one was too easy. You're losing your touch, Aunt Carol."

I couldn't stop smiling as he climbed in and closed the driver side door.

"How was your first day?" he asked as he put the car into gear and pulled out onto the two-lane road.

"Aunt Carol is amazing," I said with a genuine smile that felt really good on my face. I leaned forward in my seat, distracted by the passing trees that stretched up to touch the clouds and the endless amounts of green everything. I spotted two little brown rodent-type creatures scurrying along a mossy log. Squirrels? Chipmunks? Hedgehogs? I had no idea. "Where are we going?" I asked.

"It's a surprise," he said. "Don't worry. It's not far."

A bright yellow, diamond-shaped warning sign on the side of the road broke up the hundreds of shades of green and I squinted to read what it said.

Elk Crossing

"What's funny?" he asked when I covered my mouth to stifle a laugh.

I glanced at him, admiring the straight slope of his nose and the ridge over his lips in profile, then pointed to the sign as we passed it. "Like elk are going to cross the road right here because the sign says. Don't they live deep in the woods where there aren't any roads or people?"

His lips turned up into a lopsided smile. I loved what it did to his face, how it lit his eyes and rounded his cheeks. "Elk are all over the place around here."

I hesitated. "You're teasing me."

"I'm not," he said solemnly.

"And they can read traffic signs?"

What even was an elk? Some kind of deer, but with antlers that looked like hands instead of like fingers?

"You'd be surprised." He pulled into a rough graveled lot and shut off the car. He opened the door for me, then reached into the back for a huge picnic basket.

"We're going on a picnic?" I couldn't keep the excitement out of my voice.

"I have the perfect spot I want to show you," he said, leading me straight into the green and mysterious woods.

As we walked along the path, our feet crunching on the scattered leaves and bark and pine needles, I tried not to gape, but it was like nothing I'd ever seen. I stopped at a huge fallen tree, the roots wrenched up, forming a vertical wall, taller than me. They trailed out like a weird forest octopus, with thousands of root-tentacles stretching out, damp and muddy, seeking the connection to the earth they had lost. Some were blackened, while others were covered in a violently bright chartreuse dressing of moss. I touched one cautiously, curious if it felt as soft as it looked.

"Can I take your picture?" he asked, startling me out of my exploration.

I self-consciously pushed back my hair, instantly regretting my outfit choice—a rainbow striped T-shirt, purple skirt, and leggings with my blue sneakers. Not exactly photo worthy. "I'm a mess," I mumbled.

"You're beautiful," he corrected, holding up his phone and clicking. My cheeks warmed at the compliment. A sound like rushing water roared in my ears.

Wait. That wasn't only in my ears.

"What is that sound?"

"The surprise." He took my hand and led me a little further around a bend in the path. There, beyond a wide green clearing, a waterfall plunged down a wall of rock and crashed into a deep pool. In one direction the pool spread out into a dark lake. In the other it narrowed to a river that ran further down the mountain. The sun skipped and leaped across the surface, making bright flashes like a million winking camera bulbs.

"Oh, wow." I stood still, astonished at the sheer natural beauty of it, the endless green forest accented with the deep blue of the lake and the wild white foam of the falls.

His mouth lifted into a beaming smile, pleased with himself for the reveal. "We called it Eagle Falls when we were kids." He pointed to a hundred trees staring down at us from the top. "They nest up there, and we'd come watch them fly. We used to hike out here from the cabins and spend hours roaming around. Rumor has it the lake is bottomless." My eyes widened at that. He smiled and unrolled a thick plaid blanket. "I'll set up the picnic. You go check it out."

I perched on a large rock near the edge of the water with my feet tucked up and stared across to the rushing falls, wondering what secrets might hide underneath, and if a lake really could be bottomless.

The worry and fear of the past two days eased back to a corner of my mind, and I breathed deep, soaking up the smell of fresh air and sunshine.

My attention drifted back to the gorgeous man who brought me here. He set up the picnic, his shoulders flexing under a black, textured Henley as he smoothed out the blanket on a flat spot nearby. His serious eyes focused as he pulled containers out of the basket. He brought intensity to a simple task, attention to every detail. I loved the way his brow scrunched when he concentrated, and the way his goatee accentuated the angles of his cheeks.

I still couldn't quite believe I was here, with him, on something that felt distinctly like a date. The mean little voices in my head whispered that he just felt sorry for me, nothing more, but a new voice wanted to argue back.

Maybe it was Amber Jade. I decided to let her help me enjoy this picnic—this date—that might even end in a kiss.

He finished setting up and waved me over. Sandwiches, fat green grapes, slices of cheese and round crackers, a sealed bowl of potato salad, enormous chocolate chip cookies, a huge Thermos, and a bottle of wine covered the blanket.

"This is amazing," I said, sitting down. A bird cried out from a tree overhead and I craned my neck to find it. "I can see why you love this place."

"It's peaceful here." He handed me a sandwich and sat beside me, so close, looking straight into my eyes. I forced myself not to fidget or squirm. The clean, cedar wood scent of him blended with the crisp forest air, making me hungry for more than food. I stared at his lips, wondering if his goatee would tickle if he leaned in for a kiss.

The sandwich hung forgotten in my hand as I wondered if he would be gentle or strong, if his tongue would invade my mouth, or if he would explore my lips slowly. It had been a long time since I'd been kissed, and never with any great skill. With him, it would be different. Ethan's kiss would be ...

"—slippery with all the moss."

What? I blinked. He wasn't going to kiss me. He was talking about slippery moss.

"Umm ..."

His lips tugged up into his crooked smile. The lips I'd been fantasizing about. "You're a million miles away. Come back to me, Sophia."

I shivered at the way he said my name. "I ... uhh ..." I looked at the still-wrapped sandwich in my hand and dropped my eyes to my lap. "Sandwich," I mumbled, unwrapping it and taking a bite.

Roast beef. Delicious. Maybe chewing would give me time to pull myself together.

He looked confused, but let it go. "So, what did you do in the summertime when you were a kid?"

I stifled an inward groan. What could I tell him?

"I ... made dolls."

"Really?" He leaned toward me. "I remember some incredibly unique ones from your room."

"Yeah." I forgot he saw my bedroom in all its childish glory.

"What do you mean made? I assumed you were a collector."

"More like rescued ... I guess?" It sounded so stupid. I couldn't even remember how old I was when I found the first one, mangled on a dingy thrift store shelf. She looked so sad, with unevenly cut and tangled hair and crayon marks and glitter glue globbed across her face. I instantly wanted to help. My mother said I'd wasted my allowance on trash, but I knew I could save her.

"Rescued from what?"

"Being abandoned, I guess." I couldn't describe how it hurt to find them, usually naked, forgotten in a junk shop or at a garage sale. "I started by cleaning them up and giving them clothes. Then I learned how to replace hair. I started repainting them, transforming them, letting them express their true feelings." It sounded so silly when I said it out loud.

"That's incredibly sweet." He poured hot tea from the Thermos, handing me a cup. "You have a kind heart."

I snorted. "Well, it hasn't gotten me very far." I touched the locket around my neck. "My father calls me a dreamer."

It was not a compliment.

"Do you see them often? Your parents? Did you tell them about the assault?"

Would they care?

"I don't want to worry them." I grabbed a grape and popped it into my mouth, chewing while I thought of how to explain my parents away. "I'm kind of ... trying to show them I can make it on my own."

"Standing on your own two feet is admirable," he said. "But it's okay to ask for help too."

He'd never met my parents. Help was only for those deserving, and I'd been an unworthy disappointment almost from birth.

I took another bite of sandwich and watched the roiling froth of the waterfall. Being around Ethan was so different. He didn't make me feel stupid when I stumbled my words. He didn't expect me to prove my worth. I wished I could stay on this blanket, feeling his nearness and the sun on my cheeks forever.

"So, you're an artist," he said.

"It's a hobby." I stared at my shoes. "I'm not any good."

"I don't believe that. I saw what you can do." His eyes caught me, held me, like they had their own gravitational pull, and I was a helpless asteroid being sucked into his orbit. I wanted to touch him, hear him whisper my name against my lips. The space shrunk between us. His hand rested on my shoulder.

This time he wasn't talking about moss or anything else. He *was* going to kiss me.

The rushing water roared in my ears. I breathed in his scent and closed my eyes. I wanted this kiss so badly. I was willing to risk whatever awkward thing I might say after.

"Sophia." His voice was low and hungry, and it ignited a wild flame in my tummy.

I reached up, ready for the scruff of his goatee against my fingers. Until I realized I was still holding the sandwich.

Should I set it down? Drop it in my lap? Chuck it over my shoulder? I blinked in frustration as the moment evaporated.

He pulled back an inch, then two, his forehead furrowed with concern.

"I ... sandwich." I slumped my shoulders in mortification. "I'm sorry."

Humiliated. I didn't even get to the kiss before my mouth ruined it. My hand, still clutching the evil meat and bread, fell to my lap.

"I think we've discovered your safeword." His lips twitched with mischief.

My mouth dropped open in shock. Then I burst out laughing.

"Safeword?" I clapped a hand over my mouth, my cheeks burning. "Like whips and chains and stuff?" I kept giggling, my nerves overwhelming me, but his smirk remained. The amber flecks in his irises sparked with interest.

Suddenly, embarrassment threatened to boil me alive. "Oh, wait, is that … are you …" Oh no. Oh no. Oh no. He wasn't laughing. Which meant he was serious. Way down below, something heated and pulsed inside me. "I mean, I … I'm sorry."

I hated the old familiar apology, but I also meant it. I didn't want to offend him. Though he didn't look offended. He looked … *curious*?

"I didn't mean to make you uncomfortable." His smile remained. "I believe in being direct. I want to kiss you."

My whole body shivered at those words. He put it out there in front of me. No more guessing. I felt a rush of desire and relief.

"But it could be complicated," he added. "I'm not usually a casual guy, and I wasn't looking for a relationship when I met you."

Oh.

"No … I … never mind, I'm sorry." I tried to stand, to run away. This was so embarrassing.

He took my hand, refusing to let me pull away. "Sometimes wonderful things come along when you aren't looking. That's not the problem."

"But there is a problem." I shouldn't even care. He was right. Getting into a relationship was the last thing I should be doing. I was on the run from a man who wanted to kill me. And I couldn't even get to the kissing part without making a fool of myself. I wasn't ready for complicated, whatever that meant.

"Not a problem, sweet girl." He brushed his knuckles against my cheek. The feathery touch sent sparks everywhere. His eyes were warm and steady, easing my scalding embarrassment. "But, if we went through with that kiss, we would need to have a conversation." He leaned in close again, looking at my lips with a raw hunger that made me almost faint with need.

"A ... safeword conversation?" My voice tipped up on the last syllable.

He chuckled. The things that chuckle did to my tummy made me seriously consider whether whips and chains would be so bad.

"Not nearly as scary as you're imagining."

I looked down. "I'm sorry."

"You apologize a lot."

"I'm sorry." I grimaced. "Habit."

He nodded, as if he understood me. Beyond my worry. Beyond my awkwardness. In his eyes, the smallest parts of me felt seen. "This isn't a topic we have to explore until you're ready. No pressure. We have plenty of time." He patted my hand and leaned back, giving me space.

But did I want it? And more importantly, how much time did we have?

11

ETHAN

*T*he ride back to the cabin was quiet, but not uncomfortable. I wanted to kick myself for not kissing her. She'd been right there, her lips so ready, so ripe with possibilities.

But the safeword joke stepped in like an unseen force reminding me to take my time. We needed to talk about it first. Make sure I wasn't pushing her in a direction I wanted to go because she was vulnerable and easy to lead. If I didn't control the situation, one kiss would open a door, and if we didn't talk first, the urge to run through that door might be irresistible. For both of us.

A movement off the road caught my eye, and I grinned. Coincidence was giving me an assist. I glanced over at her, but she was chewing on a fingernail, looking out her window. I eased the car into the turn and slowed down.

The decreased speed caught her attention. She looked around, curiosity lighting up her face. "Is this the way we came? I don't remember this little neighborhood. It's so cute, nestled right in the middle of the woods—"

Her voice cut off when she saw what I had spotted. She scooted up on her seat a little, her hands braced on the dashboard. "Holy crickets, what are those?"

I put the car into park on the short, residential, dead-end street where four small houses sat tucked away on a cul-de-sac amidst the trees.

A good-sized herd of elk, about ten or twelve, mostly females and older calves, milled around in the open grassy area between the street and the first house's yard. They moved slowly, some ignoring us completely, focused on the tender young grass shoots. Others lifted their wide heads and stared directly at us as they calmly chewed. Two began a slow approach toward the car.

"Oh my gosh, are those *elk?*" she squealed, her eyes shining with unadulterated joy.

"Yep." I leaned back in my seat, enjoying her delight.

"And they're ... right there? On the *road?*"

"Yep." I pointed to a nearby metal post. "Looks like they read the sign."

Her hiccuppy little laugh bubbled out of her throat, and my heart squeezed tight at the sound. One of the bigger females, easily the height of the Rover, loomed a few feet closer.

"Can I roll down the window?" She looked to me, awaiting instructions. "What should I do?"

I nodded. "The car is in park, so you can unbuckle and get a good look."

She snapped off the belt and scooched up to the edge of her seat, tucking one foot under and staring out the window.

I pressed the button, and the window slid down. The elk stretched her nose out to investigate the sound with a thick, curious snort. Sophia let out a squeak. "Oh ... look at her eyes! What should I do? Can I take a picture?"

"Sure." I checked the rearview mirror for any cars coming and noted the rest of the herd's movements before returning my attention to the beauty in the seat next to me. She fiddled with her phone, clicking photos like mad as the elk watched with somber, patient eyes.

The big animal snorted again, and Sophia squealed in delight. "They're so big," she whispered.

The bold female looked just as enthralled with Sophia as she was of it. I kept an eye on her for signs of aggression, but we were inside the car and not threatening the calves, so the encounter stayed under control. After contemplating us a few more moments, the elk meandered back toward the herd, flicking her tail and snorting her goodbyes as she went.

"Well, what did you th—"

I was cut off by the assault of Sophia's arms flinging around my neck and her face burrowing into me in a fierce, happy little hug across the console. I caught her by instinct, loving how perfectly she fit against my chest.

"That was amazing! Thank you! How did you spot them? She came so close! I ... holy Toledo, that was unbelievable!" She leaned back to find my face, arms still clamped around my neck. Her eyes sparkled, and her lips stretched into an utterly unselfconscious grin.

And then they pressed tight against mine.

She kissed me with an exhilarated abandon that lit me on fire, lips firm at first but then softening, opening to me like a flower. Her heart pounded against my chest, her lush body molding against mine. I cradled her, stroking her back and pulling her over the console to my lap. She gasped out a little groan into my mouth that blurred my thoughts and drove me to take her deeper into the kiss. I shifted her tighter against me, my dick responding to her heat.

Resistance flew out the window. I wanted to claim her right there in the truck. Her fingers traced the back of my neck, raising up the little hairs there and obliterating my lofty thoughts about patience and control. Conversations could come later, but this kiss was too perfect and raw and sweet not to drink it deep.

But then, as fast as it started, it was over.

Her lips were gone, pulling away, her eyes wide with shock and embarrassment. "I'm sorry," she muttered, scrambling back to her seat. "I'm sorry." As if she'd broken something, overstepped some boundary.

I ached with the loss of it, the loss of her sheer, bright joy, her unabashed surrender to me, her strawberry sweet lips, but the controlled part of me returned.

Don't lose this moment.

I cleared my throat and kept my voice light, my smile easy. "So, I take it you liked the elk?"

She blinked back surprise, like she expected a reprimand. "I ... yes ... that was incredible." A shadow of her former excitement drifted back onto her face. "I ... you said we needed to ... wait, and talk, and ... I shouldn't have—"

"Do not apologize for what you just did." I captured her hand and put it over my heart. "Feel that?"

"It's pounding," she whispered.

"That's right. No matter what conversations we should have, that kiss was amazing." The corner of her mouth pulled into a tiny, shy smile that sped up the pounding in my chest all over again.

Someone pulled in behind us, so I pushed her gently back and pulled the seat belt over her, snapping the metal into place with a little click. I put the car into gear and steered us back onto the main road toward the cabin. She didn't say another word, but that little smile remained. Just like the sweet taste of her happiness on my lips.

SOPHIA

Amazing.

I kissed the most perfect guy on the planet, and he called it amazing.

My body was floating, full of bubbles and confetti, my brain pinging wildly at all the little snapshots of the most perfect afternoon I'd ever experienced as I walked back into the cabin.

The the elk, the picnic, the waterfall, the *amazing kiss.*

So what if he wanted to have a conversation? So what if it was complicated? So what if there were safewords involved?

My Kindle had more than one book with that sort of relationship in it. Captain John Harlow, the incredibly sexy but stern pirate in *A Ruthless Choice,* wouldn't even offer Ruthie a safeword before having his way with her. And to be honest, that made my tummy twitch in all kinds of dark and delicious ways. I just never considered a safeword relationship as a real-life possibility.

I slipped into the bathroom to clean up after the picnic while he made a few calls for work. A shower would give me time to think before I had to face him again.

I turned on the water and adjusted the temperature. The walls of the shower were covered in natural rocks in a million shades of pebbled grays and blues, and the water cascaded out from a rainfall shower head above. I caught a few drops on my fingers and ran them over the smooth stones.

He said he didn't do casual. Was he saying he wanted a relationship? I just met him, but we had spent a lot of time together these past two days, and he never made me feel uncomfortable or unsafe. He listened. He made me feel special. My hand left the wall of rocks and found my locket, rubbing the familiar letters with my thumb.

I shook my head and dropped it back against my neck, refusing the old familiar thoughts away.

What kind of relationship did he want? I tugged off my clothes and stepped into the steamy heat of the shower.

Not nearly as scary as you're imagining.

I could imagine ... things, and I could read about ... things, but could I *do* ... things? That magical, amazing kiss had been a fluke. An overflow of happiness that shut off my tongue and shoved me into blind action.

I squeezed out a big dollop of shampoo and rubbed it into my hair, luxuriating in the rich, berry-scented suds.

I wasn't a virgin. I had a boyfriend in high school who took that off my hands amidst a lot of fumbling, awkward elbows, and friction. It had been more embarrassing than erotic.

I even had a one-night stand once, after tequila made me stop caring what silly nonsense might come out of my mouth. We danced and laughed and went back to his place, and I felt rebellious and grown-up. I didn't remember much of the sex, but the next morning, back to my normal self without tequila's blur, I made a very awkward exit, and he didn't try to stop me.

Ethan made me feel so different from any of that.

I lathered up a bath pouf with soap and started scrubbing, remembering his arms tightening around me, pulling me closer and urging me on when we kissed. It had given me butterflies. Serious butterflies. Really tingly, lower-than-my-tummy butterflies.

The water poured down around me, just like the waterfall had poured down into the lake. When I kissed him, his goatee tickled my chin, his lips parted mine, and I barely tasted his tongue before I pulled away. He'd wanted to kiss me before, too, on the picnic blanket. He could have pushed me down, tossed my stupid sandwich into the lake, and shoved my legs apart with his knee. I would not have resisted.

"Mine," he would growl when his hand took possession of my body, a finger slipping inside and curling up to stroke the spot that made my eyes squeeze shut with pleasure. "No," he would correct me. "Look at me."

Those gray eyes of his, lit with amber flames, would pin me down and hold me open, exposed, and vulnerable to him.

"Please," I'd whisper as his fingers moved faster, pushing me further.

"Beg," he would command, lowering his head, tracing the ridge of my throat with his tongue, tickling my collarbone, kissing down the curves of my body.

I panted into the steam, my hands enacting my fantasy, my legs straining at the need rising up, my toes clenching the rough pebbled shower floor.

"Sophia." He would growl out my name, making me squirm against his hand as his fingers plunged deeper.

"Sophia." He would demand my attention as I gave myself over to him, releasing a cry of satisfaction.

"Ethan," I sighed out loud, my legs shaking, my whole body trembling.

"Sophia? You okay?" He called again from the other side of the bathroom door. His real voice, not my fantasy, calling me.

My eyes flew open, and I dropped my hands to my sides like a guilty child.

"Umm ... yes, sure, be right out!" Did I actually call out his name? I rinsed the last of the soap off and watched it swirl down the drain, envious of its escape.

So what if he did hear?

The new little voice challenged me. Maybe it was Amber Jade, and maybe she was right. He *wanted* to kiss me. He hadn't allowed me to be embarrassed, even after I clung to a sandwich then threw myself into his arms. If I wanted to do the things he had in mind, if I wanted to do complicated, I would have to be bold. Maybe this was a good start.

12

ETHAN

I made my calls, but my mind kept wandering to her, wet and naked in the shower. Nothing but a flimsy bathroom door between us. I wanted to be in that hot water with her, learning more about her body than the first sample I got when she jumped into my lap and kissed me, her sweet mouth opening and letting me in.

When she pressed tight against me, I knew.

No hesitation.

She would be mine.

Based on her reading preferences and all of her reactions, I was even more convinced she had a delightful Little side longing to be coaxed out. But she also seemed vulnerable and alone, for reasons I didn't yet fully understand. If I was going to pursue this, I needed to be careful. She needed gentle handling.

She opened the bathroom door, fresh-faced and dewy, and my heart skipped. She wore a navy-blue, slouchy T-shirt with a minimal outline of a sleeping cat's face and matching blue drawstring shorts edged with white scalloped lace.

"Sorry ... I was just taking a shower," she said. "No need to worry or anything. If you thought you heard something." Her cheeks turned that delicate pink that delighted me. She was flustered. And sorry. Always sorry. That was something we'd need to work on.

"What do you think I heard?" I asked.

"I ... we ..." She twisted her hands together, looking around the living room, avoiding me.

Suddenly it clicked.

Had my naughty little Sophia been replaying our kiss in the shower? My dick roared to life at the possibility. Her sweet embarrassment only made it hotter. She was so fucking adorable. I smiled at her without comment, letting her suffer for one more delicious moment before letting her off the hook.

"Wine?" I offered.

"Yes, wine would be good." She trotted over and sat on the couch, tucking her feet beneath her and clutching onto the armrest like a shield while I grabbed one of the bottles Evie brought over. I poured two glasses, the dark red liquid sparkling in the late afternoon light.

I sat on the other end of the couch, leaving space between us, stretching my legs out toward the coffee table and crossing my feet at the ankles.

She clutched her glass, taking a big swig then grimacing and offering me a comically fake smile. "This is yummy," she gasped out.

Adorable little fibber. I stifled the urge to call her out and threaten a spanking. Patience.

"So ..." She swirled the wine around in her glass, watching it like a kitten watching a twirling feather. She was exquisite.

"Would you like to play a game?" I asked. Her eyes flicked to the stack of old board games on a nearby bookshelf. My lips twitched up. "A getting-to-know-you kind of game. Sometimes it's easier to learn about someone with games. And wine." I tipped my glass at her and took a drink.

"Okay." She mimicked my sip then wrinkled her nose.

"Have you ever played Would You Rather?" I rested my elbow on the arm of the couch. When she shook her head, I continued. "I'll give you a choice, and you have to say which you'd rather. Then we switch." She clutched her glass and held it up to her mouth, watching me, not drinking. I forced my face to stay serious. "Want to try a practice round?"

She nodded and bit her lip, her teeth making tiny little indents.

"Would you rather ... drink wine? Or water?" I smiled and gently took the wine glass from her hand when she gave me a rueful smile.

"Sorry," she said in a small voice.

"No need for that," I said, going into the kitchen and filling a wine glass up with water for her. "You can be honest with me."

She took the glass when I returned and enjoyed a big, quenching drink.

"Much better," I said. "Now, ready to play?" I tapped my chin, considering an easy first question. "Would you rather live where it's always cold and snowy, or always hot and humid?"

Her brow wrinkled and her lip twisted as she thought. "I've never been in snow. It looks fun, but I'd miss the heat." She hummed under her breath. "Still, I do love sweaters." She was taking it so seriously. I fought the urge to pull her into my lap. "Is it *always* cold and snowy? Like I'd never go to the beach in summer again?"

I nodded my head. "That's the choice."

"So, it's a sacrifice?"

"Most choices involve giving something up," I acknowledged.

She chewed her lip then shook her head, coming to a decision. "I couldn't give up the sun. Sorry."

"No need for sorry." I sipped my wine and shifted sideways on the couch to face her better.

She took a swig of water. "Is it my turn?" A patch of fading sunlight expanded across the worn, plaid rug and she stretched one leg out, flexing her little pink toes into the warmth of its rays.

"Your turn," I agreed, resisting the urge to reach out and stroke that leg and run my hands up to the lacy edge of her shorts.

"Umm ... would you rather ..." She tapped her chin like I had before her eyes brightened at an idea. "Eat only comfort food? Or only fancy food?"

"Health consequences not a factor?" I clarified.

She shook her head. "Nope. But you couldn't ever have the other again."

"You're picking up this game pretty fast," I said.

She pulled her legs back in and sat crisscross on the couch cushion, leaning toward me, waiting for my answer.

"Hmm, tough choice. I've only just discovered the joy of spaghetti tacos. I'd hate to give that up."

She laughed.

"But I couldn't give up a really fine steak either."

"Is that your choice then?" She blinked, tilted her head and leaned back. I tried not to notice the curve of her breasts beneath the kitty cat T-shirt as she stretched.

I nodded. "Fine dining. Final answer."

She propped her chin in her hand in disappointment. "So far, I'm on the beach eating spaghetti tacos, and you're in the mountains eating filet mignon."

"Opposites attract," I said.

That shy little smile tickled the corner of her mouth. "That's true."

"My turn," I said. "Would you rather follow or lead?"

She snorted. "Well, I hate making decisions, so that's an easy one."

"You never like to lead?" I set my glass down on the table, watching her.

She pushed at a stray strand of hair, like she regretted her words. "That sounds terrible, doesn't it? Like a pathetic puppy without a mind of her own."

I shook my head. "It sounds like you know your own mind pretty well. That's self-reflective, not pathetic."

She tilted her head, considering. "Something tells me you always lead."

"Does that sound terrible?"

"No." She sounded wishful. I could see the tiny pulse in her throat. "Is that the kind of relationship you ..." Her words faded away.

"Yes." I leaned forward, encouraged when she didn't pull back. "When I'm with someone, I take the lead. Does that bother you?"

"No." She set her glass next to mine and stared at me with those deep, dark eyes.

"I'm a Dom." I decided to put my cards on the table. "Do you know what that is?"

She took a breath in and nodded. "You said you weren't looking for ..."

"A relationship? I wasn't. My plan in coming here was to focus on the resort." My family needed something to pull us back together after Uncle Joe died. That was my plan. But Sophia wouldn't stop that. I could do both. "Sometimes coincidence has other plans. I'm okay with that."

I watched her reaction. She didn't flinch about me being a Dom, which was good.

"So the problem is ... you want a ..." Her mouth twitched, shaping and reshaping like it couldn't quite form the word. I let her sit with it. She needed to be able to talk about things. "Submissive?" She finally let it out in a breathy little whisper that sent a thrill through my gut.

I nodded. "A special kind of submissive. Someone I can care for and lead."

"I've never ..." She trailed off like she was afraid of the questions forming in her head. "I don't know what kind of ... anything ... I am."

"Are you curious?" I sat up toward the edge of the couch but kept my eyes on her.

"Yes," she admitted. She was clearly nervous, but there was excitement in the way she licked her lips and tried to keep her breathing steady.

"That's the first step." I shifted so my knees slightly separated. "Come to me."

"What?" Her eyes filled with alarm ... and something else. "I don't ... what should I ..." Her words stammered, but she stood up, stepping carefully in front of me.

"Good girl. Now, get down on your knees." My voice took on the weight of command, and I relished the cascade of emotions it brought across her face. She let out a little sound, and her hand flapped opened and shut at her side, while the other slid up to clutch her locket. "You're safe. Don't overthink it. I won't hurt you. That's a promise."

She glanced over each shoulder quickly, as if someone might be watching, then dropped so quickly her knees smacked on the wood floor. She winced. "Sorry," she mumbled. "I don't know what I—"

"Shh." I eased her body between my legs, guiding but not closing her in, placing her hands on top of my knees. Her eyes stayed glued to mine, her chest rising and falling with the heat of her breath. I waited, letting her work through the nerves. "You always have the choice to stop anything that scares you or pushes you too far. You have control. Understand?" She nodded. "That's what the safeword is for. Remember yours?"

She dropped her eyes self-consciously. "Sandwich."

"Good girl." That shy smile met me back, and I loved it. Loved the way she looked, breathless and scared and excited between my knees. "Are you frightened?"

She ran her tongue against the edge of her front teeth and looked down, trying so hard to be brave. I could almost hear her thrumming heart.

"The number one rule is honesty. That's crucial." I tipped her head up. "You must be honest with me, always. And I'll be honest with you." Her hands tightened slightly on my knees. "Now, are you afraid?"

"A little." Her voice was so small.

"Are you excited?" I asked. Her cheeks took on that delicious, rosy glow, her lips parted slightly as she nodded.

"Me too," I said.

Her eyes widened. She hadn't been expecting that. Her eyes dropped from my face to my lap, and she sucked in a breath when she saw the tight bulge in my jeans.

"I'm sorry," she squeaked.

I took her chin in my hand again and rubbed my thumb across her bottom lip. "You have a little naughty streak. Don't ever apologize for that. I love it." She relaxed and let her mouth open slightly at my touch, her eyelashes brushing against her cheek. I tipped her chin up with one finger to make her look at my face again. ""Now, naughty little Sophie, ask me what you want to know."

She hesitated, then looked at me with pleading eyes. "Are you ... do you ..."

I waited, my hand resting on hers.

"Do you tie people up?" She finally blurted out the words. "I'm sorry, that's stupid."

"Don't speak about yourself that way." I gave her a stern look. "I said you could ask anything, and that's a perfectly good question. Bondage can be fun, but it's not my main thing."

"What is your main thing?" she gulped. "Do you ... like to ... hurt people?"

"No," I said. "I'm not a sadist. But my brother Vincent is." She gasped. I patted her hand reassuringly. "It's not as scary as it sounds. He only hurts people who like pain. That's never been my main thing either."

"Wait, didn't you say he owns a club?" she asked.

"I did."

"Is it a ..."

"It is."

She quirked her mouth to the side. I almost burst with wanting her, but I maintained my composure.

"Okay." She took a deep breath and looked at me directly. "If you aren't into tying people up or hurting people, then ... what?" She dropped her eyes.

I stroked her fingers. "Not all Doms are harsh or scary. I take the lead, but it's more about guidance and nurturing for me."

"That sounds so ... nice." Her voice was wistful, her eyes intrigued.

"That doesn't mean I don't discipline when it's warranted," I added. "Fibbing about liking yucky wine for example."

She rocked from one knee to the other, peeking up at me like she was gauging if I was serious. I winked to say I was teasing. Mostly.

"Want to take another step?" I asked.

She sucked her lip in, then released it and nodded her head.

"Come up on my lap."

Her breath hitched and she looked briefly at the fly of my jeans again before she stood up, hesitating only a second before putting out her hand and sliding forward onto my thighs. I guided her, turning her body so she curled against my chest. I tucked her into the crook of my arm and rested my chin on top of her head. She snuggled in, pressing herself against my body.

It was heaven.

"Comfy?"

"Mmhmm," she murmured, heaving a contented sigh.

I reached my other hand around to stroke her still-damp hair. "Still frightened?"

"Um ..." she paused. "No. This is nice. I got scared before because you were so stern, and I didn't know what to do, but this is cozy."

"Do you like following my lead, letting me guide you?"

"Yes." Her answer was a whisper. "And ...you ... called me little Sophie." She blinked up at me. "I liked that, but I ... don't know why." My dick got even harder at her admission. There was the Little I knew she hid inside.

"No one's ever called me that." She chewed on her lip.

I tugged her lip from her teeth with my finger. "Never?"

"Callie calls me Soap." She huffed out an embarrassed little laugh.

"But no one calls you little Sophie? Only me?" I traced the delicate curve of her rosebud mouth. "And you like that?"

A tiny, affirmative whimper escaped her throat.

"That's exactly what I like too." I found her hand and interlaced our fingers. "A sweet little girl, eager to follow my lead."

She shifted, squeezing my hand and placing her other hand against my chest. "You make me feel ... small." Her eyes left me to stare out the nearby window while she worked on the words. I let her process, running my nose along the top of her hair, relishing the summer berry scent of her. "But not like" —she flicked her fingers like she was dismissing something before bringing her fingers back to my chest— "insignificant ... small. You make me feel ... special small." Her fingers curled into my shirt, and she stared up at me like she discovered a truth about herself in that instant. Watching her connect with that Little part inside her, maybe for the first time, made my body flicker and thrum with electricity.

I shifted more so she was almost lying across me. "I'm going to ask you a question, my naughty little Sophie. I expect a truthful answer."

She stared up at me, her mouth turned up in a shy grin, her eyes wide and starting to trust.

"When you were in the shower, and I knocked on the door and called your name, what were you doing?"

"Oh." She squirmed, sending all kinds of sensations through my lap, her cheeks immediately flushing. "No, I ... I can't ..." Her struggle confirmed my earlier thoughts, and I gave her a triumphant half grin.

I leaned over her until only a few inches separated my mouth from hers. "Tell me."

She squirmed harder, her body rubbing against me. I called upon every ounce of my restraint not to tear off her pajamas and fuck her right there. She looked perfect. She smelled perfect. I wanted to make her confess and take her over my knee more than I'd ever wanted anything in my life.

"I can't," she whispered.

"You can't?" I gave her a stern look.

"I don't want to say it."

"You can do naughty things, but you can't say naughty words?"

"I wasn't—"

"Remember," I stopped her with a finger on those luscious lips. "Honesty."

She made a little 'eep' sound and squeezed her eyes closed.

"Do you want me to help you?" I prompted.

She opened them again, puzzled and helpless. So cute.

"I think you took off all your clothes and got into the hot water," I touched the edge of her jaw. "I think you slid your hands down your body." I ran a hand down to her shoulder, following her arm then across her belly to rest at the top of her shorts.

"You got to about here." I tugged at the drawstring, slipping a finger inside the band. "Then you started thinking about something." Her body lifted slightly to meet my hand on her belly. "What were you thinking about, naughty little Sophie?" I hovered over her.

"Our kiss," she breathed out, the words barely taking form. "I thought about our kiss."

"Good girl. Did you like that kiss?"

She nodded, eyes wide, and I couldn't resist anymore.

"Do you want to kiss me like that again, sweet girl?" I traced my finger along the edge of her belly button.

Her nod was big and fast and exaggerated.

"Then do it, baby."

13

SOPHIA

$\mathcal{H}$is command opened something inside me. Something I wanted ... craved ... but didn't even know existed until that moment. He opened a door in me, and I burst through with no more hesitation. I didn't just kiss him, I inhaled his mouth, sucking in his bottom lip and moaning a little sigh of pleasure at his taste, his smell, the bliss of his arms shifting and pulling me closer.

He growled into my kiss, his hand flattening against the rise of my tummy and sliding lower into my shorts. "That's my girl."

Amber Jade quietly purred her approval in my head, polite enough not to distract me. She even suggested I arch my back to get his hand closer to my panties. Something awkward would probably tumble from my lips soon, but in that moment, I knew exactly what I wanted. I wanted to say dirty words to him. I wanted to obey him on my knees. I wanted to confess my sins and have my flesh forgiven by his caress.

Suddenly, he pulled back, cursed, and leaned his forehead against mine. I huffed out a protest and lifted my lips up, hungry for more.

Why was he stopping?

Heavy knocking at the door broke through my haze and made me understand why he'd stopped. Who was there? How long had they been knocking? How would I ever forgive them for interrupting the single best moment of my life?

He untangled himself from my clinging arms, stroking my cheek and tucking back a strand of my hair. I flounced into a more normal seated position, waffling between embarrassment and frustration. As I adjusted to the loss of his heat, a trickle of fear slipped down my spine and pooled in my tummy, chilling the excitement that lingered there.

What if Mr. Roscoe sent the moon-faced man to finish the job?

Ethan opened the door with a sigh. "Hey Rook, come on in."

"Not interrupting anything am I?" Rook stomped in, tossing a sly glance at the glasses of wine and water on the table. Heat flushed my skin as I tried to be normal. Was my hair rumpled? Were my shorts hiked up?

Rook's heavy footsteps echoed through the cabin as he entered the kitchen and pulled a cold beer from the fridge. "Ah, Finchie brought supplies," he said happily.

"Help yourself," Ethan said, mouthing the word 'sorry' before sitting next to me and taking my hand. The connection to him sent tingly electricity up my arm.

"So, good news, bad news." Rook cracked open the bottle and sat heavily in a chair opposite us. His dark eyes moved to our interlaced hands, and he tugged at the beanie covering his coal black hair, a grin warming his face. "You sure I'm not interrupting?"

"You are." Ethan leaned forward, resting his elbow on his knee, keeping my hand in his. "So it better be all good news."

Rook released a thunderous laugh. "Wish I could oblige you, brother."

"What's going on?"

"Bats are being vacated tomorrow. That's the good news."

"And the bad?"

"Design team issues. I'm not sure they're going to meet the first set of deadlines."

Ethan sighed, scrubbing his hand against his goatee. "What's going on?"

Rook took a long pull from his beer and began to describe what sounded like a lot of drama within his interior design team. Ethan kissed my hand and gave me an apologetic glance before asking a few more questions.

I felt awkward, listening to business I didn't know anything about, so I stood up and wandered over to a bookshelf next to the door, with its dusty stack of board games. As I perused the boxes, I glanced furtively over at Ethan, now deep in discussion with Rook about how the weather would also impact the construction schedule. I could hardly believe I'd just been kissing him, experiencing a wonderful, reckless loosening inside that might have led to all kinds of questionable decisions.

He said he wanted a sweet little girl to lead. Why did that sound so amazing? He called me his naughty little Sophie, and that had sent fireworks through every part of my body.

I stared at the games on the shelf while they talked. Monopoly. Had there ever been a stack of board games anywhere on the planet that didn't include Monopoly? What else? Chess. Checkers. Two boxes were puzzles.

After a few more minutes, Rook stood up. "Well, I'd love to stay, but I have a date."

"The yoga instructor?" Ethan stood up and walked him to the door.

"Nah, she wasn't the one. But this one could be." Rook pulled the door open, and a chilly breeze blew in, raising goosebumps on my arms. He turned to look at Ethan. "One more thing."

Ethan tilted his head, listening.

"The security system is complete shit. Nothing is working. I know Griff's coming out to work on it, but I wanted to let you know. It's bad. Good thing we're out in the middle of nowhere." He laughed his big booming laugh. "I doubt there's a line of criminal types looking to infiltrate our empty resort."

I shivered and rubbed my arms. The tiniest hint of a frown crossed Ethan's face, and he glanced at me before looking back to his brother. "Thanks for letting me know."

Rook lifted his chin to me, saying, "See ya, little dove," before closing the door and stomping off down the porch.

I turned back to the bookshelf, staring at the last game box on the pile. My mind kept echoing Rook's words and thinking of one very specific criminal.

But he couldn't follow me here, right?

"Find something you like?" Ethan's deep voice rumbled behind me.

I straightened up with a little jump, trying not to look guilty. I glanced at the games again. "Um, Clue?"

Amber Jade cringed inside my mind, wanting to get back to the kissing, not playing Clue.

"Well, I must warn you, I'm pretty good at solving the murder." He wrapped his arms loosely around my waist.

A shiver ripped through me at that word. That was the real reason I was here, and it had nothing to do with board games or kissing. I needed to remember that. Rook's words played over again in my mind. I should have been thankful it wasn't a hitman knocking at the door.

He felt me trembling and turned me around so he could look in my eyes. "Sorry about that." He gestured toward the door. "Rook is ..." He shrugged, smiled, and rolled his eyes all at once.

"Oh ... sure, no, of course," I babbled, not knowing what else to say.

He let me go. "Have we lost the mood?"

I looked down at the hardwood floor. As much as I wanted to go back to kissing him, as much as Amber Jade was pouting and stomping her feet, I needed a moment to process.

"Let's make dinner," he suggested, leading me into the kitchen. "We can discuss our options better on full stomachs."

He kissed me on the forehead and directed me to pull mushrooms, a red pepper, and two tomatoes out of the refrigerator crisper. The worry, the bad memories, and the confusion all faded away as he guided me through the steps to making something he called Chicken Scallopini. It was fun, following his directions and watching the meal materialize like magic. I didn't have to worry about making a wrong decision, and I was thankful for the break in fretful thoughts.

He asked more about my dolls, and how I got the ideas for my transformations. He asked me about school, but he didn't push or make me feel bad about quitting after two lackluster semesters.

When we finished dinner and the kitchen was clean, I blinked, wondering how the time had passed. I hadn't felt foolish or embarrassed. He was just *easy* to be around. He paid attention. Listened like I was the most interesting girl on the planet. Looked at me like he really saw me and liked what he saw.

The conversation lulled, and a wave of shy nerves started to roil in my tummy. Would he kiss me again? Where would I sleep? The couch again ... or his bed?

"Let's sit on the deck." He opened the creaky French doors that led out to a covered seating area overlooking an endless ocean of trees standing like silent sentinels. I followed him and breathed in the cool evening air. Sunset played out across the big mountain, staining the snowy top a fiery orange that drained into lavender and violet shadows.

I leaned over the railing, marveling at the vast, open space.

"Careful," he warned, putting his hand on my shoulder. "I can't vouch for that railing."

I scooted back and collided against him. Before I could apologize, his arm slipped around my waist, holding me there. His chest rose and fell with steady breaths. That woodsy scent of his enveloped me.

"What's going through your mind, little Sophie?" His question floated around me in the growing darkness. That version of my name on his lips caused a decadent flutter in my tummy.

I had no clue how to put my feelings into words. How I felt fireworks bursting in my brain when our lips touched. The giddy acceleration flashing through me when he commanded me to kiss him. And most of all, what happened inside me when he purred the diminutive *little Sophie* into my ear.

"Tell me," he prompted.

My mind spun. "I ... you ... really want someone who ..." My words failed and my hands flopped in a vague, hapless gesture.

He pulled my hair to the side, tracing the slope of my shoulder with his thumb. "I want a girl who can trust me, who lets me take charge. A girl I can cherish and spoil."

I leaned my head back against his chest, helpless to resist.

"Close your eyes," he whispered, right above the edge of my ear.

I let out a tiny groan and obeyed.

"Do you want me to take control of you?"

"Yes," I breathed, the tiny hairs along my neck charged with his electric touch. That glorious whoosh of acceleration rushed through me, heady and strong, but then a nervous laugh bubbled out followed by my most random thought.

"It just sounds too good to be true."

I opened my eyes, sucked air through my teeth, trying to take it back and cursing my stupid mouth.

"Does it?" His hand slipped from my neck to my waist, and he pulled his body back an inch. An inch that felt like a chasm opening between us.

"Well ..." I hesitated. "Isn't that the fantasy? To be taken care of by a big, strong, handsome man?"

His low laugh filled the chasm. "Giving up control is a gift." He stroked my cheek. "A precious one. Not always easy." He pulled me snug against him again, his fingers stroking my tummy and sending the butterflies flying everywhere. "Letting someone else take control takes a different kind of strength."

I rested my hands on his, our fingers barely interlacing. His thumbs continued tracing my skin. I almost swooned at the feathery touch.

"Are you ready for another step?" He leaned in, close to my ear again. I stopped breathing.

"Yes," I whispered.

He kissed my temple and let me go, turning to go back inside. "Then it's time for bed, baby girl. Aunt Carol needs you early tomorrow. If you're good, I might have a little surprise for you after your shift."

Dazed at his abrupt change, I could only repeat one word. "Surprise?"

"Yep, but only if you behave," he said over his shoulder. "Now, go make up the couch for bed."

The couch? I was sleeping on the *couch*? What just happened? I wanted to spend the night in his bed. I stood in the doorway, blinking back my disappointment.

"See?" His rich chuckle brought my eyes to his. "It's not so easy to submit when you have other ideas." He took my hand, pulled me into a warm hug and whispered, "There's plenty of time for fun and games. Now go and do as I said." He kissed me quickly, enough to make my heartbeat double up but not offering anything further. "If you hurry, we can get a chapter or two of *A Ruthless Choice* in before lights out."

I scurried to comply, my mind churning. I wanted to argue. To complain. To pick up where we left off. But the lesson wasn't lost on me. Taking control was about more than taking me to bed. Not what I expected, but I had to admit I liked it.

14

SOPHIA

$\mathcal{I}$ was still thinking about Ethan's lesson the next day in Aunt Carol's back office when her cheerful voice broke through my thoughts. "Finishing up, Sophia?"

I stared at my notebook. There were at least a million things we needed to do to get the café up and running. Being a waitress had been hard, physical work. This was hard too, but different. Keeping track of things. Managing details. And I was starting to suspect I might actually be good at it.

"Yes, ma'am," I said as I tucked my notes in a desk drawer and joined her in the kitchen.

"Just in time," Aunt Carol said. "Ethan's here for you."

I couldn't stop the grin from expanding across my face.

"You guys look happy together," she commented, her hands tucked into the back pockets of her jeans.

"Oh," I said quickly, "I'm not sure if we're ... together."

"Well, you should check a mirror. It's written all over your face," she said kindly. "And I can't remember the last time he's looked so happy."

"He wants to take things slow." I blushed and picked at the drawstring of my cropped, black-and-white-striped pants.

"That's wise." She shifted on her feet. "But don't you worry, honey. Ethan's a good man, and I'm not only saying that because he's my son."

"It's amazing that you took them all in." I meant it, and it was a convenient way to steer the conversation away from Ethan and me.

"Those boys are our pride and joy. Joe and I were lucky to have them." Her bright blue eyes went soft when she spoke her late husband's name. No more than a moment, and then she blinked, giving me a shooing motion. "Now get out of here. Go have some fun while the sun's still shining."

I surprised myself by giving her a hug on my way out to the front of the café. She hugged me right back, warm and full of affection I didn't even know I'd been missing.

Ethan sat at the counter, one foot casually propped on the barstool's footrest, the other on the floor. A crisp black dress shirt accented his slate gray jacket and charcoal slacks, bringing out the layers of gray in his eyes and highlighting his broad shoulders. His goatee, trimmed neat and sharp, contrasted against the planes of his cheeks, and his hair in that perfect tousle smoothed into a fade. He looked like confidence and sex appeal got together and had a baby demi-god. I had competing urges to kiss him and sketch him out in graphite.

"Hey sweet girl." His full lips turned upward when he saw me. My insides whooshed up with heat like a furnace turned up to maximum. "Ready for your surprise?"

I nodded happily.

He looked over my shoulder as she pushed through the swinging door behind me. "Did she do a good job for you, Aunt Carol?"

"Are you kidding? I'd be lost without her." Aunt Carol beamed at him. "She's a real find."

"I agree." He pulled out a round, cherry red lollipop from his pocket and presented it to me like an award.

I bounced on my toes and snatched it from his hands. "Do you always carry lollipops?"

"Of course," he chuckled. "I need to know your favorite flavor."

"Cotton candy," I said without missing a beat. "But cherry is a close second." I popped the red orb of deliciousness into my mouth.

"Good to know." He tapped a finger to his temple as if tucking the information away.

Ethan put an arm around my waist and guided me to the door. A familiar song whistled strong and clear behind us.

"Guns N Roses, 'All I Need is a Little Patience'," Ethan called over his shoulder. "I hear you, Aunt Carol."

Her merry laughter mingled with the bell over the door as we left.

WE DROVE THE OTHER WAY, along the two-lane road. I chattered about working with Aunt Carol, and he listened, smiling and asking questions as if my work was the most interesting thing in the world. We stopped at a tiny gas station halfway down the mountain. Ethan hopped out to fill the tank and clean the windows while I watched him, still not quite ready to believe this fairy tale. I'd never had attention like this before.

The Bad Boyz theme rang through the front seat, interrupting my happy thoughts. It was his phone, buzzing in the center console.

"That's Hayden," Ethan called out through the window, his long arm reaching across with a squeegee to clean the windshield. "Can you answer it and tell him I'll be there in a second?"

Unease pulsed through me. Hayden, his brother. His detective brother. I tentatively picked up the phone. "Umm ... hello?"

"Hey, it's" —Hayden's voice stopped then started again— "Sophia? Is that you?"

"Yes," I said. "Ethan's ... squeegeeing." My dumb tongue struck again. "He'll be here in a second."

"Okay," Hayden sounded amused. "Actually, I wanted to talk to you too."

"Me?" I squeaked out the word, my stomach flipping. Hayden wanting to talk to me couldn't be good.

"Yeah, I wanted to ask if you saw anything unusual on the night of the club raid."

"Unusual?" My voice went choppy and weak, like someone playing a garbled note on a flute for the first time. "Like what?"

His sigh came through the phone. "It's a long shot, but I have to ask. Follow up on every possibility and all."

"Umm ... I don't—"

"A body turned up yesterday, and there's some preliminary forensic evidence connecting it to Renaissance. It could be nothing, but it might lead us somewhere. Did you witness any arguments or unruly customers that night? Anything that sticks out?"

My black denim jacket constricted around me, and I started to sweat, even though cool afternoon air blew into the car. "A body? No, I didn't see a body. I mean, there was the dentist's son. He was unruly when he grabbed me and spilled beer in my shoes, and all of that was unusual. But not sticky-outie unusual, and I don't think any of that would have anything to do with a body ..." My mouth panic-babbled and then ran dry.

Hayden stayed silent for a beat.

"It's okay if you didn't," he said finally. "I just wanted to make sure."

Ethan climbed back into the driver's seat and looked at me, puzzled. I tried to smile at him, but my face had forgotten how. "No, I'm sorry, detective. I don't know anything about that guy."

Hayden paused and made a tapping sound. An image of his notebook and pen flashed in my head. "I didn't say it was a guy."

My eyes bulged.

Oh shoot.

"I meant body. Was it a guy? I guess I assumed." I let out a half-hysterical little laugh and forced myself to stop squeezing the phone like a stress ball. "That's so sexist of me."

"Yeah," Hayden said skeptically. "Does the name Nik Vasili mean anything to you?"

"Nik Vasili means nothing to me." My voice shook. "I mean ... that name ... means nothing." What was I even saying? "I didn't see anything. Sorry, detective."

Ethan's eyes narrowed, his whole focus on me.

"Yep." Hayden blew out a resigned sigh. "I have some other news." He paused, long enough for my tummy to imitate a free-fall off a cliff. "There was another break-in at your apartment."

Oh no.

"Callie? Is she—"

"She's safe," he said quickly. "And we got a partial print this time. I should get the results later today."

I couldn't make sense of the details through my panic. "Great. That's ... so great. Umm ... thank you?" Ethan cocked his head, waiting for me to pass him the phone.

My mind raced. The police knew about the murder. Someone broke into the apartment again, and now the police had a fingerprint. Ethan said Hayden was a good detective. He would connect those dots, and I hadn't been honest. Would I be in trouble? Would they think I was hiding something? Especially after that slip about the body being a guy. What if they thought I was in on it?

And worst of all, a second break-in meant Mr. Roscoe was still very interested in finding me.

I half-handed, half-threw the phone at Ethan and stared hard out the window as he pulled out onto the road, chatting with his brother.

I couldn't follow what they were saying. Panic flashed around in my brain like a disco ball gone berserk. What should I do? What about Callie? I dashed out a quick text, but she didn't respond. It didn't even look like it was delivered.

Calm down. Hayden said she was safe.

But Mr. Roscoe knew we were roommates. How stupid was I to think she wouldn't be in danger if I didn't tell her anything? I had panicked and run away with the most ridiculous half-plan in the history of poorly-thought-out plans.

Mr. Roscoe was powerful and well-connected. He murdered

someone without batting an eye. Why wouldn't he have the same casual attitude about finding and killing some nobody waitress and her friend?

"Sophia? Hey? Where did you go?"

I jerked my head around and let a lame smile limp across my lips.

"There you are." He flipped the turn signal and switched lanes. "Thought I'd lost you?"

"I'm sorry ... I was ... wondering where we were going."

The number one rule is honesty. That's crucial.

His words seared into me, burning like hot smoke in my lungs, making it hard to breathe.

"Hayden thinks he has a lead on who attacked you," he said after a few minutes of silence. "That must be a relief?"

"Mmm, yeah, mmhmm," I mumbled.

Concern rippled across his face. "Have you thought about what you'll do when they catch him?"

More like what I'd do when they didn't catch him. Or when they figured out it wasn't a random attack.

"I don't know."

"You'd be safe," he said quietly. "You could go back to L.A."

Was that sadness in his voice? That avocado lodged itself back in my throat. This was all so new and overwhelming, and completely overshadowed by the reason I could never go back to L.A. even if I wanted to. Which I didn't.

I made a weak little scoffing sound. "And miss Aunt Carol's grand opening? Not a chance."

His smile returned, but it didn't reach his eyes. We got on the freeway, headed away from the mountain, toward the city. "Where are we going?" I asked.

He shook his head in a not-telling motion. "I think you're going to like it."

Guilt nibbled on my insides. He was trying to surprise me, and I was ruining it. There was nothing I could do about Hayden's information in the moment. I would call Callie, make sure she was safe and figure out what to do then. For the moment, I shoved it all down, tied it up with a bow and marked it with a tag that read 'To Worry About Later.'

Resolved, I reached out and rested my hand on his shoulder, comforted by his steady warmth. "I don't want to go back to L.A.," I said, inwardly pleading with my mouth not to screw this up. "And not just because of Aunt Carol's grand opening."

His lips twisted into a smile, exposing that dimple in his left cheek. "Is it the clean mountain air?"

"Well—that, and the views *are* spectacular," I added, laughing. Here was my chance. I could do this. I took a breath. "Besides, I ... think you have another step to show me?" I left my mouth slightly open and dared a glance at his eyes. They lit up like bonfires on a crisp fall night.

Amber Jade beamed her approval.

He grabbed my hand and kissed it, filling me with tingling electricity. I clamped my mouth shut. Best not to push my luck.

A SHORT TIME LATER, we pulled into a public parking lot in a vibrant and busy area with shops and restaurants lining the streets. People sat at tables on outside patios, chatting under colorful awnings.

"We're a little early." He checked his watch. "Let's get out and stretch our legs."

He opened my door and helped me out, interlacing his fingers with mine. Our hands fit together so naturally. He said he wanted someone to cherish, and that is exactly how I felt. Special. Cherished.

Incredible.

We strolled along, passing music stores, used bookstores, vintage clothing shops, and too many restaurants to count. An old man with a weary face and a striped stocking cap played a saxophone on a street corner, his eyes closed as he connected to his music. Ethan dropped money in the instrument's open case as we passed.

The city was vibrant and alive, Ethan's hand was strong and warm as he led me down the sidewalk, and for a moment the box marked 'To Worry About Later' shrunk the tiniest little bit.

That's when I saw them. I was peeking through a window of a store full of half-antiques, half-junk, emphasis on the junk. Behind the window display in a dusty crate that wasn't supposed to be for customers' eyes, two tiny heads poked out. One had greasy, straw-yellow hair, the other had none, just rows of tiny holes where hair had once been. My heart gave a familiar thump.

They need you.

"Could we ... go in here?" I rested my fingertips on the glass.

"Of course." He pulled the door open, and we entered the dim shop.

"You don't want those," the shopkeeper insisted a few minutes later, glaring at the box he had grudgingly pulled out onto the counter at Ethan's request. "You a collector? I have four Holiday Barbies, mint-in-box condition. Two '95s, a '97, and an '89. You'd like one of those much better." He was an older man, with thin, pale eyebrows that arched when he talked and a perpetually sniffy nose. He barely looked at me, but he eyeballed Ethan up and down several times.

"That's up to her," Ethan replied mildly, nodding his head toward me.

The shopkeeper tossed a look my way. "They're very pretty," he said, then looked back at Ethan. "Valuable too."

"I'm sure they are," Ethan agreed. "But she asked about those." The old man scowled at me and sniffed, his nose flaring.

I stared into the box of damaged dolls, their smudged little faces staring up with hope in their eyes. I counted at least five. One had no legs, but I could already see her in my mind, transformed with a bit of sculpting into a mermaid.

"These are trash," the shopkeeper said. "You'd be wasting your money."

I flinched at the echo of my mother's words.

"Let me get the others." He sniffed and turned away from me to limp toward the back of the shop muttering, "Never been played with. Perfect condition."

"I'm sorry," I said to Ethan, feeling ridiculous. "We can go. This is a waste of time."

He traced my cheek with the tips of his fingers. "Your face brightens every time you look at those dolls." He glanced at the box and then back to me. "I told you before, happy looks beautiful on you."

The shopkeeper returned, carrying four brightly colored boxes. "This one is very rare." He pushed one in a white dress toward us. She looked almost as sad as the broken ones, strapped down on the cardboard inside a display box.

"How much?" Ethan asked.

"On eBay? I could get one-fifty. Easy." He shifted his eyes and darted his tongue out of the corner of his mouth like a lizard. He was lying. I could tell, so I was sure Ethan could too. I was mortified to be the reason some shady shopkeeper tried to scam Ethan out of a hundred-fifty dollars. Ethan looked at his watch.

"That's too much," I said. "And I was more interested in—"

"Told you, those are trash." The man took a significant sniff and looked at me as if I were screwing up his deal. "This is the one you want."

"Thank you for your time," I squeaked out, desperate to get away from the situation. Ethan was probably annoyed. I should never have asked to come in.

"I'd love to bargain with you," Ethan replied, his voice silky, but with a hidden edge I'd never heard before. "But we have dinner plans. I was going to offer five for her if you included this box." He gestured to the box of mangled dolls.

"Five ... hundred?" spluttered the shopkeeper. His mouth twisted up into a delighted grimace. "You got yourself a—"

"But now you've insulted my girl. Repeatedly."

My heart sped up and a little shiver ran through me when he called me that.

The shopkeeper blinked, his mouth turning down into a sour frown.

"So now, the deal will be three." Ethan smiled at me, his dimple showing through his goatee.

The shopkeeper took a deep sniff and started to answer, some of the frown going away.

"For all four." Ethan pointed to the display boxed dolls. "And those." He moved his pointer finger to the broken dolls.

"All four?" the shopkeeper exclaimed, his mouth staying open in an outraged snarl. "I couldn't possibly—"

"Price just dropped to two seventy-five." Ethan cut him off and tapped his watch. "As I mentioned, we have dinner plans."

The shopkeeper glared at me, making it clear this was my fault.

Ethan gave me a sunny smile then looked back at the angry old man. "And an apology to my girl."

My heart gave another flutter.

The shopkeeper twisted his face, looking like a dog baring its teeth. "So sorry if I offended you, *miss*," he gritted out.

Ethan coolly pulled out his wallet and laid out several bills while the old man dumped the broken dolls into a large plastic bag and handed it over to me. I took it, speechless, unable to believe we were leaving with them. Ethan scooped up the four boxes and guided me to the door. A furious sniff followed us as we left the gloomy shop and emerged onto the street.

15

SOPHIA

We stopped at Ethan's SUV to drop off the dolls. I still couldn't believe he rescued them all—for me. Because he liked my face when I saw them. My heart squeezed like he'd ridden in on a white horse and scooped us all—the dolls and me—up and whisked us away to a castle in the woods.

That's kind of exactly what he did.

I couldn't resist a tiny smile at that.

The door to the restaurant proclaimed itself a 'Fine Fondue Experience' and opened into a dimly lit and cavernous expanse with exposed ceilings and rich, dark, brick walls. High-backed booths set each party apart in separate little spaces, offering coziness and privacy.

The hostess led us through a maze of rooms toward the back. A blond woman and a tall man wearing a beanie sat in the farthest booth, their backs to us as we approached. The woman laughed and flipped her hair in a way that seemed ... familiar.

I knew that flip.

"Callie?" I cried out, half-running the last few steps.

"Soap!" She swept out of the booth and entangled me in a wonderful, perfume-scented, Callie-hug that took my breath and filled my heart with pure joy.

"Callie," I said again, but it came out in a ridiculous little squeak because she was still hugging the daylights out of me.

"Take it easy, Chickadee, you'll squish her," Rook's deep voice admonished. He stood up and gave his brother a quick nod and grin, his arms folded easily over his green and black flannel covered chest.

Callie released her grip and banged her hip against me before scooting back into the big round booth. Rook slid in next to her while Ethan and I sat on the other side.

"Are you surprised?" Ethan dipped his head down to kiss my cheek, his fingers finding mine.

"I don't ... how did ...?"

"I told you two days," Callie said. "Hot detective brother told me where to find you and suggested I come up for a visit." Callie leaned up against Rook's shoulder, batting her eyelashes like a pro and earning an appreciative smirk from him. "He had this steamy double latte pick me up from the airport, and I've been in heaven ever since."

"I'm ..." My tongue twisted along with my gut. "I'm so glad you're safe."

"Hey, girl." Callie looked across the table into my face, her green eyes serious for once. "I'm right here." After a second's pause, she turned her gaze to Ethan, then to Rook. "And right here is"—she tipped her head and dropped her voice to a silly stage whisper—"seriously full of hot men."

A bubble of laughter burst out from my throat.

A waiter approached the table. "Can I get you started with something to drink? Perhaps one of our handcrafted Mojitos?"

"Talk to me about margaritas," Callie said.

"Blood orange or watermelon?" the waiter asked.

She shot a grin my way. "Watermelon?"

I nodded happily. The waiter made a note and looked to Rook and Ethan.

"Do you have Manny's?" Rook asked. The waiter smiled and nodded.

"Pinot noir," Ethan said.

At that moment, a huge, bald stranger loomed up behind the waiter, with eyes boring into us like drill bits. I shivered, clutching Ethan's arm. The waiter startled, then quickly stepped out of his way.

"Water," the big man grunted at him before shoving into our booth beside Rook, crossing his arms, and giving us all a baleful stare. The waiter scrambled away to comply.

"Hey, Griff." Rook gave the scary man a good-natured shoulder-shove as if he were an old friend. I blinked, trying to resist the urge to hide behind Ethan's shoulder.

"Sophia, Callie, this is our brother Griff." Ethan squeezed my hand reassuringly.

I squeezed back, doing my best to stifle my fear. "Um ... hi?"

Another brother. The one coming to work on the security system.

"Charmed," Callie purred to him, not in the least frightened by his size or glare. She nudged me and whispered, "They just keep getting hotter."

Griff barely nodded his bald head. Callie arched her neck at his lack of response but then did a hair flip and turned her attention back to Rook.

When the waiter returned with our drinks, I took a cautious sip and discovered watermelon margaritas tasted delicious, like a grown-up Slurpee.

I swirled the sweetness around in my mouth, then turned to Callie. "So, I still don't understand. Detective Valero told you to come?"

"Yep." Callie licked at a frozen drop of margarita that had dribbled down the side of the glass, her eyes darting to Griff, who still hadn't moved or said anything, before she looked back to me. "After the second break-in to our apartment—did you know we got hit again?"

I tried to keep my face neutral and took a bigger-than-I-meant-to gulp with none of Callie's casual finesse. "Were you hurt?" I asked.

My tummy clenched at the thought of her getting hurt because of my mess. I took another gulp, letting the frosty pink juice calm me down.

"Nah, I was at TJ and Crystal's. Nothing was taken. They just trashed the place. Like they were looking for something."

The conversation paused again while the waiter brought the first course, a cheese fondue with bits of bread and veggies and apples for dipping. He mixed the cheese together skillfully, but my mind could only focus on the break-in.

"Looking for something? Like what?" I asked when the waiter was safely gone.

"Fuck if I know." Callie dipped a bread chunk into the cheese, twirling it around then popping it in her mouth, closing her eyes and moaning as she chewed. She turned her head toward Ethan and continued. "Anyway, after that, your dashing detective brother thought me coming here would be a good idea, and I have to agree."

She threw a suggestive look to Rook, then to Griff, who leveled a stare at her that would have shriveled me like a forgotten raisin in a hot car. She just grinned, her lips watermelon glossy.

"Hayden thought Callie might be safer here for a while," Ethan explained. "Just a precaution."

"Are you running a resort or a witness protection program?" Griff growled.

"With such handsome protection, who am I to argue?" Callie squeezed Rook's arm, but her eyes locked on Griff.

Rook beamed at her and sipped his beer. "Maybe it could be part of the resort's sales pitch? Tired of dealing with stalkers? Stay with us."

Griff rolled his eyes and glowered at his brother.

Callie snickered.

"I'm so sorry, Callie." My dry throat cracked on the apology. I grabbed my drink and sucked in a frozen mouthful that caused a slight spinning sensation behind my eyes.

"You don't need to apologize to me. You didn't break in and trash our place." Callie tossed a piece of green apple drenched in cheese into her mouth. I wondered if she was even aware of her gestures anymore. Her lipstick was still perfect, despite the fondue and the lovely watermelon margarita. And she shamelessly flirted. Rook was eating it up. Griff looked increasingly infuriated, which only egged her on.

When the main course arrived, the waiter offered another round of drinks, and Callie nodded enthusiastically, pointing to our glasses. I didn't stop her. Somehow the frozen goodness and Callie, safe and sound, made things warm and fuzzy and shrunk the box marked 'To Worry About Later' even more. Ethan tapped his fingers on the table and asked the waiter to bring water for everyone as well.

The conversation bounced along, and I tried to focus, avoiding Griff's glare even though it grew harder and heavier as we ate.

"We need to discuss security." He cut Callie off mid-sentence, as if he couldn't hold it in any longer. "Your system is shit."

"Maybe we need to discuss manners," she threw back at him.

The table was silent. My nervous tummy clenched, and I took another big gulp of watermelon to diffuse the tension.

"Two hits on your apartment isn't random," Griff growled, completely ignoring Callie and turning his glare on me. "So what's the real story?"

I looked helplessly at Ethan. He rested a hand on my knee, patting it and giving Griff a dark look. "Is there cause for concern?"

"A stalker on the loose? Yeah, it's a concern." He shot another piercing look at Callie. "Even if you refuse to take it seriously."

Callie stabbed a meat bite with a fork and flicked it into the fondue pot. "Detective Hottie thinks it's Brad."

My head jerked back involuntarily, and a tiny wave of dizziness hit. Brad? Why would Hayden think it was Brad?

"Who the fuck is Brad?" Griff asked. His voice only had different levels of growl.

Callie waved another skewer at him. "A bartender from the club who's been hassling me to go out for a while now."

I grabbed for my glass, licking absently at the rim and taking another big gulp. That wasn't right? How could it have been Brad? It was the moon-faced man. Why was my head so mushy?

"Ridiculous, right?" Callie poked her long red nail at me. "Brad's a dickhole, but not ... I can totally handle him." Griff's mouth turned down into an even deeper scowl. "Whoops, I lost my meat." She stared between the community fondue pot and her empty skewer. "Hate it when that happens." She winked at Rook, who snorted and fished her steak out of the pot, dropping it on her plate with a flourish.

"Enough of this bullshit." Griff's coal dark eyes turned back on me. "Who's after you?"

My throat tightened. I shrunk in my seat, desperate to escape the glare and the question behind it.

"Easy, Griff. She's had a rough time." Ethan's face, etched with concern, only made things worse. I took another sip because I had no idea what my mouth might say if I didn't keep it busy.

"How the fuck should we know who it is?" Callie saved me by snapping at him. "And even if we did, why do we have to tell you?"

"Because Sophia was attacked, and your place has been broken into twice." Griff's eyes were daggers aimed at Callie. "And I don't believe in coincidence."

"You should. It hates me."

Oh no, did that come out of my mouth? My tongue felt numb, but it definitely sounded like my voice. My tummy started to churn unpleasantly.

"Sophia." Griff's gaze lost its sharpness and his tone softened. "I know you're scared. And maybe not telling us everything."

"Griff just wants to make sure you're safe." Ethan rolled his thumbs along my knuckles. "We all do."

"What else do you want her to say?" Callie snapped. "You're acting like this is her fault. She's the *victim* here, right Soap?" She turned to me, her face full of loyalty. Totally misguided loyalty.

I froze in fear for what my muddled mouth might say. The jig was up. The lie clear as Sharpie on my face. I opened my mouth. "I ..."

"Sophia?" Ethan's voice was warm, kind, unsuspecting.

Honesty is crucial, the number one rule.

How could I tell him he brought a liar home to Aunt Carol?

"I ..." The restaurant began to tilt and spin. Everyone at the table's eyes were on me.

My heart squeezed out a single beat, and my tummy churned again, more urgently. My eyes flicked down the aisle to the vintage signs at one end of the hall—over one door a man on a unicycle wearing a top hat, over the other a woman wearing a long Victorian dress holding a parasol.

"I ... gotta go. Excuse me." I shoved out of the booth and left the table.

ETHAN

I STARED after her as she retreated to the bathroom.

Her secret bubbled close to the surface, and she was fighting to keep it from spilling out of her. I could see it, no matter how hard she fought to keep it down.

Griff stood up. "I'm going to gather some more intel and start working on the system upgrade. Keep your girl close. Try to get her to open up." He pointed a finger at Callie, who was fishing in the fondue pot for a potato. "You. Do not leave the resort till we know what we're dealing with."

Callie let out a snort that stopped Griff in his tracks. "Uh, no, but fuck you for trying." She patted Rook's shoulder and gave him a wink. "I may stay for a while though."

I tried not to smirk. Very few people talked to Griff like that.

He glared at her, hard. "Not up for discussion."

"Look, buddy," Callie snapped back at him. "I don't know what authority you think you have, but you've been misinf—"

Griff walked away leaving her stunned and blinking rapidly. "Wow," she muttered. "That guy has issues."

Griff had that effect on people.

"Well, I guess that's dinner," Rook said after an awkward silence, patting the table and standing up. "Shame. The chocolate's my favorite part."

"Is there a cabin ready for Callie?" I glanced down to the bathroom again, worry tugging at me.

"Yeah." Rook pulled his keys from his pocket. "I got another one functional since you told me she was coming. And in case *your couch* wasn't comfy." He smirked. "The hot tub even works at this one."

"Ooh." Callie clapped her hands together.

Rook held out his hand for her. "Chickadee?"

She took it, sliding out from the booth before glancing toward the bathroom. "Maybe I should check on Soap? She seemed upset."

I shook my head. "I'll wait for her."

She nodded, still subdued from Griff's shutdown.

I watched them leave, then walked to the back of the restaurant to take care of my girl.

I knocked on the bathroom door and slowly pushed it open. I made sure no one else was inside and stepped in. Little sniffles were coming from the far stall.

I tried to focus on her and not worry yet about what had sent her running in here. Whatever it was, we would face it.

"Sophia?" The sniffles stopped. "You okay?" The sniffles started again. I walked to the stall door. Her feet and a sliver of her form were barely visible through the spaces between the partitions. "Baby, let me in."

Her voice drifted out, soft and small. "I can't."

"Yes you can. Let me in, sweet girl."

A hitch in her breath. Shuffling. The metallic sound of the lock sliding loose.

I pushed open the door.

"I threw up," she sobbed. She was kneeling on the floor next to the toilet, her eyes red, her face blotchy. She looked so lost and forlorn. I made a mental note that we should discuss drink limits once she was truly mine and we'd had a talk about rules.

"Shh. Daddy's here." It slipped out before I could catch myself.

She was too distraught to notice, and I wouldn't take it back even if she did.

She whimpered as I helped her up, holding her steady. She looked up at me in horror. "I can't go back out there."

"Let me do the worrying." I slipped off my jacket and wrapped her up in it.

"I still can't—"

"Don't think. Don't worry. Just obey." I put a little firmness in my tone to gain her compliance. She stopped talking and stared miserably at the floor. I scooped her up and cradled her in my arms, tucking her head against my shoulder.

"I ruined your surprise," she muttered into my shirt.

"Not possible," I said into her ear, pushing my way out of the stall.

She snorted. "You can't say this is how you wanted it to go."

"You're in my arms, right?"

She nodded, her dark silky hair sliding against me.

I placed a kiss on top of her head. "Then I consider it a success. Now, close your eyes." When I was sure she was sheltered, I walked briskly toward the door.

16

SOPHIA

*T*hings couldn't be much worse. I was about to be carried out of a fancy restaurant after vomiting all over their fancy bathroom. I felt humiliated, dirty, and ashamed. On top of that, a killer wanted me and my best friend dead. And I lied about it all, tossing aside all possibility of help. I lied to the cops. To Ethan. That part hurt the most. And there was nothing I could do about any of it. I dug myself so deep there wasn't any way out.

So I did as I was told, closed my eyes and tried not to think. I breathed in the clean cedar wood scent of his shoulder pressed against my nose and let him take control.

"My girl isn't feeling well. Can you bring me the bill, and can we use this side door?" His voice rumbled against me. I barely heard the worker's muffled response. "Thank you." Ethan said.

My cheeks burned, but somehow the embarrassment dulled with me hidden against his chest, wrapped in his jacket, secure in his arms.

I felt him shifting me as he pulled out his wallet and paid. Then cool spring air rushed over me. He must have opened a door and stepped outside. After a few strides across the parking lot, he stopped. I peeked out and saw his SUV. He tucked me inside and safely buckled me in before I could blink. I let myself pretend no one had even noticed.

Ethan walked around and climbed into the car. "How's your tummy?"

"Okay." I dropped my head in my hands. He must be wishing he never talked to me in that police station. "I'm so sorry, I—"

"Hush. None of that now." He handed me a bottle of water. "Drink some of this, then keep your eyes closed. We're going home. We'll clean you up. And then we're going to talk."

I took a sip, closed my eyes and rested my head against the cool glass of the window. Home. He called it home. But he also said we had to talk. What was there to say that wouldn't end in him asking me to pack up and get out?

When the car finally came to a stop and he shut off the engine, I cracked my eyes open. At least my tummy had stopped churning and my head felt less fuzzy.

"Where's Callie?" I asked when he opened my door, unbuckled me, then lifted me up in his arms again. His embrace was so warm, so safe and comforting. I couldn't help curling in against his broad chest and burying my face deeper into the folds of his jacket still draped around me. The embarrassment of being carried faded, replaced by a longing I didn't recognize.

"She's well looked after, I'm sure." He brought me into the cabin, through to the bathroom and set me gently down onto the counter, pulling his jacket up and around me before turning to the tub.

A deep, old-fashioned, copper claw-foot tub sat on a pedestal next to the shower. He turned on the water and started pouring something that smelled like tropical flowers and summer rain into the basin. The water sloshed, and bubbles began building up in white soapy peaks.

While he adjusted the water, I grabbed my toothbrush and scrubbed the taste of stress and retched-up margarita out of my mouth. Shame combined with the general awfulness of my situation, making my heart race.

I dropped my toothbrush back on the counter, swigged and spit some minty mouthwash, and forced a shaky breath.

He left the tub and stood in front of me, his gray eyes mesmerizing. "How are you feeling? Are you still woozy?"

My cheeks burned, and I dropped my head. With the alcohol buzz gone, all that remained was the humiliation. "I'm okay. I guess. I … got it out of my system."

He stroked my cheek. I leaned into it, surprised. His fingers curved around my chin and tilted it up until I looked into his eyes again.

"I'm so sorry. I ruined—"

"Shh." He tapped a finger against my mouth. "I want you to listen. Carefully. We talked about what I want. A sweet submissive girl I can take care of."

I blinked, trying to focus on his words. The humid heat from the tub made his hair curl slightly at the tips over his fade, adding to his generally tousled yet controlled look.

"I don't do casual," he added.

I wrapped my hand around his wrist, daring to connect with him, to hold onto him. What was he saying?

"So I need to know what you want." He traced his finger along my jaw, sending little electric pulses from where he touched me to the base of my spine and up through the top of my head.

"What I want?" My words came out hazy, even though I felt sober. I pressed my lips together, barely comprehending his words. He wanted to know what I wanted?

"You don't have to decide everything right now," he said. "I don't mind taking my time. But I want to take care of you. I want to undress you and bathe you and take control so you can let go." He tucked a strand of my hair behind my ear. "If I misread this, or you changed your mind, say so, and I'll leave you to your bath."

He took a half-step back, giving me the space to choose. His hands fell to his sides, and my body wilted at the loss of our connection.

This was it. He was offering me a way out. Or a way in.

He stepped over to the tub, shut off the water, then returned to me, still leaving that bit of space between us. "Tell me what you want."

Heat flushed in my tummy. I could feel my belligerent tongue tangling. He asked what I wanted, and I had no idea what nonsense might come out of my mouth.

"I ... want ..." I swallowed. Took a breath. Amber Jade hovered in the back of my mind, her eyes wide with suspense.

For once in your life, spit it out right. Say what you want.

My mouth opened, closed, opened again.

He took another step back, his posture stiffening. He dragged his fingers through his hair and squeezed the back of his neck. "I can give you time to think." His hands dropped to his sides. "This probably isn't the fairest question right now." He blew out a breath and took another step away.

A falling sensation whipped through me, as if I were plunging off a cliff, past the rope that would save me, too scared of rope burn to reach for it.

"No," I practically yelled the word. "You," I added unhelpfully.

He tipped his head, waiting for clearer words, the gold flecks in his cashmere eyes glowing.

"I don't ... You, I mean ..." My eyes widened in horror at how badly my tongue was betraying me. "I don't need time to think." I gasped out the words, watching his face as he tried to understand my babbling. He looked wary, but he waited.

"You." I tried again. "I want you ... to take control." I shivered at my admission, but it was true.

He took a big breath, his face brightening, his lips relaxing into a smile full of sunshine. Then his arms wrapped around me, and he leaned in. His fingers traced the dampness of my hairline in the steamy bathroom, found the edge of my jaw, and tipped my face up to him.

He kissed me, slow and sure, taking charge, not letting me go, pushing me for more. I slid my arms around his neck and let him pull me off the counter and guide me to the tub, reveling in the velvety texture of his lips claiming mine, even as the scruff of his goatee tickled my chin.

"I want you too." His words were a whisper as he tugged his jacket off my shoulders, then my jean jacket, dropping it next to his on the floor. He pulled my tank top up and over my head, finally breaking the kiss as he tossed it aside. "Take off your bra."

I took a shaky breath, revisiting every critical thought I ever had about my boobs all at once.

"Don't think. Do as I say." His words soothed my fears. I took another breath, unhooked the clasp, and dropped the bra to the ground. I wrapped my arms around my chest, trying to prolong the moment before facing his judgment.

"Hands down by your sides."

"I'm sorry," I mumbled then dropped my arms. He could probably see my heart beating through my chest, it was thumping so hard.

"You're gorgeous." He rested his hands on my hips, slipping his fingers into the waistband of my pants. I sucked in a breath and my tummy clenched as he slid them down the length of my legs, slowly, gently.

I stepped out of them, wiggling my toes and noticing I needed a pedicure. I scrunched them up, trying not to fidget as he stared at me.

"Take off your panties."

I moved my hands slowly to the simple black underwear I wore. When I removed them, and stood bare before him, something settled in my heart. I told him I wanted him to take control, and he had. He commanded, and I obeyed.

He looked at every inch of me, laser focused, taking me in. "You're fucking perfect." He undid the first button of his dress shirt, its fabric starting to cling to him in the humid air.

"Get in the tub."

Two quick steps and I was sinking down into the delicious, soapy mountains. The tropical-scented steam enveloped me, and my body relaxed.

"Good girl."

I basked in the praise, even as I pulled the bubbles around me protectively. He scooped up a handful and playfully dolloped my nose before wiping it clear. The nightmare of the past few hours faded away.

He rolled up his shirt sleeves, and I savored his tan, muscular forearms and the tiny blond hairs highlighting their shape as they flexed. He grabbed a washcloth and started scrubbing large, slow circles on my back.

"Does that feel good?"

"God yes." I let my head hang forward, giving myself up to the heavenly bath.

"Sweet little Sophie. I want to take care of you."

The avocado lump formed fast in my throat, taking me by surprise. I wrapped my arms around my knees and forced a swallow that made me grunt in pain.

"Does this hurt?" He paused in the circles, his voice concerned.

"No." A small laugh worked its way out, making the lump throb even more. "It's just ... I really like it when you call me 'little Sophie.' That's so stupid, but I can't help it."

"It's not stupid." He tipped my head back and poured warm water over my hair, shielding my face from the splash. Tingles spread across my scalp, and I let out a guttural sigh.

"Know what I like?" he asked.

I shook my head, leaning my chin carefully on my arms and flexing my toes in ecstasy while he massaged shampoo into my scalp. "I like calling you *my* sweet little Sophie."

My heart thumped. A brave thought popped into my head. "But what should I call you?" When I heard it out loud, I immediately regretted it. Still ... he said something earlier that I couldn't get out of my head.

His fingers trailed down through my hair to trace the lines of my neck. "What do you want to call me?"

"At the restaurant ... you said ..." I stopped. I had been in the middle of a breakdown. Even if I had heard right, I was a grown woman. He wouldn't want me to call him—

"I said 'Daddy's here,'" he said. No hesitation.

A little sigh snuck out of me, and I dropped my hands into the water with a sploosh. Suddenly it all made sense. He wanted to take care of someone, to cherish them. I'd read a book like that, my heart swooning at the words, but I never imagined I would meet a man like that in real life. "Is that ... what you want?"

The warm air of his breath raised goosebumps on my wet shoulders as he leaned in close to my ear. "That's a title with a lot of meaning to me. You should only use it if you mean it." He rinsed the shampoo away, running his hands through my hair along with the stream of warm water.

"But yes, my little Sophie, I would love it if you called me Daddy."

I clutched the locket around my neck. What he said should feel impossible, but it didn't. It was overpowering and decadent and so right and real.

"Tell me about that." He traced the chain along the back of my neck. "Who gave it to you?"

I tapped my teeth together, considering. He'd think I was pathetic. Or worse.

"Your father?" he prompted. "Are you two close?"

I snorted. "I didn't ... my ... father ..." the last word caught in my throat. I looked at him, miserable in my battle to speak.

He rubbed his chin for a second, then stood up. "I have an idea. I'll be right back."

When he left, I squeezed my arms around my body, trying to process the last few minutes. So much could go wrong with this. So much could humiliate me and dash my heart to pieces. And that was before I factored in my bigger problems. They were practically a guarantee this whole thing would end badly.

But holy crickets, I didn't care. My whole body was thrumming with delicious hunger, and I wanted this ... wanted *him*, more than I ever wanted anything. If I didn't take this chance, I would regret it forever. Letting him take control already felt worth all the inevitable embarrassment and pain.

Could I take the next step? Could I be brave and claim what I desperately wanted? I might spend the rest of my life humiliated and alone, but being his sweet little Sophie would be worth it, even if only for one unforgettable day.

I was going to do this.

He returned holding something red and ruffled.

"Sometimes, when you have something difficult to say," he said, easing himself back down next to the tub. "It's easier to say it to a friendly face. A face that will listen with no possibility of judgment. A face who might even be grateful to you."

He handed me one of the Holiday Barbies, freed from her box and looking ready for a gala event in her red-and-gold plaid dress. "She looks happy to be out of that box, wouldn't you say?"

I took her with one hand, turning my body in the tub to stare at him. "But I'll mess up her dress with my wet hands ... and she's not as valuable out of the box," I protested, the grouchy shopkeeper's disdain ringing in my ears.

"Do you care about that?" he asked.

I shook my head hard back and forth, my wet hair slapping softly against my neck. It had nothing to do with money for me.

"Then I certainly don't."

I stared at the doll, then at him, afraid my heart might actually crack open and melt into a puddle. He grabbed the washcloth again. "Do you have a name for her?"

A silly thought popped into my head, but somehow, in this small, steamy space, it made perfect sense. "Ruthie?"

"Oh?" He chuckled, eyes twinkling. "You mean the brave young heiress, Ruthie Luddington? Currently tied up in the captain's quarters awaiting her punishment in *A Ruthless Choice*?"

I giggled.

"That's a great name. If anyone can relate to challenges from her past, it's Ruthie." He settled back into scrubbing my shoulders. "Now, tell Ruthie about your locket."

I took a deep breath and looked at the doll. My tongue relaxed. "Well, Ruthie, ever since I was little, my parents ... my father especially ..." I paused, resisting the memories. I didn't feel silly talking to a doll in front of him, but I did feel the pinpricks of pain my childhood always brought back.

I took another breath. "Well, he had expectations. He's a professor. So is my mom. Their kids were supposed to be prodigies. But ... I was a daydreamer. I rescued dolls and didn't really like school. He was disappointed. They both were."

I propped Ruthie up on a low shelf next to the tub and swirled my fingers around in the bubbles, breathing in their sweet scent and staring into her bright eyes. I was already planning how to give her a more spirited expression, more suited to a pirate wench.

"Keep going, baby," he said, his voice so low I barely heard him.

I sighed. "It got worse when they found out I would be the only child they could have. I don't know the details. I was maybe six or seven? But I remember them arguing, and him saying they wasted their chance on me."

Ethan sucked in a breath. His hands stopped rubbing. They rested lightly on my shoulders.

"I tried to be what they wanted. But I wasn't great at school. He took all my toys, my dolls ..." The avocado shifted in my throat. "Said I could earn them back with good grades, but they were never good enough."

I picked Ruthie up again, plucking the little plastic strings from the packaging in her box out of her hair. "*I* was never good enough."

I blinked hard and continued. "He's written six books on genetic engineering, which is impressive, I guess. My mom's a board chair for a behavioral neuroscience center. Eventually they stopped hoping I'd ever be anything they could be proud of."

I sighed. I hadn't even gotten to the locket. "You're a good listener, Ruthie. I'm sorry this is so depressing." I set her back down and dropped my forehead onto my knees.

Ethan reached around and took my hand, stroking the palm then kissing each finger. When I finally looked up at him, he said, "Your fingers are like prunes, baby girl."

I looked at the swollen ridges in my fingertips.

He pulled me to my feet, wrapped me up in a towel and helped me out of the tub, an arm slipping around my shoulders. "Your parents are fools," he whispered into my ear. "I don't care how smart they are."

The avocado in my throat doubled in size, and I burrowed down into his embrace. He lifted me into his arms, carried me up the stairs to the loft, and laid me down on his bed.

I should have been nervous, stammering, awkward, but I wasn't. "Am I sleeping on the couch tonight?"

He sat down, reaching for me, and his thumb grazed my bottom lip. "We can sleep on the couch or in my bed, but I'm not sleeping without you again."

Happiness poured over me, and I watched, wide-eyed but unafraid, as he stood up and undressed for me. His abs flexed as he unbuttoned his shirt and slipped it off, then pulled off his belt with a swishing sound. Shirtless, in dark gray dress pants, he looked even more gorgeous. His body came together at exactly the right angles, strong and sinuous, his abs well-muscled, his waist tapering to a sinful promise below.

I blushed and looked away when he took down his pants, a giddy shyness making me cover my eyes, but not before I saw his black silk boxer briefs. They rode his hips superbly, and I couldn't help licking my lips.

Beyond his raw sex appeal, though, something else made my lower parts heat. The pain of talking about my past, the embarrassment at the restaurant, even the fear about the secrets I still kept, all felt smaller around him.

He made it easy for me to just be. He took me seriously, gave me space to be myself, no matter how silly or ridiculous. I guess Ruthie wasn't the only one he released from a display box.

And those forbidden-sounding words, the ones I only ever read in books, woke something up inside me that definitely wanted to come out and play.

Call it Amber Jade, call it whatever you want. Something new unfurled inside me, reaching out a hesitant tendril to his awaiting touch.

I'd love it if you called me Daddy.

The more that echoed in my mind, the more I admitted that I might love it too.

17

ETHAN

When she asked me, with such a mix of innocence and hunger, about sleeping on the couch, my control seriously wavered.

Images of taking her straight to my bed, spreading her open, and showing her just how much I wanted her to call me Daddy flew through my mind. She asked me to take control, and that lit me up in a deep and primal way.

But I wanted to do this right. Desire for her had been building ever since I saw those gorgeous espresso eyes at the police station. But this sense of investment was new. Sophia was beautiful, and absolutely perfect for me, but she was also tender and needed me in a way that no one else ever had. She was real.

She'd been through a lot. I burned to protect her, but I needed to maintain control. The guy in me wanted to dive in and explore every inch of her delicious body on the spot, but the Daddy in me knew I couldn't do that when she was still so vulnerable.

She hadn't said where that locket she clutched came from, and I was pretty sure it wasn't her fucking neglectful father. But when she asked about calling me Daddy, besides sending me over the edge with desire, it also told me there hadn't been a Daddy in her life before me.

She was still holding back about the attack in L.A. too. I needed a lot more info on that. I needed to build her trust. Show her she could tell me what happened. Show her she didn't have to carry it alone.

She shifted slightly on the bed, pulling her legs up and squirming under her towel. I watched her, enjoying the view.

"I'm naked," she whispered, sucking a corner of her bottom lip under the edge of her teeth.

"You're perfect," I whispered back. I wanted to peel the towel away and have her truly naked. I wanted to touch her skin and kiss the perfect breasts she trusted me enough to show when getting into the bath, but I wasn't going to rush her.

She smiled at the compliment, her eyes taking a quick trip up and down my body. She gasped when she saw my dick's reaction to her nakedness.

"See?" I said.

She let out her cute little hiccuppy laugh and turned away, cheeks pink. "Are we going to ..." She squirmed as her words failed her.

"I have some questions that need answers." I paused, studying her. "But there's time. We can take another step if you're ready."

She looked up at me with those rich, dark eyes, the beginnings of trust lighting a fire. "I am."

If she was ready to follow, I needed to be ready to lead. "Good girl, show me."

Her brow furrowed; her eyes blinked as she thought through my request. She plucked at the towel's edge, teetering on the edge of a decision. "It's wet."

"Sounds uncomfortable," I answered. I held out a hand to take it if she was ready.

She wiggled on the bed, opened her mouth, drew a big breath, and pulled the towel away, putting it in my hand. I tossed it aside and soaked her in, memorizing the arch of her knees and the slope of her calves.

"So fucking perfect," I murmured, the sight of her laid out on my bed heating my desire to a fever.

Her legs were long and slightly askew, her toes clenched. Because she was on her back, her stomach dipped flat, the little curves accentuating her hip bones, and her breasts rested heavily over her near-panting chest.

I dropped my knee onto the bed beside her, forcing myself to move slowly, easing next to her. "I want to touch you."

She sucked in the corner of her lip and bit down with her pretty little white teeth. Her head nodded. Her eyes watched every move I made. I stretched onto my side and propped up my head with my hand. I stroked her cheek. She pushed it against me, her skin soft, seeking my touch.

"Close your eyes," I instructed. She pressed her eyes closed tightly, scrunching up her nose.

So cute.

I dragged my fingers across her furrowed little brow, pressing gently against the ridges. "Relax."

She inhaled deeply, her hands fidgeting at her sides before going still, her face relaxing.

"That's better," I crooned. "Now, tell me what feels good."

"That feels good," she mumbled as I drew my hand down from her face to trace along her collarbone and down her arm. I made the strokes feather light, so she had to concentrate to stay connected.

I eased my hand onto her stomach, two fingers tracing the bottom edge of her breasts, loving that smooth curve. The tingling sensation against my fingertips as I stroked her skin made my dick harder than I thought possible. She whimpered then arched her back.

When I found her hip, she let out a soft little moan. Her knees pressed together, so I leaned down and kissed her neck, whispering, "Let me in, baby girl."

Her legs relaxed apart, and my fingers crossed her thigh, sliding downwards. "Do you like that?" I murmured.

"Mmm," she hummed in answer.

"Tell me." My finger found her sensitive skin, teasing her open, tracing her folds, slick and soft. "Tell me what you want."

"I ... I want ..." she squeaked, and her eyes scrunched tight.

I kissed the furrows of her brow till they eased again. "Breathe. Remember your safeword. You control this."

She nodded, her eyes opening. I fell into their depths, overcome with the need I saw there. Overcome with the matching need brewing inside my chest. The need to protect her, to claim her, to make her mine.

"Do you want me to keep going?" My hand lingered at the edge of her sweet little pussy.

"Yes," she gasped. "Please ..." Her mouth stayed open like she had more to say, but the only other sound she made was a delicious little moan.

"That's my good girl." I pushed forward, sliding my finger in, mapping her, learning the first secret her body shared with me. I found her clit and teased her, making lazy circles.

"I like that." She groaned and opened her legs a little wider.

"I can tell," I murmured, loving how responsive she was to my touch.

"No. I mean ... I do, like that too, but I like ... I want to be ... your good girl."

"Daddy's good girl?" I bit the bare edge of her ear, teasing her, testing her.

"Yes." She gulped, turning her head and seeking my mouth with hers. Her kiss a plea for more. Her lips velvet soft and pliant. Her words made my already-straining cock even harder against her leg.

I sped up my hand, pushing a finger in deeper, then adding another, stretching her, stroking her from the inside, learning the places that made her squirm. She gasped, releasing the breath she'd been holding, her legs sliding down and her arms lifting up on their own over her head. It was intoxicating how naturally she submitted to my touch.

I kissed the round of her breast, tasting her sweetness, dragging my tongue around in a slowly closing circle until it found the hard tip of her nipple. She hitched in a breath, and I thought she might pull back, but instead she arched toward me, pushing the little peak farther into my eager mouth. I sucked it in, pulling it taut, stroking it with my tongue. I kept up a steady pattern with my fingers inside her, building the intensity, taking her higher.

My heart pounded, and my hip pressed into the mattress as I rolled toward her, wanting to touch her with every inch of my skin. Her silky folds were tight around my fingers, sending zaps of electricity down my arm and straight to my balls as I imagined what she would feel like around my cock.

Her hips rocked with me, no longer hesitating, greedy with need. As sensation consumed her, she let her doubt go, her body taking over, sharing her true desire with me. Gorgeous, hungry sounds hitched out of her throat, and her long eyelashes fluttered.

I pulled my mouth away from her nipple. "Keep your eyes closed." She bit her lip again in adorable frustration.

I leaned in, sucking it free from her teeth, and caging it with mine, biting slightly then easing into a sweet kiss. I wanted to taste her as she gave in to me, to drink in that moment she truly let go. "Are you ready?" I whispered against her lips.

She nodded, the movement almost frantic. Her toes clenched tight in anticipation. Her legs vibrated with need against my leg, sending shivers through my body. The velvet-soft walls of her pussy began to squeeze around me, forcing my control to its limits.

My fingers moved faster, finding her rhythm, pushing her over her edge.

I leaned in to nuzzle just between her hairline and the back of her ear, breathing in the sweet scent of her. "Come for me, baby girl. Come for Daddy."

She bucked up against my hand, her tight body gripping me, her hips thrashing and her pussy pulsing hot and wet around my fingers. My dick throbbed hard as she rolled toward my body, pressing her chest against me. Her gasping and groaning louder and even more delicious than I expected before finally trailing off into a sigh of relief.

Fucking incredible.

I kissed her again, my tongue pressing her lips open. I pulled back to watch her as I brought my fingers up from her pussy and pushed them gently into her mouth. She opened her eyes and stared up at me before starting to suck. My dick pounded, thick against her bare skin, the thin material of my briefs the only thing between us. I took a ragged breath then kissed her hard, tasting her sweetness smeared across her lips, breathing in her scent.

"Daddy loves your taste," I whispered.

"You do?" she whispered back.

I nodded, her acceptance of my title flushing me with heat. "Next time, I'm going to use my tongue."

"Next time?" she asked in that soft bedroom voice that threatened my thin layer of composure. "But what about ..." Her cheeks turned my favorite shade of pink again, but she pressed tight against my hardness between us.

"Me?" I asked, my brow hitched.

She twisted her face into my chest then peeked back up, her damp hair rustling as she bobbed her head in a nod.

If she only knew how tempting that was. But the controlled part of me, the Daddy that knew she needed to take one step at a time, cooled my thoughts. "You don't worry about that. I'm in charge and now it's time for you to sleep." I kissed her forehead and stood up, tucking her into the blankets.

She stared up at me, resisting the sleepy relaxation taking her. "Are you coming back?"

"I'm going for a quick shower before bed." A shower that would involve me jerking off hard to the image of her body writhing and squeezing my hand between her legs.

"Okay," she mumbled and closed her eyes.

"Good night, baby."

"Good night ... Daddy."

I sucked in a breath at the word coming from her mouth, soft and half-asleep. My dick throbbed, making the shower even more impera- tive, but at the same time, an unnamed need settled inside me. A sense of contentment with this sweet girl falling asleep in my bed. Everything about her cried out for nurturing and love. And every-thing in me wanted to give her just that.

18

SOPHIA

Murmuring voices and the sounds of movement downstairs pulled me from sleep. I blinked, scrunching my eyes closed against the morning light. I stretched my legs, reaching my arms over my head. I was in his bed. Alone.

The memory of him still lingered. Wrapped around me, holding me close. He came back, just like he said he would, fresh from a shower in another pair of black boxers, his hair damp and still perfectly tousled. I hadn't been quite asleep, so he tucked me in with Ruthie, read a chapter of *A Ruthless Choice*, then slept next to me all night, holding me, shifting with my movements, with no expectations beyond a few nuzzles to my neck. No whips, no chains. Nothing scary or embarrassing. Just him taking care of me.

Part of me had wished for more. Amber Jade pouted about when we would move past cuddling and get to the good stuff. Although she was very pleased with him touching me in all the right places last night.

Good night ... Daddy.

I said those words. And I wasn't embarrassed. I was excited. I felt ... special. Treasured. It felt as easy as taking a deep cleansing breath.

"System still uses VCR's for fuck's sake." A deep, angry, growly voice floated up to the open loft bedroom from the kitchen below.

Griff, the scary brother. I sat up in bed, straining to hear.

Kitchen noises muffled Ethan's response. Cabinets opened and closed and something metallic kept clanging against something else.

"—could follow her here." Griff's admonishment was sharp.

I flinched. Oh no. Griff was talking about me. I brought all this trouble right to their doorstep. I tugged the top blanket around me and crept to the stairs at the edge of the landing so I could hear a little better.

"Whatever it is, she's really scared." Ethan's concern made a bubble rise in my tummy, both warm and painful at the same time. "Did Hayden tell you—"

I missed the rest thanks to more shuffling and the coffee pot's cheerful gurgle.

I slid down another step.

Something sounded like a mug sliding across the counter as Griff sighed. "It's going to be bad."

A spoon stirring, the fridge opening.

I risked going down another step.

"You need to—" The fridge slammed shut so I missed Griff's suggestion. The sound of a fork whipping eggs in a bowl made it indistinct. I only caught the end.

"—brat in need of a hard spanking if you ask me. Then she might start taking this seriously."

Ugh. The criticism stung, but it also rang true. How had I thought I could run away up here and not tell anyone that a hardened criminal wanted me dead? Why hadn't I told the police? How could I have been so stupid?

I pulled up my feet, the need to get away driving me back up the stairs. Twisting around on the step and standing up at the same time tweaked my balance. I tripped on a trailing corner of the blanket and fell upward, grabbing the railing and managing to hoist myself ungracefully back to the top step.

Noisily.

I stood, heart pounding, hands clutching the blanket around my naked body, frozen, listening to the sudden silence coming from the kitchen.

"Sophia?" Ethan sounded concerned.

I scrunched my eyes closed. "Umm ... I'm okay. A ... blanket tripped me."

"Be careful, blankets can be unpredictable." His chuckle resonated up the open stairs. Why did I love that sound so much? "Breakfast is about ready. Come down and eat."

"I'm ... not dressed." I looked desperately around, but my clothes were still downstairs in my bags by the couch. Great. I just broadcasted my nudity to big, scary Griff. The man who called me a brat in need of a spanking and didn't think I was taking this seriously. Now he knew I was dancing around upstairs naked in a blanket.

"Sounds like you've got your hands full," Griff's voice echoed up the stairs. A chair scraped, and his heavy boots thudded across the kitchen. "Thanks for the coffee."

I let out a tiny, relieved breath when the front door closed. At least Griff was gone.

But he was right. I should take this seriously and have a conversation with Ethan. Tell him everything. Give him the chance to back out of whatever we started last night. He didn't need me and my problems while trying to get this resort up and running. I could move back in with my parents, go back to school. Admit that I had no business being on my own. Do what I should have done from the beginning.

The creaking staircase made me spin around, the blanket whirling out around me like a superhero cape.

"Need help taming that blanket?" He stood on the second step from the top, looking like an underwear model, shirtless, in black pajama bottoms, the tight lines of his bare chest sculpted like a perfect work of art. Like a giant piece of man candy that I wanted to taste.

All the *shoulds* in my head fell silent while I admired his sleek abs, his bed-tousled, sandy hair, and his utterly kissable dimple flexing as he grinned up at me.

When I told him the truth, all this would be over. Was I being a brat, not taking things seriously because I wanted a few more minutes before this all disappeared?

That new, tiny rebellious spark inside me shook its head.

No.

He took the final step into the loft, crossed the room, and lifted the edges of my blanket like a net, ensnaring me and tugging me into his arms. "Are you hungry?" His voice was a low, sexy grumble in my ear.

I was, but not for breakfast. I reached up to touch his rough cheek, the sharp stubble sending sparks through my fingertips. He nuzzled against my neck, and I saw fireworks behind my eyes.

"I'm not ... I'm hungry, but ..." There went my mouth again, screwing it all up. Saying something embarrassing. Ruining this moment that might be our last.

But the moment didn't really belong to me, did it? I needed to tell him the truth. "I ... can't." I dropped my hand to his chest, half-caressing and half-pushing him away.

His muscles flexed as he shifted, still holding me but giving me room. The look in his eyes cooled from desire to concern.

"What is it?" He let go of the blanket, and I stepped back, hating the space spreading between us. "Have you changed your mind?"

"No ... I ... you might."

He took a step toward me. "Talk to me baby girl. Want me to get Ruthie?"

I blew out a sad huff of air and pressed my fingers to my forehead, straining for words that didn't want to come. If only Ruthie could solve this problem.

I needed to say it.

Tell him.

Rip off the Band-Aid.

"Griff sounded angry ..." I trailed off. God, I was such a coward.

"Griff?" He sounded relieved. "Did he scare you? There's nothing to fear from him, even if he does come off like a surly prick most of the time. He wants you to be safe. I do too."

I pulled the blanket tight around me. This was impossible. "I'm sorry."

He frowned. "Why are you sorry? What is it you think you need to apologize for?" He took my hand. "None of this is your fault."

I jerked away, frustrated. If only that were true.

"I should get dressed," I said miserably, walking past him to the head of the stairs and looking down over the railing to the cabin below, full of morning sun even though my heart felt gray.

He let out a heavy sigh and stepped over to the dresser to pull out a crisp white T-shirt. "I'll meet you in the kitchen. You need to eat your breakfast before it gets cold."

He pulled the shirt over his head and turned away. I bit the inside of my cheek to keep from crying and padded my way down the stairs, blanket trailing behind me, still like a cape but not at all heroic.

ETHAN

I POURED juice into her glass and set it next to her plate. She poked aimlessly at the eggs with her fork. Even pouting, in denim shorts and a tight blue T-shirt with a smiling rainbow heart emblazoned across her breasts, she took my breath away. Her hair was up in a ponytail, and if I wasn't so concerned with her mood, I'd suggest we go into town to find a ribbon to tie around it.

But I was concerned.

At first, I thought she changed her mind. Maybe she decided she liked reading about Daddies but having one in real life was too much.

But she'd said no when I asked, and here she was, dressed even more like a Little.

She asked about Griff. Maybe she was scared about the possibility of somebody being after her. So why couldn't she tell me that? She had opened up about her parents. What was holding her back?

"Do you not like eggs?" I asked.

"Oh. No. They're really good." Her voice was flat as she stabbed a bite and dragged it around the plate, letting three-quarters of the food break off before bringing a minuscule bite slowly to her mouth. "I'm sorry."

She forced the remnant between her teeth and started chewing.

Sorry. Always sorry.

"Look at me," I said. Her head snapped up at the firmness in my tone, her eyes a combination of wariness and heat. I held her gaze. "Give me your fork."

"Wh-what?"

"You heard me, young lady. Give me your fork."

She handed me the fork immediately. If I'd been wrong about her Little side, she would have told me to fuck off.

She didn't.

"If you won't eat like a big girl, Daddy will feed you."

She stared at me for a moment, gauging my seriousness. Her eyes dropped to the plate. "I'm sorry. I shouldn't be wasteful."

"Three bites." I pulled the plate over and broke off a small chunk of egg. I held the fork up to her mouth.

"You don't have to—"

"Are you arguing?"

"No," she whispered, her eyes going wide, her bottom lip sucking in under her teeth.

"No what?" I pushed her a little further.

"No, Daddy."

"Good girl." I kept my face serious. "Now open your mouth."

Her breath hitched, but she complied, sitting up straighter and leaning in slightly.

I slid the fork in, then let her chew while I set up another bite. "Open."

She took the second bite.

"Good. One more. Open for Daddy."

She took the last bite with more enthusiasm than before, a faint, almost hopeful smile curling her lips as she swallowed the last morsel.

"Very good. Put your dishes away. Then come into the living room. It's time Sophie and Daddy had a little chat."

19

SOPHIA

I slid the plate into the dishwasher rack like it had been the most normal breakfast in the world. From the outside, no one would guess anything life-changing happened. But inside, my body snapped and sparked. When I'd called him Daddy again—no, when he had *commanded* me to call him Daddy—something inside me clicked firmly into place.

"Sophia," he called from the living room, his voice sharp.

I hustled out of the kitchen to obey, a flutter starting in my tummy. "Y-yes ... Daddy?" It felt more right each time I said it.

He was sitting in the big, rounded chair next to the couch. "Right here. On your knees." He pointed to the floor in front of him.

I had knelt there once before, but then he'd been teasing. Playing with me. Now he was serious. And my whole body vibrated with the thrill of it.

"We need to talk, don't we, little Sophie?"

My pet name usually gave me happy bubbles, but this time it filled me with fear and heat. "Yes, Daddy."

"Do you remember your safeword?"

I nodded, stepping toward him and slipping to my knees. He had changed from pajama bottoms into well-fitting black khakis and a dark gray Henley over the white T-shirt.

"And you understand how to use it?" He rested his hands open on his knees, his fingers beckoning to mine.

I nodded again, laying my hands in his.

"What did Daddy say was the most important thing for a relationship like this?"

"Honesty." The dreaded word felt like ash on my tongue.

"That's right." His words cut like knives piercing my heart. "Trust can't grow around secrets. And you have some secrets you're scared to tell me."

My breath caught. I shifted on my knees, wishing he wasn't right, but knowing he was.

"You can tell Daddy *anything*. But you have to take a leap of faith. That's your lesson."

He rubbed his thumbs along the edges of my palms. Waiting. This was not how I imagined my confession would go.

"What would you like to do?" he asked.

"I ... want to tell you the truth." My heart galloped, a wild animal in the throes of fear and hope and something like ecstasy all at once.

"I'm listening."

My mouth opened.

I took a breath.

And told him everything.

I poured out my whole heart on my knees before him. About the murder. About lying to the police, lying to him. About hoping to escape my problems, and how, by not telling anyone, I'd put Callie in danger.

He said nothing, only listened.

When I finished, I took a deep breath and dared to glance up at his face. "So, now you understand. I'm so, so sorry, Da—Ethan."

This time with him had been amazing; nothing had ever been so right in my life. But now he knew the truth, so I forced myself to break that habit before it started.

He didn't correct me.

I understood why, but I wasn't prepared for how bad it hurt.

"Stand up."

I did, my hands sliding away and down to my sides. My nose started to sting, and I squeezed my fists closed at my sides, determined not to cry. My eyes drifted over to my still-packed bags. "I'll get my—"

"Why are you sorry?"

The question took me by surprise. When he didn't elaborate, I tilted my head. Had he not been listening after all?

"Well, I told you everything and ..." I lifted my shoulders in a miserable shrug.

"Is it better, with no secrets between us?"

"It is." Even though it would hurt to leave, I did feel better.

"Now, *why* are you sorry? In all of that, what did you do wrong?"

Oh.

My brain picked through it all, trying to find the answer he wanted.

"Well, I lied. I mean, I wasn't completely truthful to Hayden."

He nodded, one finger tapping on his knee.

"And I wasn't truthful to you either," I continued. That one hurt a lot to say. "Or Callie, so now she's mixed up in it too."

Why was he making me say it like this? It sounded so awful.

"And did keeping it secret make things better?"

"No," I croaked, the avocado in all its glory clogging my throat. "It only made things worse."

"What should we do about it?" He leaned back and folded his fingers loosely together, pulling them apart then back together in thought.

I blinked hard, dropping my eyes from the motion of his hands to the rounded white toe tips of my Converse. He wanted me to set things right before I left. I could do that.

"I'll tell Hayden everything ... and I can"—I tried to swallow down the lump, but it only got bigger— "call my ... p-parents and go back home. If I agree to go back to school, they might let me—"

"No, my sweet Sophie, you misunderstand." He shifted slightly on the chair, his knees coming together, his muscular thighs flexing under the fabric of his black pants. He held out a hand to me. "Your place is here. With me."

My head jerked up, and I stared at his outstretched hand. I took it like I was in a dream, my skin tingling as our fingers laced together.

"And we can deal with what you saw together." He leaned forward, his eyes locked on mine. "We can talk to Hayden and make sure this bastard goes away forever so he can never hurt you again." Then he patted his lap, slowly and deliberately, his brow furrowing. "I meant, what should we do about your misbehavior?"

This stern side of him heated my insides despite all my guilt. "My ... misbehavior?"

A passage from *A Ruthless Choice* popped into my head. Ruthie, confessing her plans to steal Captain John Harlow's logbook in an escape attempt. He told her he would deal with her misbehavior by turning her over his knee for a thrashing. A thrilled little snake of excitement and fear slithered through my tummy and then slipped lower.

But then Griff's words rang in my head, and the feeling cooled. "Is this because Griff thought I was a brat, and I wasn't taking this seriously?"

"Griff?" He leaned back again, looking confused for a moment, then his lips quirked up, his eyes crinkled in amusement. "Griff was talking about ... someone else. And now we need to add eavesdropping to your list."

Oh shoot.

My cheeks burned. "I'm so sorry." I hated the words. Their empty familiarity.

"Exactly." He pointed for emphasis. "And you carry that guilt around like a bag of bowling balls around your neck. It's my job to help you with that."

It was? I turned the idea over in my head. How was that possible?

"Pull down your shorts."

The little thrill spread through me like watercolors. Holy crickets. He was going to spank me. Just like Ruthie in my book.

Except this was really happening.

"Do as Daddy says," he encouraged.

I unbuttoned and unzipped like I was dreaming, hyper aware of little details. The tickle of denim strings as my shorts slipped down my thighs, the smell of coffee lingering from breakfast, a bird outside warbling a happy chirp as if I weren't standing here in my underwear about to submit to a real live spanking.

"Panties too."

Holy Toledo.

Another detail flashed in my mind—the wetness of those panties, which would be obvious when I dropped them. Tremors ran through me, and that little rebellious little voice inside whispered a thrilling thought.

So what if he sees?

The memory of him pushing his fingers, still wet from making me come, inside my mouth ... then kissing me, shimmered in my mind.

I shoved the white cotton eyelet panties down in a rush, before my courage could fail me. The air found my bareness, increasing the sensation of vulnerability and exposure.

He patted his lap once more, and I shuffled the step and a half that separated us. The restriction of my shorts and panties wrapped around my ankles heightened my arousal.

I took his hand, and in one quick movement he laid me across his thighs, my head down, hands holding his leg for support, feet crossed nervously together, panties and shorts dangling, and my butt ... well, it ended up front and center on his lap.

He rested a hand on my back, which was strangely comforting. "Now, what did you do wrong?"

I recited the list again, staring at the rustic pattern on the thick rug beneath me.

His fingers traced my spine. "Don't forget the eavesdropping."

I shivered, suddenly aware of his hardness pressed against my belly.

"And eavesdropping," I added, my voice barely a whisper.

"What's the most important thing in our relationship?"

"Honesty." I wobbled on his thighs, the word coming out choppy as I shifted and clenched my hands tighter around his calf, my heart pounding so hard it might break out of my chest.

"Good girl," he said as he steadied me. "Now let's clear the slate."

I focused on the exposure of my bare behind, so vulnerable to him, so … visible. The first strike took me completely by surprise.

Bright, burning pain seared across my whole backside, and I let out a great big gasping cry. The second and third fell fast after the first.

Heat flared out, singeing my skin and making me squirm. His hand on my back secured me as his other moved around methodically, covering the entire area with stinging smacks. I couldn't decide which was worse—repeated slaps on places he'd already visited, or new spots that only served to spread out the scalding agony.

I couldn't suck in a breath to cry or beg, and I couldn't stand the fire on my bottom anymore. That's when he began to lecture.

"You kept a secret from Daddy, one that put you and your friend in danger. You kept your troubles to yourself instead of letting me help you solve them. Did that make your problems better? Or worse?"

"Worse," I squeaked out, squirming and kicking in earnest. I couldn't help it.

"That's right."

He held me securely despite my wiggles, while he kept up his relentless, methodical assault on my tender flesh. "I can't help you if you don't talk to me. I can't keep you safe if you keep secrets from me. And I can't help you get free of your guilt if you don't share your feelings with me."

A helpless, whimpering cry clawed its way out of my throat, but worse than that, my heart cracked over his words. He was right. I should have told him. I shouldn't have tried to hold it all inside.

"Please, Daddy, please," I blurted out, my breath coming in shorter and shorter gasps. He extended his aim to the tender area across the tops of my thighs, and I squealed and wriggled against the sensation. My shorts and panties fell from my ankles onto the floor from my kicking as the flaming heat raged across my tender skin.

It burned everywhere. Worse, a different kind of heat rose between my legs, both delicious and confusing amidst the scorching sting on my poor, poor bottom. His length pressed hard and thick against my belly, and each punishing slap drove that point home.

Tears I didn't know I'd been holding back broke through, and I let out a sob. The words poured out like a mantra between my jagged, tearful breaths. "I'm ... sorry, Daddy ... I won't ever ... keep secrets from you again."

His hand stopped landing, and I lay limp across his lap. My bottom radiated heat like the sun. My forehead pressed against the side of his calf.

He stroked my back with the hand that had chastised me. "*This* is the right place for you to be sorry." He pulled me up so carefully, turning and tucking me into the crook of his arm, letting my raging hot bottom stick out so no fabric or pressure touched it. "And now, baby, you can let that go."

I rested my face against his chest and let my tears flow into his shirt, drinking in his scent to soothe my hitching breaths. He held me close, placing tender kisses along my forehead while murmuring things like "Good girl" and "You did so well" against my skin.

Time passed, and my tears slowed. My breathing regulated, leaving my head strangely clear. A new sense of peace wrapped around me, along with his arms, and I felt ... lighter somehow.

"Tell me what you're feeling," he said gently after I'd clung to him in silence for a while.

"Better," I said, marveling at the truth of it. "How can that be?"

He ran his fingers along my forehead, tucking a loose strand of hair behind my ear. "When you make the wrong choice, keeping secrets or breaking rules, your heart can get heavy."

I nodded. "I felt alone."

"Yes," he continued. "And the best way to lighten your heart back up is to face that wrong choice. It's my job to help you do that."

I wanted to believe that so bad. But worry started to creep in. I touched the little letters engraved in my locket, feeling the scratch of them against my fingertips. "I don't understand why you would—"

"No." He pulled my hand away, brought it to his lips and kissed each finger. "You deserve a light heart and a clean slate. You are worthy of forgiveness, and I want to help you feel it. That's what Daddies do."

He hadn't dismissed me, hadn't given up on me. I sobbed out my apology against the punishing strokes his hand doled out, and it worked—like it never had before. In all the years I tried, apologizing had never given me peace, never relieved any of the crippling, inescapable guilt. At his hand, the absolution I craved poured over me. I felt forgiven. My heart really was light.

"Thank you, Daddy." I nestled deeper into his arms, my mind floaty and peaceful. He reached down and gently rubbed the painful heat on my bottom. I flinched at first, but he knew what he was doing, and the stinging eased a little.

The circles he rubbed drew my attention to the other heat building inside me. I carefully shifted on his lap. My body, naked from the waist down and completely exposed, grew slick and wet with excitement.

Part of me was embarrassed, but a bigger part was exhilarated. That part wanted him inside me, thrusting deep while he squeezed my burning bottom, melding the sting and the glorious friction into a sensation I wanted with every cell in my body.

Amber Jade beamed.

He wanted that too. I could feel him still diamond hard beneath me. Only the fabric of his pants separated us. I turned my face up to his, and our lips connected. The kiss intensified, filling my lower parts with an almost painful need. He shifted me easily, hands sliding along my body and pulling me against him, matching my growing hunger with his own.

"Daddy," I whispered when we stopped to breathe.

"Yes, baby girl?"

"Did you ... enjoy spanking me?"

He laughed, low and gravely, as he guided my hand onto the bulge that had been growing ever since I first lay across his lap. I shivered with excitement and gave him a squeeze that made him groan against my lips.

"Are we going to ..."

He leaned his head back against the chair, watching me, his gray irises rimmed in warm gold. "Naughty little Sophie," he purred. "Do you need to come?"

I bobbed my head up and down vigorously.

He cocked his head and offered his crooked smile. "Too bad little girls don't get to come after discipline spankings."

I whimpered in frustration. The chastisement did nothing to cool me off. In fact, it turned the flames up higher. Was spontaneous combustion from unresolved lust a thing? I guess I was about to find out.

"What about Daddies?" I whispered, squeezing him again.

His eyes sparkled, and his hands slid down to grip my burning bottom. "Do you want to please Daddy?"

I nodded my head up and down again.

"Then get on your knees."

I slid down his lap, melting against his body as I moved to my knees on the floor between his legs. Somehow, I pulled off the move with absolutely no embarrassing flubs.

High five, Amber Jade.

"Unbuckle my belt and take down my pants," he commanded, sliding up to sit on the edge of the chair.

I found his belt and buttons and tugged them open. He watched my fingers work, his eyes like ash and fire, ready to consume me. His hips thrust up as I pulled his khakis and boxers down. My face and hands were just inches from his rigid cock. The word felt delicious and dirty in my mind, and I didn't flinch away.

I tore my gaze away and searched his face, ready for direction. He nodded, reaching one hand down to caress my cheek. He slid his thumb under my chin to hold me steady, sending a thrill down my spine.

He ran the fingers of his other hand into my hair.

"Open your mouth, baby girl."

I did as I was told, and he guided me right to the tip of his cock, thick and ready. I extended my tongue, running it slowly along his ridge before sucking him straight into my mouth.

He let out a groan and tightened his fingers in my hair. I sucked harder, letting my tongue explore.

Callie had given me more blowjob descriptions than I could count, and I had enthusiasm on my side, if not much practical experience. I relaxed my throat and tried taking him deeper, relishing the feeling of him swelling bigger as I sucked.

"That's so good, baby girl," he crooned.

His praise lit me up and urged me on. I let my mouth drench him as I took him deeper down my throat. Warning signals made my eyes water. I'd gag if I went much further, but I wanted to take him all the way down. I wanted to do that for him.

He guided me with his hands but let me have some control. Let me ease into it. His hips rose slightly every time I pushed my lips down his shaft, meeting my effort and working with me, enjoying my mouth around him.

Those little thrusts thrilled me. My butt still burned from his hand; my nerves buzzed and tingled. My thighs slipped against each other, desperate for friction I knew I couldn't have, but my heart pounded with the desire to please him. A feral little pleasure hum rumbled in my throat as my lips glided faster.

He evened out my pace, not pushing past where I could go, but showing me what he liked. I loved accepting his control and relaxed my throat a little more. He slid slightly deeper and hit my limit. I gagged as my throat closed up. He let me recover, and I sucked harder to cover my embarrassment.

"Good girl." His voice was thick and rough, pleased and unrelenting all at once. "Keep going."

I found the place I could manage and took him there, fast and eager, needing to please him more than I needed air. He stopped thrusting, letting me work to bring him over the top. He swelled between my lips, his hands gripping my shoulders, his control retreating with a guttural moan as he gave himself over to me, and I drove down and took him deep one more time.

"Yes," he hissed, his thick cock pulsing in my mouth, streaming down my throat as he came. "Oh, fuck yes, Sophie."

Pride swirled through me as I swallowed him down, heat flaring when he moaned my name.

I made sure I took it all before gently releasing him as he eased his grip on my shoulders. "Christ, sweet girl," he groaned. "You're fucking incredible."

I laid my head against his thigh, still buzzing from the thrill of making him come in my mouth. He stroked my cheek lazily, his breath evening, his body relaxing.

"I gagged a little," I started, but he tapped my lips with a finger.

"That was the hottest thing I've ever experienced. You will not apologize for that, or I'll have you over my knee till your ass is on fire and I won't let you come for a week."

His sinister threat made me squirm. I kissed his inner thigh, feeling absolutely naughty and thrilled all at once. "How long *do* I have to wait?" I asked. "If I'm good?"

He played idly with a strand of my hair.

"You took your punishment well and what you did with your mouth was stellar. Behave the rest of the day, and I promise you'll go to sleep satisfied tonight."

My tummy flipped and my lower parts pulsed in sweet anticipation.

20

ETHAN

I left a message for Hayden. We would need to get Sophia's statement on record and figure out a plan so her murderous ex-boss went away forever. Sophia wouldn't be truly safe until that asshole was behind bars, so I was eager to make that happen.

While I waited to hear back, I went over some of the financials for the resort. Sophia sat on a pillow by my feet, humming to herself and patiently removing the matted hair from one of the broken dolls.

The rest soaked in a special solution she had passionately explained as the best way to get them clean without damaging them. Her depth of knowledge fascinated me. My lovely little Sophie had more skills than she gave herself credit for.

A lot more skills.

After her spanking, she'd been a different girl. She hadn't gotten tongue-tied or stammered. My instinct would always be to spoil her, but she also responded to firmness and discipline.

And what she did with her mouth was fucking incredible.

She talked softly to the doll as she removed its hair, comforting it and promising to be gentle with none of the embarrassment that so often weighed her down. She was adorable and absolutely perfect for me.

A sharp knock on the door broke my happy train of thought. I told Sophia to stay put till I knew who it was then opened the door to Evie, surrounded by boxes on the porch.

"Sophia's items arrived." She walked in with a cardboard box and dropped it heavily on the dining table.

"Great." I grabbed another and brought it in. "Sophie, the rest of your stuff is here."

"Yay!" She jumped up then caught herself, her eyes on Evie. I hoped she would soon learn she didn't have to hide her Little side around any of my family. And Evie was practically family.

"This one was damaged." Evie pushed a half crushed, punctured box toward Sophia. "You'll need to open it and check for anything that needs to be replaced so I can file a claim."

"Oh," Sophia said. "I'm sure it's fine, I don't—" She broke off when she saw the list of names on the box.

"Why does it have a bunch of girls' names on it?" Evie asked.

"They're my ... dolls." Sophia opened the box carefully.

"You collect dolls?" Evie adjusted her glasses and leaned in to peek inside the box.

I tucked my arm around Sophia. "She doesn't just collect them, she rescues them. She's very talented at restoration."

"No, I'm not," she said quickly, pulling out several and unwrapping them, scanning for damage.

"You did this?" Evie asked, gingerly picking up a doll that looked like she'd been a Barbie in another life, transformed into a forest fairy with skin the color of sun-dappled leaves. Her face radiated an ageless wisdom, compassion, and a slight sternness so different from the ones in the display boxes. Gossamer wings cleverly crafted from wire and tulle stretched behind her back, continuing the mesmerizing, dappled pattern on her body.

"Oh, yeah ..." Sophia smiled fondly at the doll. "That's Elowen. I found her at a thrift store. Now she's a tree guardian. It took forever, but she looks happier now to me at least. I mean ... I guess ..." Her eyes dropped to the table.

Evie examined the doll's dark hair, intricately woven with tiny flower petals and little crystal dewdrops dispersed throughout. "You painted her?"

"I did it all." Sophia carefully unwrapped another doll. "She started off a lot like those." She pointed to the dolls soaking in the cleaning solution.

Evie pushed her glasses back on her nose. "Ethan." She looked at Sophia then back to the forest fairy doll. "She should take a look at Caroline."

"You're absolutely right," I said, amazed at the suggestion. "She should."

"Who's Caroline?" Sophia asked.

"The doll Uncle Joe gave Aunt Carol when they first started dating," I explained.

"Oh. I'd love to meet her." Sophia's eyes brightened, and she gave a cautiously hopeful glance to Evie before picking up another doll. A warm bubble of happiness swelled in my chest to see her comfort with her Little side increasing.

"She was damaged in a fire." Evie was still staring down at the doll, Elowen, her finger tracing the doll's hair. "Now she's sitting in a box. Aunt Carol can't bear to look at her but can't stand to throw her away."

"Oh no," Sophia exclaimed. "Poor Aunt Carol and poor Caroline."

"Do you think you could do something with her?" I asked.

Sophia tipped her head to the side, thinking. "I'd need to see her to understand how badly she's damaged, and what materials I'd need. I couldn't make any promises, but I'd do my best to bring her back." She chewed her lip, considering possibilities to rescue the doll.

"Can you get her from the storage facility?" I asked Evie.

"Of course, Ethan," she said. "Let me make a call, and I'll have her delivered this afternoon."

SOPHIA

EVIE WAS STILL unsure of me. That much was clear on her face, but hope for Aunt Carol's doll might have softened her mask. I had a wild moment of optimism, imagining we might even become friends.

When my dolls were put away, Evie and Ethan settled down in the kitchen to go over some quarterly reports.

"I think I'll go ... check on Callie," I said after a few minutes. "If that's okay?" I added, unsure if I needed permission, or how to ask for it in front of Evie.

"Good idea. You need to have a conversation with her." Ethan raised an eyebrow, and I nodded. "Be careful." He pulled me in for a kiss. Evie didn't bat an eye. She even smiled at me. Maybe we really could be friends someday.

"I will," I said with a hopeful grin. "Her cabin is only a few yards away."

Callie practically leaped out her door when I knocked. "Let's explore. I'm bored out of my mind, and Rookie's construction crew is working at the big building today."

We walked down the path toward the main building, me in my trusty Converse, Callie in highly impractical burgundy Dior sling-back pumps. Somehow, she managed to look perfectly at ease wearing a super short, navy shirt dress only half buttoned, a blue silk scarf wrapped around her waist, and multiple bangled bracelets.

We walked toward the sound of hammers and coarse laughter while I worked on how to tell her about the murder.

The huge flight of steps toward the main building loomed before us. We walked up, past the swing, and through the cavernous doors into the main lobby.

"I can't believe you've been up here by yourself with all this yummy manliness." Callie sauntered past two men working on electrical outlets. "I've been back in L.A. shaking my ass, and you've been here with so many possibilities." She gave a flirty hair flip to the guys, who grinned, leaning back and elbowing each other.

We wandered over to a seating area near an ancient bar. She

scrunched her nose at the old, floral couches and several black and white photos that looked like shots of skiers from some long-gone Olympics event.

"Jesus, who decorated this place? It looks like my grandma's basement."

"It's been around a long time," I said. "Ethan and his family came here when they were kids."

"I mean, the elements are all here, grand staircase, stone fireplace, amazing view. But it's all wasted. That window should be three times bigger." Callie tugged at dusty curtains in mock horror. "Are there any amenities?"

"I think there's an indoor pool," I offered. "We could go find that."

"Perfect, we can scope it out for a skinny-dipping party." Her eyes sparkled. "Down that hallway maybe? Can you believe this carpet? It's like that creepy old hotel movie with the guy with the ax. You know that was based on a real hotel? The Ahwahnee in Yosemite. It's gorgeous in real life." She ran her hands along the old, lacquered bar, her eyes appraising. "Rustic but classy, soaring windows, painted details, practically gothic in its reverence to the mountains around it. This place has so much potential."

After a few wrong turns, we found the pool, and it was lovely. There were a lot of chips in the tiles around the edges, but it was big, quiet, and serene. Our voices echoed in the huge space. Callie immediately kicked off her shoes and sat on the edge, sliding her legs into the heated water.

"So. Tell me all about life in the woods with Ethan." She extended one leg and wiggled her toes, making tiny ripples. "And when I say life, I mean sex. Preferably in the woods."

I snickered and sat next to her, untying my shoes and setting them to the side. "It hasn't happened ... yet."

"Jesus, Soap, what's with the slow burn?" She leaned back on her elbows and held up one foot, watching the water drip from her toes. "He's hot, you're hot, he's obviously into you. That was clear at dinner. What's holding you up?"

"Well, we've done a ... I mean, I ... did a—"

Callie sat back up abruptly and dropped her foot back into the water with a splash. "Sophia, you dirty girl! Did you swallow his babies? I'm so fucking proud right now. Amber Jade takes the wheel!"

I buried my face in my hands, laughing. I'd missed her.

"And what did he do for you?"

I took a deep breath. Which was harder, telling her about the murder? Or telling her about what Ethan had done for me? "He"—I covered my eyes then peeked at her through my fingers— "spanked me." I dropped my hand to my mouth and chewed my thumbnail, waiting for her reaction.

"Ooh ... he's kinky? I love it," she squealed. "Did he spank you like a dungeon master? Or like a Daddy Dom?"

I blinked at her, shocked but not shocked. Of course, Callie would take this in stride. No judgment. Only excited curiosity.

"More like a ... Daddy Dom," I muttered, my cheeks flushing.

"Aww, Soap ... he's perfect for you."

"But what about ... girl power and being a seductress?" I asked. "You don't think it's stupid that he wants to take care of me ... and I want to let him?"

"Fuck, no. Daddies are super-hot." Was that a hint of wistfulness in her voice? "I can't believe I didn't pick it up myself." She dipped her fingers in the water then flicked them at me, her green eyes bright and happy. "Amber Jade is a sexy Little."

The acceptance was overwhelming.

"I love you, Callie."

"I love you too." She leaned over and gave me a hug. "Now tell me about the rest of these brothers. Are they all kinky?"

I took another breath. I could tell her about Mr. Roscoe too, but I needed this moment of girl talk. I wanted it to last just a few minutes more. "Well, there's five of them altogether. Ethan, Rook, and Hayden, the detective." I counted with my fingers. "Griff, the scary one at dinner, and ..." What was the fifth brother's name? "Oh yeah, Vincent. He owns a club that caters to ... uhh ..."

"Oh my god, we've hit my fantasy jackpot, Soap." She threw her hands up in the air with glee. "Well, except for Griff. He's a grumpy ass." She rolled her eyes.

"Yeah, he's scary," I agreed.

She snorted. "He didn't scare me. He pissed me off." She puffed up her shoulders in an exaggeration of Griff's big muscles and pulled her face into a scowl. "*I wasn't asking.*" She snorted back a laugh. "Who does he think he is?"

"The guy who has to keep your bratty ass safe, apparently." At the sound of his deep growl behind us, I came embarrassingly close to tipping myself into the pool. Callie froze, her eyes expanding like balloons.

We whipped around to spot Griff, all broad shoulders, shaved head, glowering eyes, and arms crossed over massive pecs, standing in the doorway of the pool area.

"Oh look, Soap, did you order some big brooding biceps? Cause I didn't." She kicked her foot through the water with a splash of annoyance.

I gaped at her sass then looked apprehensively at Griff.

He hadn't moved. "Do you always have such a smart mouth?" he snapped.

"Do you always skulk around, listening to people's conversations?" she threw right back.

He stomped past us and pointed to a camera in a corner. "I wasn't skulking. I'm working on the security system. Because we're harboring a couple of girls in more trouble than they seem to realize."

Callie scowled at him, uncharacteristically lacking a smart answer. Before she could recover, Griff's phone buzzed.

He glanced at it then flipped a hand at us. "Let's go," he snapped and stalked toward us, pointing to the door.

"Excuse me?" Callie stood up and grabbed her shoes but refused to move. I was not as brave as her. His command had me tugging my socks and sneakers back on as fast as I could.

"Ethan's looking for you," Griff growled. "Let's *go.*" His emphasis hinted he wouldn't ask again.

A small flicker of doubt flitted through my mind as I wondered why he would be looking for us.

Callie crossed her arms and glared at Griff. "Well, I don't answer to Ethan, and I certainly don't answer to—"

He cut her off with his body, propelling her forward with sheer force of will without touching her at all. He swept us up in his wake, opening the door to the pool and shooing us through.

"Fine. I wanted to talk to Ethan about the awful décor in this place anyway," Callie grumbled, sulking through the door with me following close behind.

21

SOPHIA

*W*e came back into the main reception area where Ethan, Evie, and Rook stood around a large white box laid out on the front desk. Callie, Griff, and I joined them, forming a circle of six. At first, I was confused, but when Ethan carefully opened the box, I remembered.

It wasn't pretty.

She lay inside, wrapped in white tissue, the box a doll-sized coffin. It was difficult to see much of her face because of the soot and ash. Her hair had melted into a charred, solid clump and her once-fancy, now-discolored dress reeked of smoke.

"Oh no," I whispered, my hand hovering over her, unsure until Ethan pushed the box toward me.

"Shit." Rook blew out a sad breath. "I forgot how bad she looked."

"I never saw her," Griff said. His voice so soft I didn't recognize it as him at first.

"What is this?" Callie asked, her eyes gauging the seriousness of everyone's expressions.

"Caroline," Evie said.

"Aunt Carol's doll," I added, gingerly exploring her little burned face, trying not to disturb her brittle clothes. "She was in a fire." I thought of Mrs. Helmsley's unicorn, broken by the moon-faced man. I knew what it felt like to lose a treasure from the past.

"You can fix her, right?" Callie asked. "Soap's amazing. There isn't a doll she can't fix." Her confidence warmed my heart.

I glanced at her, grateful for the praise, but daunted at the hope everyone was placing on me. "I'd need some supplies ... but ... I think I can do something."

"Whatever you need," Ethan said.

"You have to understand." I looked carefully at each of the faces around me, worried about all the hope I saw. "She won't be the same." I lifted her from the tissue and turned her over gently. "She's too damaged for a simple restoration. Will Aunt Carol be disappointed if she's different?"

"I trust you," Ethan said.

I could feel Caroline reaching out under all the ash and soot. She wanted to heal. To be out of that box and back with Aunt Carol again. "Can we go into town tomorrow?" I asked. "I need new wefts, epoxy sculpt, fabric, oh, and elastic too." I stopped talking, but the list kept growing in my head.

"Shopping day," Callie squealed. "And after we get the stuff for Caroline, I have an idea."

LATER, as Ethan and I strolled hand in hand back up to the cabin, we paused on the porch to take in the sunset. It was nothing like the oranges and browns of the L.A. skyline. The colors were more vivid, closer somehow. The sky swirled with outbursts of purples and oranges and pinks mixing around swollen gray clouds outlined with a fiery yellow light.

Ethan wrapped his arms around my waist and pulled me close against his chest. "I left a message for Hayden." He rested his chin on top of my head, the rumble of his voice vibrating through my back. "He's going to need to talk to you. Did you talk to Callie?"

I dropped my head, and he turned me around to face him. His hands found my shoulders and gently stroked up and down my arms.

"I … didn't get the chance. I meant to …" The words felt like excuses. I dropped my eyes to the weathered planks of the cedar porch.

"Tomorrow then." His voice was kind, but firm. "You'll be with her most of the day. I expect you to make the chance happen. Can you do that?"

"Yes." He was right. I needed to tell her.

He tipped my chin up, and a little thrill rippled through my core. "Yes what?"

"Yes … Daddy?" I still hesitated, but each time I said it, it felt a little more natural.

His eyes glinted in the dusky light of the sunset. "Good girl."

My whole body filled up with butterflies taking flight. Thoughts of his promise from before flickered in my mind. That I would go to sleep *satisfied*.

I had been on my best behavior all afternoon.

"Want to play a game?" He let me go and leaned against one of the stone pillars holding up the porch roof, a mischievous smile tugging up the corners of his lips.

I never imagined a man who could be so playful, indulging the imagination my parents always held with such disdain. Ethan wanted me to play and be myself. It was freeing, and the more I tried it, the more I loved it. "What kind of game?"

His grin turned slightly evil, and the golden flecks in his smoky eyes glittered. My insides started to melt. Would this game end with us naked in bed together? I hoped so. The irony amazed me. Playing games and calling him Daddy brought out the sex kitten in me that never appeared working at the club.

"I'll wait here and count to ten," he said. "You go in and hide. When I find you, the price for your freedom is one article of clothing. Ready?"

"Wait, what about—"

"Set … go!"

I squealed, my tummy flip-flopping at the sensation of being prey, and dashed toward the door of the cabin.

"One," his voice boomed out.

I grabbed the doorknob and twisted. It didn't budge.

"Two."

"No fair," I cried out. "The door's locked."

The jangle of keys made me look over my shoulder. They hung from the tips of his fingers.

Shoot.

I dashed back to him and made a grab for them, but he pulled them up and out of reach with a diabolical smirk.

"Three."

"This is cheating," I exclaimed, but my heart was pounding in the most thrilling way. "How do I get in?"

"Keys cost one article of clothing." He grinned like a hungry wolf. "Also, four."

"This is extortion."

"Well, now it's two articles. And we're at five."

"Noo," I cried, but my feet were already slipping out of my sneakers. I picked them up and shoved them at him, jumping and reaching for the keys with my other hand. He let me catch hold of them but kept them high, forcing me up on my toes.

"Shoes are one item. I need something else." He leaned into my ear and whispered, "Six."

"Why are you such a tough negotiator?" I groaned and quickly inventoried my items in my head. Socks, T-shirt, shorts, bra, and panties. That was it. My hair was in a scrunchie. Would that count? Then an idea struck. A marvelous, flirty, Amber Jade-inspired idea.

"Would you accept the shoes with a kiss?" I bit my lip and even risked batting my eyelashes. Just once. No need to push it.

His lips twitched up to his dimpled half smile.

Bingo.

The arm not holding the keys wrapped around me, swooping my lips up to his. His fingers clutched my waist as he slowly took my kiss, tugging my lips apart and breathing me in while his tongue explored.

I sighed into him, forgetting the game for a moment, until the keys shifted into my hand. He let them go to cup my face, and a sense of triumph shot through me.

Sucker. Those keys were mine.

He whispered through the kiss, "Seven."

Shoot!

I pulled away, my lips still buzzing from his delicious, deceptive kiss and ran back to the door in my socks.

The key turned, the bolt catching and grinding in its hole, resisting the key.

"Eight."

Finally, it gave way, pulling back with an aggravated clacking sound. I was in.

I ran across to the fireplace, my eyes darting around the room, looking for the perfect spot. Spare room? Bathroom? Too obvious. Kitchen? Too open. My brain fizzed with adrenaline.

"Nine."

Focus.

A tiny broom closet near the hall. Could I even fit? Maybe, if I tucked up very small.

It wasn't ideal, but it could work.

"Ten."

The closet would have to do. I sprinted toward it.

It was empty except for one old broom and a dustpan, so I could fit, but my panting would give me away if I didn't control it. The bottom half of the door was solid, the top half had slats, creating diagonal lines of light and shadows above me.

I curled in tight, trying to be small.

The porch creaked with his footsteps. The front door closed slowly. *Snick.*

Like that night.

Hiding in my bedroom closet.

Listening to a monster creep closer and closer.

Panic bubbled in my chest.

"Ready or not, here I come."

Ethan's voice.

Playing a game.

He wasn't going to hurt me.

My brain got it, but my body suddenly did not.

"Where are you, little Sophie?" His voice was low, moving farther away.

My chest burned, and I realized I had clamped my hand over my mouth to stop my breath.

My throat closed up. Dots of light danced behind my tightly closed eyes.

I couldn't move. A whimpering moan filled the closet. I didn't even recognize it was me.

"I'm gonna kiss you all—" His voice cut off at the sound of my moan. "Sophia? Where are you? Come out now." His playful tone had switched to worried. The closet door flung open, and then I was in his arms, sucking in great, choking gulps of air.

"I'm sorry," I said when my tongue could form words again.

"Baby, what happened?" He rocked me till my breathing somewhat steadied. "What scared you? Your heart is racing."

"It's stupid." I burrowed my face into his chest, taking in the safe scent of him. "I heard the door ... and it was like ... that night."

"Oh fuck," he growled, squeezing me closer. "I'm so sorry." He tipped my head up gently. "Hey, look at me." I focused on the warm amber flecks in his cashmere eyes, the safety of his arms around me. "It's not stupid, and you have no reason to be sorry." He stroked my cheek with his finger. "*I'm* sorry. It was stupid of me to forget what you just went through."

"But I ruined the game."

"You ruined nothing. I'm the Daddy. I shouldn't have put you in a position to be scared." He paused. "You know the best thing about that night? You ended up in my arms for the first time." He kissed my forehead and gave me a squeeze. "And now here you are again. Right where I like you."

I relaxed into his embrace. "I guess you're right," I said, trying to sound normal. "It wasn't all bad. We met that night."

"You know what else?" he asked, his words like magic spells cast to ease my fears. "That was when I saw you in your cute little Eeyore pajamas for the first time."

I snickered. "I'm sure those were super exciting."

He leaned back with a shocked expression. "Are you kidding me? It was so inappropriate, wanting to kiss you in them after what you went through, but I was dying to."

I let my hand rest on his arm, my heart starting to slow back to its regular speed. "I figured after seeing my bedroom and my pajamas you thought I was a big baby."

"Nope." He settled down against the wall and shifted me up onto his lap. "I saw a gorgeous little girl in serious need of a Daddy to cherish and protect her." He rocked me slowly back and forth. "And I started hoping I might get that privilege."

"I'm such a mess." I laid my cheek on his shoulder, trying not to tear up.

"I wanted you then, and I want you even more now," he whispered. His kiss was soft and reverent, his scruff-covered chin sending electric tingles zinging through my body. The adrenaline from my scare turned into something else.

"I want you too, Daddy." It sounded kind of breathy and sexy, which made me proud of myself, but more importantly, I spoke the truth. I wanted him. Wanted this. I wanted to be his cherished little girl. I wanted him to play with me, care for me, and keep me more than I ever wanted anything in my life.

"Daddy?" I whispered against his lips. Calling him that was like hitting two live wires together at the base of my spine, and I couldn't get enough.

"Yes, baby?" He kissed me, his fingers running up my neck to tangle in my hair.

"I behaved myself."

"Yes, you have," he chuckled, shifting me over so he could stand, lift me up, and lead me to the stairs.

I dropped my eyes and embraced being small, following him,

giving myself over to his control. When we got to the top of the stairs, he pointed to the edge of the big bed.

"Have a seat."

I scurried over and sat down, nerves tickling my tummy. Was this it? Was he going to take me?

He stood in front of me, arms crossed, his face stern—except for a tiny upward twitch of his lips.

"I think it's time for some rules, young lady." He tilted his head.

"Rules, Daddy?" My heart thumped, and a surge of heat flared between my legs.

"That's right." He stepped up close, until the toes of his shoes touched the tips of my socks. "We've got your safeword, but we need to have clear rules, so we understand our boundaries and limits." He reached down and tugged the scrunchie out of my hair. "From now on, Daddy does your hair every morning. You wear it the way I like it."

My hair fell loose around my shoulders, and he stroked it, plunging his fingers in deep and tugging slightly, so my head moved with his hand. Gentle but firm. My heart accelerated, my blood whooshing through me, but my mind calmed. I loved feeling his control over me.

"Every day?" My voice trembled with excitement.

"Every day, baby girl." He tipped my head back so I was looking up at him. "Your turn."

"I get to pick a rule?" My eyes widened.

"You get to make a suggestion," he said with a smirk. "I have veto power."

"Umm ..." I searched for an idea. "Spaghetti tacos for dinner once a week?"

He laughed. "How about once a month?"

I stuck out my lip for a moment, making him grin, but couldn't hold it because of my own grin. "Okay, once a month. But then, I get to do your hair too?"

He pushed me backward on the bed and stood over me, his legs pressed against the edge. "I've seen you with your dolls' hair. You use sharp instruments and hot glue—no deal." He lifted my leg so that he could kiss my inner knee while one hand slipped off my sock.

I shivered and squirmed back.

"Be still," he warned, his goatee scratching my skin. He switched legs, tugging off my other sock while nibbling along the bend of my knee. "Next rule. Daddy dresses you. And undresses you."

His hands found the buttons of my shorts and undid them, the muscles of his forearms flexing with each popping release. His thumbs grazed my tummy before he hooked them into the belt loops of my shorts, easing them over my hips and down my thighs.

I let out a shuddering breath. "Okay." I lifted my legs up, my toes pointing.

"Yes, Daddy," he corrected as he pulled my shorts the rest of the way off and tossed them to the floor.

"Sorry. Yes, Daddy."

"That's another rule." He pushed my legs apart and stood between them, staring down at me, bare except for my panties from the waist down. "No saying sorry if you haven't done anything wrong."

I tensed, worry starting up like a cranky lawnmower in my head. "I c-can't—"

"Non-negotiable." He reached out for my hands and pulled me up to sitting, extending my arms over my head. "It's a habit, and it's harmful to you. It's my job to put a stop to that." He slid my T-shirt over my head where it quickly joined my shorts on the floor.

My hands rested on his chest. My face an inch from his hard abs and hard ... other things just below. I pressed my forehead against him, trying to absorb his words.

He stroked my back and bent to place a gentle kiss on top of my head. "Let me lead you."

That silky command quieted the grumbling motor in my mind. I sighed with relief into the warm cotton of his shirt. He shuddered and pulled me closer. He unclasped my bra and slipped it off my body.

I slid my hands down to his belt buckle, but he stopped me, taking my wrists and slowly laying me back down on the bed. His pants rubbed against my inner thighs, raising goosebumps and making me tremble. I was spread out before him, in only my panties. He remained fully dressed, his power somehow magnifying my nakedness.

He crossed his arms and tilted his head, a crooked smile tugging his lips up. "Such a good girl. Do you like following my rules?"

"Yes, Daddy." I squirmed under his praise. My nipples tightened, and I felt a rush of arousal. Knowing I was on display for him only made me wetter.

"Do you need a warm bottom before Daddy makes you come?" He grabbed my hips, rolling me over onto my tummy, my hips bent, legs hanging off the edge of the bed.

I squealed in surprise, but his hand pressed the small of my back, steadying me.

"Ask me," he commanded.

"Please, Daddy," I said, my face pressed into the sage green comforter. I hesitated. What did he want me to ask? I closed my eyes and opened my mouth, hoping the right words would come. "Please ... warm my bottom ... before you make me come."

He groaned his pleasure at my request, his fingers tracing down my spine to find the edge of my panties. He pulled them off roughly —firm, demanding, but not hurting me.

"Perfect," he growled over my naked body. "You truly are my perfect, sexy little girl."

My inner thighs were slick with my response.

A stinging slap across my bottom relit the fire from my recent spanking and made me gasp, more in surprise than pain. The aftershock warmed my skin and connected directly to my core.

"I knew it from the moment I first saw you," he said, laying down another strike against my flesh. "I wanted to make you mine."

Another smack heated me more, and I groaned and wiggled into the bed, unable to help myself.

"Wanted to hear you call me Daddy," he said, bringing down three more, fast, with exactly the right amount of sting.

"Please, Daddy," I begged. He gave me all the delicious flush of heat without the burning intensity of my punishment spanking. This time, I didn't feel sorry at all. I rode a wave of exhilaration, and I didn't want him to stop.

He nudged my legs further apart with his knee, rewarding me with another light slap when I complied. His fingers trailed up my thigh, tickling me close but not close enough while another smack landed. I sucked in a breath. That one smarted. My whole bottom glowed as I teetered on the edge between pleasure and pain.

His hands gripped my hips, and he rolled me again, flipping me onto my back. My breasts bounced, heavy and exposed, my bottom burned against the comforter, and my tummy clenched when I looked at him, looming over me, so hard I could see his pants straining.

I wanted that. Wanted him. I stared at his belt, wondering if I could undress him with sheer force of will.

Instead of undressing, he sank down to his knees before me on the bed, that devilish smile dancing on his lips. He pressed against the bed and propped my legs over his shoulders. I froze. He was right *there*. I blushed, embarrassed with his face so close to me, but also burning to beg him in closer.

"What are you doing?" My legs tried to pull together, self-conscious, squeezing against his neck.

He slapped my outer thigh, just a corrective little sting. "What did I say about next time?"

I gulped. "You'd ... use your tongue?"

"That's right. I want to taste you properly." His fingers reached up to grip my hot bottom as he pulled me closer, arranging me for his pleasure. "Let me in."

My knees slipped wider apart, giving in. A sweet sense of surrender overwhelmed me. My legs bent, my heels resting on his back. His cheek rubbed along the sensitive skin of my inner thigh, his lips kissing a trail right up to my edge.

"Good girl." His breath blew across my bareness, my wetness, and I squirmed, blushing fiercely at how much I wanted him to kiss me there.

"So beautiful." His finger opened me first, sliding up easily, teasing me apart, sending tingles up my body like lightning as it moved around. "My girl has such a pretty little pussy."

His tongue touched me next, slowly gliding up the path, circling, opening, lighting up the circuits in my brain with a long, deliberate lick, ending in a focused swirl before the finger retraced its steps, exploring lower areas with his tongue right behind.

My legs clenched with the sweet torture of it, wanting to resist, but also wanting to splay wider so he could bury his face against my body. I opened my knees a tiny bit wider, shocked at how that bare fraction of an inch brought his tongue in deeper.

"Oh yes ... Daddy," I breathed out the words that ignited me, that lit me up for him like the morning sky.

My whispered words affected him too. His fingers squeezed my bottom harder, pulled me closer, his mouth pressed tighter against my sex, claiming it, taking it over, and making it obey his tongue.

The slow, incessant gliding up and down drove me half-crazy, each stroke better than the last. His tongue found the perfect spot, then located another, even better place, then returned to the first again.

"Please," I begged.

His tongue pulled back and his lips pressed into a firm kiss against my body.

"Please what?" he growled against me before sending his tongue back to the business of setting me on fire. Any embarrassment I had melted away, and I dropped my legs wider, needing his mouth to take me all the way.

He let out a little hum that made bursts of colors explode behind my eyes. His finger pressed deep then pulled back in a steadily increasing rhythm. I was helpless, my body tilting and moving with him, wanting more.

"Please what?" he paused to ask again, making me sob with need. "Tell Daddy what you want."

His tongue settled on my nub, pressing, circling, flicking, and stroking, slow enough to keep me right on the edge of bliss. I arched and panted for each incredible sensation, desperate for that final push to send me over.

"Please ... I want ..." Pressure built up from the bottom of my spine and radiated out across my chest. It sparked in my fingers and toes, bathing my whole body in a glistening prism of exploding color and light. I couldn't take much more. "Please, Daddy, I want you to make me come."

"My pleasure, baby girl," he hummed against my clit as his tongue settled into a ravenous pace of unending strokes matching the thrusts of his fingers. Faster and faster, until everything blurred into a bolt of electricity that shot through me. My muscles clenched and spasmed in ecstasy. My back arched, and I shuddered and pulsed until I thought I might splinter into a million pieces.

"Daddy ..." I hovered like a feather rocking in a warm breeze. My brain planned a whole sentence about how amazing I felt, but my body was too full, too happy, too blissfully floaty and free.

I lay on his bed slowly coming back down from the orgasm clouds. I was dimly aware of him joining me on the bed, holding me close, kissing my neck, and pressing his body hard against me. His hand stroked my belly then the underside of my breast. Everything tightened up again, and I was ready for more.

He kissed me, sharing my flavor with me, running his tongue along my lips before pushing inside.

I reached my hand up to touch his cheek when a blood-curdling scream echoed through the woods.

22

ETHAN

"Stay here," I commanded, leaping off the bed and taking the stairs two at a time. The scream sounded like it had come from the cabin Callie was staying in.

I was almost to the door when I heard footsteps pounding up the porch. I threw the door open to find Callie, wild-eyed and gasping for breath. Her hair was disheveled and she was tugging at it frantically.

"A fucking ... gang ..." She panted.

A gang? What the fuck?

"In the ... cabin ..." She pointed back the way she'd come running.

"Callie?" Sophia came running down the stairs.

"F-fucking gang of BATS," Callie yelled. "In my hair!" She kept pulling at it so hard she was in danger of ripping it out.

Sophia grabbed her hands before she could do more damage to her hair. "They're gone. There are no bats in your hair."

I scrubbed my hands down my face, blowing out a hard breath. Fucking cock-blocking bats. The exterminator must have missed some. I closed the door and grabbed the blankets for the couch while Sophia kept soothing Callie, leading her into the kitchen for a cup of tea.

Good thing I was a patient man.

THE NEXT MORNING, I convinced Rook to stand bat guard so Callie could return to her cabin and get dressed.

I set a plate of pancakes in front of Sophia. "You look so cute today, baby girl." She was dressed in black leggings, a long, slouchy lavender sweater, and those bright blue sneakers of hers.

When I brought her a cup of milk, I noticed the pink paw prints winding up one leg.

"Thank you, Daddy." She wriggled and leaned into me, then turned a worried gaze up. "I don't have a lot of business-y clothes ... like Evie."

"I'm sure Aunt Carol won't mind casual." I caressed her cheek. "Do you want to dress more *business-y*?"

Her smile was self-conscious, worried. "I want Aunt Carol to know she can count on me to do a good job."

"Then do your best work and be comfortable."

She didn't look convinced.

"Are you done with your breakfast? You didn't eat much."

Her eyes turned wary, but with an underlying sparkle. "Am I in trouble?"

I chuckled. "No, I just want your tummy full. You have a big day. Also, considering the circumstances, I don't feel comfortable with you and Callie going to the café or out shopping alone."

Not until I knew Tommy Roscoe was safely behind bars.

Her eyes widened.

"Don't worry. Griff agreed to chaperone you. That way you can get what you need for Caroline's restoration." I reached across the island and held her hand. "Thank you for doing that. You have no idea what it will mean to Aunt Carol."

"I'm happy to do something good for her." Her fingers curled around mine. "And for Caroline. She doesn't like being in that box all burned up."

That innate sweetness radiated out from her, sensitive to a doll's feelings, and a widow's.

"Go into the bathroom and bring me your hairbrush if you're done," I instructed, taking her dishes away.

Her eyes turned wide as windows. "You said I wasn't in trouble."

The wholesome laugh she brought out of me was good and I wanted more of it in my life. I wanted more of her. All of her. "You're not, silly girl. Remember the rules? Daddy does your hair."

She padded off to the bathroom, but she looked over her shoulder at me. Twice.

So fucking cute.

When she returned, I patted the barstool and took the brush from her hand. Standing behind her, I drew the brush through her silky hair, reveling in its supple glow, watching it cascade down her back as I released it.

She let out a little moan and leaned her head back. "That feels so good."

"It's supposed to." I leaned down to give her a kiss. I could kiss her all day. If my day wasn't packed, I would. Especially since she'd shared her secret with me. But I knew they would be safe with Griff.

I forced myself to focus on the task. Her hair gleamed in my hands. "So beautiful," I murmured. I split it in two, loving the silk of it in my fingers. I pulled two of the bands wrapped around the handle of her brush off to secure low ponytails that rested loose and wavy on her shoulders.

"You like it like this?" she whispered, tipping her head to one side.

"I like *you* like this," I answered, kissing her again.

She pressed herself against me.

With perfect timing, Griff's heavy knock rattled the door. She pulled away again, adorably pink-cheeked and breathless.

"Don't think these interruptions are always going to save you, baby girl," I teased. "Tonight, you are mine."

I PASSED Evie's car in the lot as I walked up the steps of the Mt.

Tahoma Lodge House and headed up to our new office. "Morning, Evie," I called out as I stepped through the door. "You're here early."

She hopped up from her desk, smoothing down her perfectly pressed charcoal gray skirt. I grinned at the thought of Sophia wanting to wear *business-y* clothes.

Evie held her hands out to collect my briefcase, setting it down on her desk. "You have a call starting in ten."

I nodded. "What would I do without you?"

She smirked and shifted her eyeglasses. "Miss about a thousand meetings?"

I laughed as I headed to my desk. "Speaking of meetings, I need you to block off some time tomorrow. Hayden's coming in and we'll need the conference room."

We'd spoken briefly, and he wanted to take Sophia's statement in person. Evie pursed her lips and made a note on her tablet.

"And did you get an estimated completion time on that request I gave you?"

She tapped a finger on the side of the tablet, giving me her best skeptical face. "I did. But ... the price was exorbitant. He's the most sought-after glass artist in Seattle. He's booked out for a year. I wasn't sure you'd authorize—"

"Do it. Cost doesn't matter."

She frowned. "But it's a cheap glass statue, not worth—"

"Whatever it takes." The look on Sophia's face would be worth it.

"Of course, Ethan." Evie shook her head. "Anything else?"

"I need to go over some details before the meeting with Rook's design team. Did we get it rescheduled?" I sat down at my desk and clicked open my email.

"About that." Evie sat down across from me, reaching out to straighten a stack of folders. "Rook left a message. The design lead fired her main assistant, and one of the other two just quit."

I rubbed my chin. Not exactly a surprise, but that could put things considerably behind schedule. "Alright. See if he needs help finding alternatives."

Evie tapped on her tablet then gave me a little salute. "Aye aye, captain."

"Smart ass," I snorted as she stood up and headed back to her desk. Her comment reminded me of the scoundrel pirate captain from Sophia's book.

Suddenly, an idea started forming in the back of my head. "One more thing," I called out to her retreating back. "Call Vincent and see if his boat's available tonight."

23

SOPHIA

"This is ... are you sure about this?" I stared into the mirror of the dressing room, my head tilted to one side.

"How does it make you feel?" Callie stood next to me, twirling back and forth in neon orange tulle fluffy pants that looked like a million mini tutus up and down her legs, a sequin-covered butterfly halter top and pink bunny ears, her grin taking over her face like the cat in *Alice In Wonderland*.

"Exposed?" I said, my eyebrow raised and my mouth quirked at the image staring back at me.

Callie laughed. "What does Amber Jade think?"

Before I could answer, my phone pinged with a text.

ETHAN

Hey baby, you having fun?

I looked in the mirror again, shocked at how much fun I was having. "Should I ask his opinion?"

Callie shook her finger at me, making her bangle bracelets clink together. "And ruin the surprise? No way. Trust me. He's going to love it."

I tapped in my response.

Hey Daddy, yes, but I miss you

Miss you too. Are you behaving?

Always :)

Thrilled little tremors erupted in my tummy at his question and at my answer. Having a Daddy—having *him* as my Daddy, was something I'd never known I needed, but it was quickly becoming something I didn't want to live without.

Have you talked to Callie yet?

My tummy sank. We'd been having so much fun, and every time I tried to spit out the words, Callie dashed off onto some other topic.

Not yet. But I will

You better, baby girl. Or you may have another punishment spanking in your future.

I looked into the mirror again, grimacing and brushing my hand across my bottom.

Yes, Sir

Good girl

My spine tingled at his praise. How was it possible those two little words could have such an effect on me?

Callie dragged me out of the dressing room. "Come on, let's see what other colors this comes in."

Griff stood nearby, a glowering, silent chaperone, looking shockingly out of place for the kind of store we were in.

As we dug through a rack of colorful, over-the-top outfits, my phone pinged again.

I have a surprise for you tonight

Callie led me to an animal ear headband display and looked at me, hand cupping her chin, lips poked out, finger tapping her cheek in contemplation. She picked up a pair of mouse ears, then put them back when I wrinkled my nose.

"You're right. You're not a mouse." She gasped, grabbing a headband with a unicorn's multicolored horn. "Oh my god! Griff, this would be perfect for you." She waved it at the dour man, and we both broke into giggles when he stuck out his thumb and pointed it down at the ground.

She returned her attention to me. "Maybe ..." She carefully set a pair of black kitten ears on my head and stood back to consider her work.

"Like all areas of life," she said, resting her hand on my shoulder as if she were imparting great wisdom. "You have to find your style, then dress for what you want."

I looked around the store, the rainbow of colors beckoning to me. Something on the far wall caught my eye. I looked down at my phone and grinned.

> I have a surprise for you too.

"What about those?" I pointed to the display in the shoe section.

Callie's eyes lit up. "Excellent idea. Build the concept from the ground up. The right pair of shoes can change your life."

"So says Cinderella," I laughed, ready for that change.

ETHAN

It had been a long day, and I was more than ready to see my sweet little Sophie and focus on her surprise. Everything was set. I only needed her.

I knocked on Callie's cabin door, noting the shadows stretching out as the sun dimmed and dusk fell. I needed to make sure Rook installed better lighting out here. I knocked again, impatient to get my hands on my girl. Feminine giggles bubbled out from inside. She said she had a surprise for me, so they were clearly up to something. That strange, satisfying happiness settled into my chest, making a goofy grin spread across my face. I tried to suppress it. I'd need to muster up some stern Daddy energy if they didn't open up quick.

Before I could knock again, Callie threw open the door, her heavily made-up eyes twinkling and her long, blond hair bouncing. "Come in, Mister Ethan, come in."

She did a dramatic curtsy and waved me inside. My mouth ticked up, fighting me on suppressing that smile. What were they up to?

"*Mister* Ethan? What's going on in here?" I tried and failed to sound gruff, happy to play along. "You two haven't been getting into trouble, I hope?"

"Us? No way," Callie batted her eyes at me, and I rolled mine at her. She giggled.

"I assume all the bats are gone?" I craned my head around, looking for Sophia.

Callie shuddered. "I made Rook check three times." She tugged at her hair absently, then bounced on her toes in excitement. "Come on down, Soap! Daddy's here!" she yelled up to the bedroom loft.

Daddy's here?

She must have confided in Callie about us. And, good friend that she was, Callie embraced it, cooking up whatever this game was. I wanted to hug her for being a safe person Sophia could talk to. If I could ever do something to repay her, it was a done deal.

I looked up the stairs—and stopped breathing.

Dainty, dark blue, sparkly shoes, complete with buckles and bows, led up to white-and-blue striped knee socks outlining her fantastic legs, past the peek of her bare thighs and directly to the blue plaid mini skirt that curved around her hips.

I dragged my hand across my mouth and down my chin, barely able to take it in.

She came down the next few steps, and I saw the short blue top that stopped right below her breasts, so her soft little belly showed as she moved. The fuzzy top had a rounded neckline, demure white collar-flaps, and two pearly round buttons. Perfect. Sweet and sexy.

Mine.

Every primitive instinct in my brain growled it. Her image burned into my memory and took my breath, shooting a high through my veins I'd never experienced before.

She did this. For me.

She made it to the bottom of the stairs and stood still, clutching the rounded banister and shifting from foot to foot. She bit her baby pink bottom lip, nervous but excited. Her glossy hair still remained in the two low ponytails I loved, but she added two blue and white polka-dotted satin bows. And kitten ears perched on her head. Fucking perfect.

"Hi ... Daddy." Her voice was shy and hopeful. I grabbed reflexively at the back of my neck and squeezed, then scrubbed at my goatee again, trying to form a coherent thought.

Out of the corner of my eye I saw Callie hopping up and down and waving a not-very-discreet thumbs up. "I tried to talk her into the see-through lace tank and the open cage bralette with nipple rings, but your Little Sophie is more of a traditionalist," Callie giggled. "Anyhoo—she's all yours."

All mine.

Two strides to the stairs and I had her, catching her as she jumped into my arms, wrapped her legs around my waist and threw her arms around me, kissing me with those baby pink lips and making a little mewing sound that might have driven me slightly insane with desire.

"My work here is done," Callie said, in the distance. Neither of us broke the kiss to respond.

Finally, when the need to breathe forced me, I pulled back and looked into her heated eyes. "All this for me?"

"Do you like it, Daddy?" she asked.

"Fuck yes I like it." I turned around and walked back to the door, still carrying her, my hands cupping the cheeks of her ass and squeezing. "Say goodnight to Callie, baby," I said without stopping my stride.

"Goodnight, Callie," she called over my shoulder with a giggle and a wave.

"You two kids have fun," Callie laughed as she shut the door behind us.

SOPHIA

Holy crickets, I did it.

Daddy was breathing hard, and not because he carried me out of Callie's cabin to his SUV. His hardness pressed big and firm against my thin panties, so I squeezed my legs around him, wanting him as close as possible. He squeezed my butt in response and whispered against my neck, "The kitten ears are a nice touch, baby girl. I want to see you wearing nothing else later when I make you purr."

I squirmed against him, giddy with my success. "Meow, Daddy."

Amber Jade threw a fist pump in the air inside my head.

He let out a big happy laugh, dropped me in the passenger seat, buckled me in, and crossed around to the driver's side while I clapped my hand to my mouth, so proud of myself. No stammering, no apologizing, no awkward, ridiculous, random nonsense that made me sound stupid. I pulled off my own version of seductive, and he responded. He would take me to the cabin, and then he would ... take me. Finally. He'd been more than a gentleman, giving me time, letting me get used to this dynamic, but I didn't want to wait any more.

He climbed in and looked at me again, up and down, savoring every inch. He rubbed his hand across his mouth and chin, as if he couldn't believe what he was seeing. "Well," he said after a deep breath, "you certainly surprised me, little kitten."

A smile burst across my face. "I'm glad you like it, Daddy."

"Oh yes, baby girl, I like it a lot." He chuckled and shook his head, started the car, and put it in drive.

"What's my surprise?" I asked, excitement bubbling in my tummy. He wore a thick, white, button-down, no-collar shirt and dark pants that weren't quite slacks but weren't jeans either. A wide cummerbund-like belt didn't make the surprise any clearer. It was an odd outfit, a strange mix between dressy and casual, but it fit him incredibly, and he wore it with his usual confident attitude that made me want to jump into his lap.

"What kind of surprise would it be if I told you?" His dimple flashed at me.

Good point.

We drove for what felt like forever. He asked me if we noticed anything strange while we were out, or if Griff seemed worried and I assured him it had all been fine. I told him about the things I got for Caroline, and then I told him about the store Callie found. "It was mostly a ... naughty kind of store." My cheeks flamed, and I tugged at the hem of my super short skirt. "But they had this whole section for ..." I hesitated.

"Littles," he finished for me, sneaking another wolfish once-over to my outfit before changing lanes.

"That's the kind of submissive you want?" I asked, my voice small.

"*You* are what I want," he said, making my heart flip-flop in my chest. "Yes, I want to be your Daddy. But it needs to work for you too. I never want you to do something you don't enjoy because you think that's what I want."

I rolled that thought around, plucking at my skirt again. "It does work for me. But there was so much in that store that I'm not sure about. And what if I'm too much of a brat? Or not enough? Or ... you don't like knee socks?" I hesitated, adjusting my kitten ears. "What if I can't do this right?"

"Not possible. Just relax and be yourself." He snaked a hand over to slide along my thigh to the top of my sock. "And by the way," his voice dropped to that gravely baritone that took my breath away, "I fucking love your knee socks."

I squirmed in my seat, my heart thumping, his touch setting fire-works off in my brain.

"As for the things in that store, they're just ideas, baby girl. Options," he said. "We choose what we take home and what we leave on the shelf." He made it sound so simple. Maybe it was.

"It does sound like a field trip is in order, though," he added with a squeeze to my thigh. "Maybe we could find a cat o'nine tails, like Captain Harlow keeps threatening Ruthie with."

My eyes widened, and my mouth dropped into a thrilled little O.

The most recent chapter we'd read taunted me in my dreams. Only, the captain in my dreams had cashmere gray eyes, a goatee, a dimple in his left cheek, tousled hair the color of wet sand, and demanded I call him Daddy.

In fact, his outfit almost reminded me of the captain's pirate garb, and I swirled my tongue along my teeth, imagining him in a heavy leather buccaneer coat with shiny round buttons and a red pirate sash. It was almost too yummy to contemplate.

"Speaking of the dashing captain and his naughty prisoner"—he tapped a few buttons on his phone— "I got it on audio so we could listen on the way."

I clapped my hands in pure delight.

"Where were we at?" he asked.

"We just finished the part with the fancy meal at the captain's table, when Ruthie stole the knife and stashed it under her skirt," I answered. "He just stripped her down and tied her to his mast," I added in a big whisper.

He grinned at me as the narrator's voice came out of the speakers:

"You'll not break me," Ruthie cried, fear and fire flashing in her ocean blue eyes.

"I don't want you broken," Harlow replied, dragging the leather down her camisole-clad back. "Just chastened enough to stop defying me."

Her treasonous body arched in response to his touch as the boat rocked beneath their feet.

"You plan to return me to Lord Borthwick," she snapped. "I'll never stop defying you."

"He'll pay handsomely for you," the captain agreed, ever the pragmatist.

"Not if I am marked by your whip," she said, desperate to convince him.

"True." Harlow squinted at her, considering. "But he may thank me for taming you for him."

Her only response was to spit at him over her shoulder.

Captain Harlow seized her hair and exposed her neck, his lips against her ear as he whispered, "Enough games, little pet. I'll take you right here, tied to my mast. I'll free the pirate vixen inside your heart and make you mine for all time. If you live with the flaccid Lord Borthwick for a thousand years, you'll spend every day of it pining for my hands on your backside and my sword inside your sheath."

Ruthie gasped at the crudeness of the man pressing against her, at the rough scrape of his beard against her tender skin and the wild way her heart beat at his words. She desperately hoped, despite herself, that he would do exactly as he threatened.

"But, Sir," she whimpered. "Your crew. They're watching."

Captain Harlow let out a dark, ominous laugh. "Sweet little pet, I'll fuck you right here, in front of my crew, and you will beg me for more."

"WE'RE HERE, SWEET GIRL."

I jumped at his words and looked around. "We were just getting to the good part," I complained.

His lips twitched up, enhancing that dimple, but he didn't say anything.

He helped me out of the car, and I realized I had dressed like a Little but had no idea where we were going. What if his surprise was to take me to the opera? Or a shopping mall? Or dinner with Aunt Carol?

He won't let you be embarrassed, the little voice in my head assured me.

I took a deep breath to relax.

And smelled salt in the air.

We were at a marina. Several huge boats floated on barely

rippling dark water, hulking beside endless wooden docks. Water lapped against the pillars, and boards creaked when the big boats nudged them. "Are we at the ocean?" I asked, confused.

"The Sound," he answered, taking my hand and leading me down toward the end of one of the docks, where a yacht twice the size of our cabin awaited. "It leads out to the ocean."

"Is that your boat, Daddy?" I asked, staring up at its sleek, shark-like lines and dark glass windows.

"It belongs to my brother, Vincent." He guided me with a hand against my lower back toward the gangplank where a smiling crew member in a black polo and khakis waited to help me on board.

"Your brother?" I squeaked, tugging my shirt down as if I might suddenly make it long enough to cover my tummy.

He wrapped his arm around me and kissed my ear. "He's not here. He loaned it to us for the night. It's just us." He nodded to the patient crew member still holding out a hand for me. "And the crew."

To his credit, the crew member kept his face neutral, his eyes carefully straight ahead. I supposed part of his job was not to have an opinion about guests. I took a deep breath, held my head high, and took his hand with a smile that only trembled a little bit.

When I stepped onto the teak deck, I couldn't hold in my delighted gasp. Tiny strings of lights twinkled like fireflies in the last bit of dusk before night truly fell. A raised area held an enormous hot tub that bubbled quietly, and a glass-topped bar filled a corner by a door to the interior.

But the table, and what stood behind it, froze me in my tracks. An awning covered a section of the deck, and under that awning sat a long, old-fashioned, wooden table. Candelabras lit up several silver platters of meats, cheeses, finger foods, baskets of bread, and bowls of fruit. Two heavy oak chairs sat, one at each end of the table.

A fancy meal.

At a captain's table.

Just like in *A Ruthless Choice*.

"Daddy? Is this ..." I scanned his outfit again, button-down, no-collar shirt with the top two buttons open, and the black silk cummerbund that resembled a pirate captain's sash the more I stared at it.

"I had a dress for you," he said as we walked toward the table. "But I like your surprise for me better."

Toward the front of the boat there was a thick, vertical, wooden pole, held in place by a bunch of wooden barrels. It was as out of place on the ultra-modern yacht as the fancy feasting table, so clearly a prop.

A pirate ship mast.

I looked up at the top of the pole. There was a heavy iron ring. And a rope.

"Your seat, my lady." Another uniformed man ushered me to the chair at one end of the table. He wore a red and white striped, long-sleeved shirt, a matching bandana around his head, and an eye-patch. I sat down and looked at my place setting. A black-and-gold name card read 'Miss R. Luddington.' A butter knife rested on a snow-white napkin diagonally across the white-and-gold embossed dinner plate.

I reached out to touch the knife, but the server stopped me. "The captain would like to remind the lady that a woman may not touch a weapon aboard this ship," he said with a wag of his finger. "Would you like to start off with something to drink? A cup of Captain Harlow's Grog, perhaps?"

Drinks arrived in heavy silver steins. Captain Harlow's Grog turned out to be something fruity and yummy and non-alcoholic, so I could drink as much as I wanted without worrying about an embarrassing repeat of the restaurant. The server warned me, again, that the captain was watching me, and under no circumstances was I allowed to do anything naughty, such as attempt to steal a butter knife and hide it under my skirt. Ethan—the captain—my Daddy sat at the other end of the table, and even though it was far away, I could see his lopsided grin.

As the boat engine roared to life and we moved sedately away from the marina and out into the open water, dinner was served. Between the watchful eye of the server and my impossibly short skirt,

I had no idea how to steal the butter knife. It would have been much easier if I had a Victorian gown on instead of a tiny plaid mini skirt, but Daddy had loved my surprise, so there was only myself to blame for that.

I finally managed to stash it in my sock during the second course, when the server made a fuss of looking away out over the water, saying he thought he might have seen a rival pirate ship. I owed him one for that.

The table was so long that conversation was impossible, so the server brought me messages from the captain at the other end, mostly reminding me that he expected ladylike behavior, he hoped I was comfortable, and that we should be arriving at *Lord Borthwick's* compound in the morning.

I sent messages back saying I was as comfortable as I could be on a ship full of pirates, and he could be assured I would throw myself overboard before going to *Lord Borthwick's* compound, tomorrow or any other morning.

I couldn't stop grinning.

Until dessert was served. In the story, Captain Harlow asked Ruthie to dance after dessert, and that was when he discovered she stole the knife.

My knife was pretty poorly hidden. If I tried to dance, odds were good it would fall right out of my sock. There was no way I was pulling this off. My tummy quivered with the most delicious kind of fear as I contemplated what would happen when he discovered my treachery.

As I took the last bite of the most decadent chocolate cake I ever tasted, a waltz started up over speakers hidden in the corners of the ship. The violins wove a melancholy web while a piano tapped out a refrain that sounded like a storm brewing.

Daddy stood up, looking perfectly pirate-like with the salty breeze tousling his sandy hair and moonlight dancing on the water directly behind him. He walked slowly toward me, the candles casting flickering shadows across his handsome face, sinister and alluring. "Dance with me," he commanded, reaching for my hand.

I took it in a trance, my heart pounding, the light breeze tugging at my hair. He pulled me effortlessly in his arms and spun me, nuzzling into my neck. "Are you having fun?" he whispered.

"This is incredible," I whispered back. The crew cleared the table in the background and turned on outdoor heaters to warm the chilly sea air.

"Remember, you're safe. If it gets scary, use your safeword." He twirled me to the haunting melody, then pulled me back, his hand sliding down my back. "If you do, the captain goes away, and it will just be Daddy holding you."

I tipped my head and let my body sink into his embrace, let him pull me along, following wherever he might lead. As we moved across the deck, my eyes fell on the pole playing the part of the ship's mast, complete with iron ring and coarse rope. My heart trembled with excitement as I parted my lips and said, "I'm ready ... captain."

The glint in his eyes darkened, and he kissed me deep, crushing me to him while never missing a step in the dance, controlling me as I floated in his arms, taking everything his mouth offered. I stepped over the edge and let myself fall into the game. If this were my last night before facing the awful fate of wedded misery to the evil Lord Borthwick, my choice was easy. I was certain Ruthie would agree.

The music changed, the tempo increased, and he broke away from my kiss. "My sweet little pet," he said in perfect pirate accent, silky and dangerous. "I warned you, more than once. A woman may not touch a weapon on my ship." Before I could protest, his hand slipped down my leg and took my knife. So much for undetected.

"You don't understand the fate you're dooming me to," I said, trying to sound plaintive.

"And you don't understand the captain's rules." He spun me around, capturing my hands behind my back and marching me forward toward the mast. "They are not to be broken."

Fear spiked down my spine, but his thumb gently stroked my palm. The deep, protective survivor response in my brain calmed with that tiny touch, and I knew I could trust him enough to let myself play, to be frightened and aroused, and know I was safe.

"Please," I whispered, stumbling forward, letting him guide me. The crew seemed to have disappeared.

"It's too late for pretty words, little pet." He snaked an arm around my chest, his hand holding the butter knife in front of my eyes before he threw it across the deck. He pushed me face first against the mast, hard enough to thrill me but not enough to hurt.

"Do not move," he growled into my ear as my cheek made contact with the rough wood.

He pulled my shirt taut, and I heard the click of a pocketknife then the rip of fabric. He slid my top off my shoulders, leaving me bare except for a white cotton bralette. The soft breeze raised goosebumps along the backs of my arms. He lifted my right hand over my head, wrapped the rope around my wrist and put the end in my hand. He did the same for my left. I was secured, but I could let go at any moment. The eerie calm in the depths of my mind tucked that away, then let my conscious mind believe I was tied.

"Please have mercy," I begged.

"I'm a pirate," He answered, his voice graveled and full of mirth. "We're not known for mercy." He pulled something from his waistband and flourished it, waiting for me to look over my shoulder at him.

A cat o'nine tails.

Fear and heat plunged down my spine and landed between my legs, but the calm, sub-conscious anchor held fast. I tugged against the ropes, keeping the ends clutched tight in my hands. "No," I pleaded.

"Oh yes, my dear." He dragged the whip sinuously down my back.

The fear turned into a torrent of excitement. I arched back, hungry for the whip's caress, hungry for his touch, and struggling to remember to protest.

I looked back at him again, full of need. From the corner of my eye, I saw the table, now completely cleared, no crew members in sight. But the mirrored glass windows of the control room stared down at me like an impassive sea god. "But Sir," I whimpered. "Your crew. They're watching."

He let out a dark, ominous laugh. "Sweet little pet, I'll fuck you right here in front of my crew, and you will beg me for more."

Those words, his body looming over me, the whip in his hand all combined in my mind and the fantasy made real undid me. I moaned and twisted my body around, the ropes pulling tighter, my back scraping against the mast. I had no coherent thought left, except that he was right. I would beg, and I didn't care who was watching.

"Please," I cried, pressing my chest forward, straining toward him with my hips.

He dropped the whip, and it clattered to the deck.

"Sophia," he murmured, his voice dropping to a heated groan.

"Mine." His hands grabbed my face, pushing back my hair, pulling me to his lips and crushing me, kissing and sucking and breathing me in, taking control of my head, leading me.

His hands raked down my body, tugging my skirt up to my waist then wrenching my panties down to my feet where I frantically kicked them away.

"Yes?" He looked into my eyes, searching for fear or doubt.

"Yes," I panted back at him, promising there was none. There was nothing but me needing him to take me.

He grabbed at my bralette and tore it open, shredding the lace, exposing my breasts to the cool night air and anyone's eyes who might be watching. I didn't care. My nipples tightened, hard as buttons.

"You're not going back," he growled, pinning me to the mast, pressing our chests together so tight I thought our hearts might collide. "Not to *Lord Borthwick*." He bit my lip playfully, then his eyes turned serious. "Not to anybody."

"Only you," I gasped, wrapping my legs around him and pulling on my ropes for leverage. His hands cupped my butt, squeezing, holding me steady. I was bare and grinding against him, writhing, trying to show him with my body what I wanted.

"I want you," his chest rumbled against me. "For real."

He was so strong, so commanding, a master I was more than ready to follow. But something else flickered in the golden flecks of his gorgeous gray eyes, some tiny hint of vulnerability. I could trust him to take control, keep me safe and make me his, but he was trusting me too.

No one had ever wanted me like that before, and the magnitude of it hit me like an explosive blast.

He pulled a condom out of his pocket and held it up between two fingers, a question in his eyes. One last opportunity to back out.

As if.

I nodded frantically, my kitten ears tilting wildly askew. He tore the packet open with his teeth, shifting me slightly in his arms as he adjusted, undid his pants, and readied himself for me. He was right there, hard at my entrance, but still he held back.

"I'm going to fuck you now, sweet little pet." The pirate gleam was back in his eyes. "But I need to hear you beg." His hand came up to my throat gently, his fingers stroking beneath my chin as if they might coax the words out. His voice lowered until I was sure we were the only two people in the world, and his eyes softened, searching mine for something. "Tell me what you want, baby girl."

His words felt like electric sparks sizzling through my body. I wanted to give him my everything. Every part of me, from my tangly tongue to my jittery tummy, from Amber Jade's blossoming sex kitten to the Little side I was learning to embrace. My body, my submission, my trust. All I could give, I wanted him to have.

"You ... I want it ... you, please ..." I huffed in frustration, needing my words to work. The tip of him pushed against me while his fingers stroked my throat. Waiting. I took a breath and tried again. "I want ... you." He leaned in to brush my lips with a kiss that was more poignant than pirate, his brow slightly furrowed against mine. His chest expanded with his breath, pinning me tighter against the mast. I squeezed my legs tighter around him. "I want you to take me ... for real ... please, Daddy."

He jerked back his head, his smokey eyes burning as he stared into mine. "Say it again."

"Please, Daddy." The words tumbled out, and before I could take another breath, he plunged inside me to the hilt.

I thrashed against him, desperate for him to pull back and do it again, again, again. He groaned deep and obliged, tilting my hips to best meet his, charging forward, impaling me, grinding me into the hard wood of the mast. Some dim, distant part of me noted I would be sore later, but the primal part of me threw that thought out the window and urged him on.

I arched and tugged at the rope around my wrists, pulling myself up and over and towards him as much as I could, needing to meet him thrust for thrust, to take him as hard as he was taking me. Embarrassment, fear, guilt, all gone. For the first time ever, I felt free.

"Mine," he said low and heated in my ear. Pure possession in his voice. His mouth made a rough trail of kisses along my neck, barely biting at my collarbone as he claimed my body.

"Yours?" It was a question and a plea, full of more hope than I meant to express before I squeezed my eyes closed and arched my back, shoving my chest against him, desperate for connection.

"Aye, lass," he purred. "Mine."

He kissed me again, moaning my name against my lips, tracing the edge of my jaw with his tongue, finding my neck, kissing and sucking and tasting me all in the same rhythm of his relentless charge into my body.

I arched back again, tilting my hips as much as I could, the rough wood of the mast holding me firm, letting him plunge even deeper. The tingling electrical hum in my core intensified, the explosion building. I teetered on the edge of anticipated bliss.

He caressed my left breast, holding it firm and pushing it up to meet his hungry mouth. His thumb stroked the bottom edge of my nipple while his teeth grazed the top. His tongue circled, then flicked. He sucked it hard, making my eyes roll back in ecstasy. His fingers squeezed and stroked and tickled all while he drove into me over and over against the mast. His mouth pulled back, taking my poor, tortured nipple to new levels of hard, aching need before letting it pop out, the cool air hitting it like an electric shock.

Then, I was there.

My eyes flew open, and I threw my head back, seeing stars, literally. A thousand tiny flashes of light glittered in the black sky as I took a gulp of sweet night air, arched my back once more and came in a long, pulsing, clenching burst of flawless joy.

I looked back at him, dazzled and dazed, just in time to see the tension of pleasure take over his face. "My baby girl," he rumbled out as he released, pushing into me, staking me to that unforgiving mast, his forehead coming to rest on mine before he peppered my mouth with tender kisses.

Our breaths slowed in sync, his rhythm leading me back to earth. Too soon, he shifted. Reluctantly I let my legs loose and my feet found the ground, though I wasn't sure I could stand on my own. He held me fast, not letting me fall, and I pressed myself tight against the safety of my Daddy's embrace.

24

ETHAN

"Let go, baby," I whispered.

She looked up at me, confused, still dizzy and comestruck. It was adorable, and I felt like a fucking king.

"Let go," I whispered again and tapped gently on her fists, still clenched around the rope ends like they were the only things keeping her tethered to the planet.

"Oh," she mumbled with a meek little smile and slowly uncurled her hands.

The ropes fell away. I scooped her up in my arms, and carried her over to a lounge area, laying her out on a big, round, cushioned couch covered with blankets and pillows. I tucked her in gently. Deck heaters combatted enough of the sea air that we could be comfortable, but the breeze was still brisk.

I tugged at her skirt. "Take this off. I don't want anything between us." She slipped it off. I straightened the kitten ears still perched on her head. "I told you I wanted to see you wearing nothing but these."

She smiled then stretched out long, grabbing a pillow and watching me.

I shed my clothes and joined her, pulling the blankets up and relaxing as the waves rocked us. She curled her whole body against mine, and I breathed in the scent of her hair, the warm glow of her skin, and the lovely gift of herself she gave me. She was so much more, so much better than I even dared to imagine.

She lay in the crook of my arms, and we gazed at the sky together, basking in the afterglow. I stroked her forehead and listened to the steady hum of the engine and the slap of water against the hull.

Her brow wrinkled, and I wondered what troubling thought she was having. "The crew didn't watch," I said.

"What?"

"If you were worried. The threat of them watching was for the scene."

She smiled and kissed my shoulder, tracing my chest with her fingers. "This surprise was ... incredible," she said softly.

"*You* are incredible," I answered.

But unease still marred her beautiful face.

"Do you remember what Ruthie does after the captain has his way with her?" I asked.

"He takes her to his chambers?" she said, the little wrinkle on her forehead returning. "And ... she tells him about her awful childhood?" She sat up and clutched a pillow to her stomach.

"That's right." I eased up on an elbow, watching her face.

She laughed, but it sounded hollow and sad. "My father didn't sell me to an evil lord to increase his spice empire, if that's what you're wondering."

I reached out to her, brushing my fingers along her collarbone until I captured the little gold locket that dangled just above her breasts. I rubbed it, testing its slight weight. "You can tell me anything."

She reached for it reflexively, something like guilt flickering in her eyes. I let the locket go, dropping my hand back down to the blanket.

She traced the engraving for a minute before releasing it and reaching for my hand. I laced my fingers in hers.

"My father didn't give it to me." She sucked a breath back through her lips and clamped them shut as though the words had escaped without her permission.

I forced myself to wait. Stay quiet. Ready for any private piece of herself she wanted to share. "It wasn't a boyfriend either." Those words came out faster, obligatory, as she looked at me, chewing on her lip. "You're the only person I've ever called Daddy."

I bit back the happiness that soared through me, trying to keep my focus on her words and her pain. But the happiness was there. I was the only one she called Daddy. It would stay that way if I had anything to do with it.

"Truth is ..." She chewed the inside of her cheek and looked away. "I stole it."

Not what I expected.

I swallowed down my questions and let her go at her own pace.

"I had a friend in fourth grade. Libby Sutton. Her parents spoiled her. Especially her dad. She had dozens of trinkets and gifts like this one. I'd go over to her house and watch how he treated her, spent time with her, and doted on her. He was never disappointed in her. Never told her she wasn't good enough. My dad ... well ..." She turned to look out at the water. "Libby's dad was a pretty stark contrast."

The shadow of her fourth-grade self, hungry for her father's love and envious of what her friend had hovered over her like a dark cloud.

"She didn't even want it. She was going through a silver phase and threw it in her jewelry box like it was nothing." She lowered her eyes, the shame of her long-ago crime paling her pink cheeks.

"Something came over me, and I just ... took it. I felt guilty for stealing it, so I hid it in my room and sort of forgot about it for a while. Libby's family moved away, and we didn't keep in touch. But a year or two later, I had been eliminated from the science fair finals, and my father was so disgusted he wasn't even speaking to me. I found this locket when I was cleaning out a drawer and the whole bitter irony came rushing in at me. So, I put it on."

Her breath hitched. "I don't even know what I was trying to say with it."

I pulled her down to me, stroking her hair and holding her close.

"I've worn it every day since. He's never even noticed. Now I wear it as ... a reminder ... that it doesn't matter what I do. I'll never be the daughter he wanted. I'll never be enough." She let out a tiny snort. "At least, it reminds me I don't have to keep trying anymore."

My fingers twitched with the urge to jerk that chain off her neck and throw the damn thing in the water, but that wasn't my wound to heal.

"I'm not your father, Sophie." I used the name no one else ever called her. No one but me. "He sounds like a fucking fool. I am your Daddy. And I'm here to tell you, you will *always* be enough."

SLEEP TOOK US, until sometime in the middle of the night, when she stirred against me. I'd been dreaming of her, and I was half-hard even before the awareness of her hand resting on my lower abdomen finished the job.

"Daddy," she whispered.

"Yes, baby girl," I said into the silky luxury of her hair.

"You said something ... before," she started, then paused.

I chuckled, trying and failing to keep my dick from twitching toward her hand. "I said a lot of things."

"But ... you said ... this one something, and I was wondering if you meant it, or if it was ... the sex-frenzy"—her hand fluttered on my stomach— "which is fine if it was, I understand—"

"Sex-frenzy?" I tried hard not to show my amusement. She was being serious, so I didn't want to hurt her feelings.

"Sex-frenzy. Where you want to do it really bad, so you say what-ever it takes—"

"No," I interrupted her, rolling half onto my side so I could see her face. "I don't just say whatever it takes. Honesty, remember?" I kissed her forehead then nuzzled into her ear, whispering, "Even when I want to do it really bad." She giggled and moved closer, one luscious leg draping over mine, completely unaware of the torture she was inflicting on my overeager dick.

"You said ..." Her voice dropped and she hesitated, her foot wiggling nervously against the back of my thigh. I waited, listening to the low hum of the yacht's engine and the sound of the water rushing against the side of the boat. "You said ... you wanted me ... for real."

"I did."

Sex-frenzy indeed. I hadn't set this little pirate adventure up intending to make any declarations, but I had zero regret. We could take our time or we could charge forward. It didn't matter to me, so long as I got her.

I didn't want to spook her though.

"So ... what does that mean?" She gasped out the question like she was afraid to let it loose into the world but couldn't hold it back.

I paused, choosing my words carefully. "Why did you dress up for me?"

"Callie said you'd like it."

"And I did." I kissed the apple of her cheek, drawing my nose along her skin till I found the edge of her jaw and planted another kiss there. "Did it turn you on?"

She puffed out a little breath. "Yes."

"What about when I spanked you?"

"Oh, yes."

"And exploring the stuff you saw at that store?"

"Mm-hmm." She wiggled against me, making it hard to stay focused.

"I'm a Daddy, that's who I am and what I want." I dragged my tongue against her neck, kissing her earlobe. She tilted her head back, giving me access, goosebumps lifting the tiny hairs on her body. Her reactions were exquisite.

"You're fucking incredible. So sweet. My perfect little girl." My hand found the curve of her hip and traced it down to her thigh. Her hand tucked between our bodies, directly next to my dick, and when her fingers tentatively curled around me, I couldn't resist a groan.

After a moment, I took a deep breath and continued. "I was in a relationship before."

She opened those deep brown eyes to me, wariness flickering

there. I hated to put it there, hated to mention another woman when all I wanted was her, but I needed to be honest too.

"She called you Daddy?"

I weighed the words I was about to say. "It was a game to her. A way to manipulate. To get what she wanted. I don't want that. I want real. I want it all."

She tensed, letting go of me. Maybe that was a good thing—it made it easier to focus.

"I don't know how to do that," she said, her eyes closing in frustration. "I just dressed up because Callie thought it—"

"Look at me, Sophie." I kissed her scrunched up eyelids and whispered, "Open your eyes."

She pulled back, her eyes open again. "Your goatee tickles," she said with the barest hint of a smile.

I stroked her cheek with one finger, hoping to ease the worry away.

She moved her head to kiss my fingertip, then sighed. "I don't know what I'm doing."

I pushed up onto my elbow, easing her onto her back and tucking the blanket around us against the chilled ocean air. "You let me brush your hair and give you a bath and fix you dinner. You talk to your dolls and wear Eeyore pajamas and curl into me and hide your eyes in my shirt when you're scared. You have this hiccuppy little laugh that you do when you're happy, and you got so excited when I showed you a herd of elk that you jumped into my lap and kissed me for all you were worth. There's nothing you have to do. It's you. It's who you are. And I want it. *That's* all that means."

She leaned up to kiss and nuzzle my chest. "I don't want to manipulate you."

"I know. That's what makes you so perfect for me. You just are who you are, and that's exactly what I want."

Her hand found me again and squeezed and I couldn't stop a groan from escaping.

I cupped her ass and pulled her up tighter. "And for the record, I want to do it really bad right now too, but this is not sex-frenzy talk."

She let out that hiccuppy laugh I adored. My fingers found her sweet little pussy, wet and ready for me, and her laugh turned into a breathless little squeak.

"I ... want that too, Daddy," she whispered into my mouth as I kissed her. "I want you for real."

My heart gave a tight, happy squeeze that had more to do with what she said than with what her hand was doing to me, although that was also fantastic.

"My little Sophie," I murmured, slipping my fingers inside her and kissing down to her perfectly peaked nipple. "You make me so happy."

I moved my thumb in quick, relentless circles against her clit till she was moaning and writhing and ready to come.

"That's so good," she gasped.

"You're such a good girl," I said around her nipple before sucking it back in.

She let out a desperate little grunt, and I sped up my thumb, ready to relish in her orgasm.

"That's it, baby girl, let it go and come for me," I encouraged her.

She tossed back her head and squealed, lost in sensation.

"Oh Daddy, I love you!"

My eyes widened in surprise, followed by worry for how she was going to handle this. Her face remained blissful, still lost in the moment until her brain must have kicked back on. Her eyes flew open, horrified.

She slapped her hand across her mouth so hard it echoed off the sides of the boat. "I'm sorry," she said through her fingers. "It wasn't ... I was ... too soon ... I don't ..."

"Shh," I pried her fingers off her mouth and checked to see if she had made a mark. Her cheek was pink, but it would fade.

Her eyes were full of misery. I traced the edge of her jaw. I couldn't let her spin out over this, not when we'd come so far. I held her hands against my chest like I had when she kissed me the first time. "Feel my heart?"

"It's going fast," she whispered.

"That's right," I said. "I'm right here with you." I hadn't planned to have *this* conversation quite yet, but I was okay with it.

I only needed the answer to one question. "Did you mean it? Or was that the sex-frenzy?" I waggled my eyebrows and dipped my head, scrubbing my goatee against her chin and planting a nipping little kiss there, trying to give her some space to laugh, to process.

She snorted and bit her lip like she might get out of this if she chewed hard enough. I steeled myself for her answer. The boat rocked gently on the waves, completely unconcerned about the weight of our conversation. She cast her eyes up at the sky like she wanted to float away. Too bad I wasn't ready to let her go.

When she realized there was no escape in the stars, she brought her gaze back to me, her eyelashes fluttering. Her head slid up and down against my arm as she slowly nodded and mumbled, "Yes. I meant it."

I touched her lips, rubbing my fingertip along the edges, loving the way they trembled and parted to give me access. "You always tell me how you really feel. I love that about you."

She twitched, eyes narrowing, then let out the breath she was holding, her expression wary.

"Talk to me," I said gently.

"I'm embarrassed," she blurted out. "It's ... true ... I meant it, but I didn't mean to shout it out like an overexcited kid at a birthday party." She squeezed her eyes shut so she didn't see my lips quirk up.

That exuberance was exactly what I'd been telling her about.

I knew what I needed to do.

"Don't move." I kissed her, then rolled over to the edge of the big couch, found my pants on the deck, and grabbed another condom. I came back to her and held it up. "See this? No matter what, we are having sex again, so nobody has to say anything they don't mean, understand? No sex-frenzy." She nodded, her cheeks turning that lovely Sophie pink.

I eased my body over her, holding her down and grounding her, pressing my throbbing dick hard against her lower belly. "Feel that?"

She nodded, kitten ears somehow still in place. Adorable.

"That's how much I want you." I kissed her nose. "Open up little kitten." She spread her legs for me, and my restraint came seriously close to breaking, my cock hovering right there by her wet and waiting pussy. I gritted my teeth. Patience.

"Remember, you're safe with me. You can tell me anything if it's the truth."

"Anything, Daddy?" she asked, her eyes so fucking sweet, her body so fucking soft beneath me.

"Anything, baby girl."

"I have that implant thing in my arm," she whispered, she bit her lip hard and looked over my shoulder, then back to me. "And I haven't ... been with anyone since before my last checkup. So ... maybe you don't have to ..." Her eyes turned toward the condom in my hand.

"You sure you're ready for that?" I asked, forcing a measured breath, my limits of control straining. "I got tested when I broke up with my ex, and there's been no one since." I traced a finger along her collarbone. "I told you, I'm not a casual guy."

She nodded, her eyes trusting, her body ready.

I kissed her, slow and easy, prepping myself for what I was about to say. It felt huge, but also completely right. There was no doubt, no hesitation, just a burning desire to make her happy, to hold her hand and take this next step together.

"Now," I said, lining up my lips to her ear and my bare cock to her entrance, shuddering as she shifted and pushed against me, absolutely nothing between us but this final moment.

I was ready. "Say it again. But only if you mean it." I pulled back my head so I could see her face.

Those gorgeous dark eyes opened wide and locked onto mine. "I love you, Daddy."

"I love you too, baby," I said and slid deep into the heaven of her, all the way home.

25

SOPHIA

*S*oft morning light tickled my eyelashes, and I stretched like a lazy cat, letting myself wake up slowly through each of my senses—the quiet slapping of water against the hull, the scent of bacon and fresh coffee and sea air, the fluffy blanket against my naked skin.

I was naked.

On a boat.

And I told him I loved him. Twice. Maybe even more than that as I went over the hazy, orgasmic memory in my mind.

He said he loved me too.

No one had ever said that to me. Not like that.

I had a Daddy, and he loved me.

I peeled one eye open, then the other, squinting into the morning light and making them focus.

"Good morning, sleepy girl," he called out to me.

I sat up, the blanket wrapped around my body, and looked at him. Bare-chested, lean-muscled, and completely at ease in his own gorgeous skin. His hair tousled from sleep and glowing in the backlight of dawn, his stubble dark and thick, his dimple showing as he grinned at me. Happy. To see me.

I gazed around the deck for something besides a blanket to wear. My shirt lay crumpled on the deck, sliced in half. A delicious shiver ran down my spine at the memory, but it was definitely not in wearable condition.

His thick, white, linen shirt dangled at the foot of the lounger so I snatched it and pulled it on, readjusted my kitten ears to help hold my hair back in the morning breeze, then joined him at the table. My chair had been brought much closer to his for a more intimate breakfast setting. Bowls of dark red strawberries and neon green grapes, baskets of muffins and croissants, and covered silver platters filled the middle. My place already had a plate waiting, with a big coffee mug ready for me. He took my hand and kissed it, then poured coffee from a silver carafe into my cup.

I stirred in sugar and cream and watched him from the corner of my eye. Would he say something? Acknowledge last night? Pretend it didn't happen?

"Did you sleep well?" he asked.

Small talk. We were going to make small talk. Anxiety flopped in my tummy like a panicked, gasping fish. I needed reassurance that I hadn't gone too far, said too much, pushed past a boundary he didn't want to cross. But I couldn't ask for that. Who knows what my treacherous tongue might let slip out. "The boat ... rocking was nice."

The rich, throaty sound of his chuckle made my heart pound in my ears. "Look at me, baby girl."

I peeked at him over the rim of my coffee cup.

His gray eyes were bright, barely crinkled at the corners. His lips parted in a smile that highlighted his dimple and brought a rosy glow to his cheeks. "I meant everything I said last night."

"You sure?" I asked, hating the neediness in my voice.

He reached out for my hand, stroking my knuckles with the tip of his finger and sending delicious little zaps of heat straight through to my spine. "We can still take our time if you need that. But I have no regrets. I know how I feel about you."

No regrets. He knew how he felt. Something warm and brave

stretched itself big inside my chest, almost painful after a lifetime of shrinking in. This was real.

Encouraging my new boldness, I stifled a giggle and asked, "No sex-frenzy?"

"No sex-frenzy." His lips twitched up. "Even though you are incredibly tempting in my shirt." He shook an admonishing finger at me, a playful frown crossing his face. "Now stop distracting me and eat. We have a busy day."

The flopping fish in my tummy slipped back into calmer waters. I had a Daddy, and he loved me.

I smeared warm butter across a flaky croissant and watched a gull coast by on a wind current, landing on a nearby dock. We must have arrived back at the marina sometime in the night.

I had a Daddy, and he loved me. The thought kept flashing in my mind, making a goofy smile spread across my lips. Amber Jade practically brimmed with glee.

"We do have some business to take care of, though," he said. I paused, mid-chew, trying to gauge his tone. "Did you have that talk with Callie?"

A flicker of guilt ran through me. Somehow, I'd never gotten around to telling her. Amber Jade froze, her hands covering her bottom.

"Umm ... I tried. We kept getting interrupted."

He made a slow, tsking sound with his tongue against his teeth, tapped a finger alongside his mouth and pulled up our texts on his phone. He pushed the damning dialogue toward me, my assurances that I would tell her glaring up at me in black and white. "What should we do about this?"

My heart fell. "Are you mad? Am I in trouble?"

His lip twitched up. He patted his lap. "Come here."

I slipped out of my chair to crawl into his lap, burrowing my face into his neck.

He kissed my forehead, and I sucked in a shuddering breath, overwhelmed by the way he enveloped me in his arms. "Did you deliberately defy me?" he asked.

I shook my head hard. "No, Daddy." Never that.

"Then I'm not mad." He stroked my cheek, and I sighed into him, warming at his touch. "But part of being a Daddy is holding you accountable. I asked you to do something, and you said you would do it. Something important. You didn't follow through, and now you're feeling pretty bad."

I nodded. "I'm sorry, Daddy." The words bubbled up and popped hollow in the air as I said them, only adding frustration to my guilt.

I shifted, looking up into his eyes. They were their usual gorgeous gray, edged with burnished amber, but I was more struck by what I didn't see. There was no coldness. No hint of disappointment. Nothing like what I'd come to expect from others when I apologized.

"What will you do to correct your mistake?" His brows were firm, steady, waiting for me to set things right.

"I'll tell Callie today."

"Yes, you will," he agreed. "Hayden too. He's meeting us at my office to take your statement."

I sat up, surprised. "He is?"

He nodded. "And you'll have to tell them while sitting on a sore bottom. That's your penance."

Tremors coursed through me. "My penance?"

"Sorry doesn't solve anything by itself, does it?" he asked.

No. It didn't. It never had.

"It's my job to hold you accountable and to help you finish the process."

"What's the process?" My heart quivered and my tummy twitched, afraid of what he was going to say but also desperate to hear the words.

"Sorry is the first step. Next comes the penance, the forgiveness, and the letting go."

Penance. Forgiveness. Letting go.

I knew about being sorry, but those other parts? No one had ever mentioned those before.

His hands cinched around my ribs as he turned me over in his lap. "Now, you've told me you're sorry. That's step one." He moved me into position across his knees, my bottom turned up for him to close the loop I never knew needed closing.

He slid the shirt up to expose my bottom, and I was bare to him again. The breeze tickled my skin. A steady pulse beat between my legs making me ache deep inside. His hand rested on my back, steadying me, holding me firm. I clenched my bottom in anticipation, squeezing my eyes closed, my bare toes digging into the deck for balance.

The expected smack of his hand didn't come.

Instead, two fingers pushed straight into me, firm and businesslike, finding no resistance. I hadn't realized how wet being bottom up on his lap made me.

The drum-like pulsing of my body intensified, squeezing around his fingers. They didn't tease or explore. They went straight to the spot that made my toes curl up and began stroking quickly. I gasped, my legs spreading involuntarily, my bottom pushing up towards his intruding hand, desperate for him to keep going, shocked at how fast I was accelerating toward a climax. The pulse became a throb as the coming explosion built up inside, making my legs tingle and shake.

"Daddy." It came out a hiss as my body ramped up.

My heart pounded in rhythm with my body's vibration around his fingers. I tensed, starbursts already forming in the darkness of my squeezed-shut eyes. His fingers slid out of me, trailing my wetness across the backs of my thighs and leaving an almost painful emptiness.

"No," I sobbed.

I spread my legs more, pushed my bottom toward the empty space where his hand had been. In that moment, I wouldn't have cared if the entire crew gathered around to watch. I needed to come by his hand more than I needed anything in my life.

"Please, Daddy," I begged.

Then his hand fell. The slap of it against my tender skin rang out across the deck, wrenching a yelp from my throat. A barrage of intense, fast-falling spanks burst against my bottom, and my nervous system lit up with the switch in sensation. Hot, stinging pain seared across my skin while the throbbing inside turned up to a blaring, frustrated denial. He continued without mercy, the heat spreading through my body like a wildfire out of control, leaving me gasping and squealing with the pain and need of it.

The onslaught paused. The breeze chilled the skin that had so recently been burning, and somehow that made the sting sharper, deeper, like a million tiny, piercing needles, tingling and mixing with the need to come. I grunted and squirmed for any possible friction against his lap, reduced to animal-like instincts begging for release.

A heavy slap fell, shocking me into stillness as he spoke. "Daddy asked you to do something important, and you chose to delay doing it."

Six more hard smacks burned across the backs of my thighs. "Now you have the proper motivation to be my good girl and see it gets done." Two more smacks fell, but his words, calling me his good girl, sent zaps of hungry pleasure to my desperate core. I squirmed harder against his lap, unable to help myself.

"Do you need to come, baby girl?" One finger lightly tapped against my entrance.

"Yes, Daddy. Please." I shuddered, pushing toward him, trying for more contact and crying out when he withdrew. I was empty of shame. I would beg if he would only touch me again.

"When you've corrected your behavior, I'll give you your release." He tapped once more, and I moaned at the shock of electricity that zipped up and down my spine. "That's your penance."

He slid me off his lap and onto my feet. I stood before him, panting, the fog of need swirling around my head. I turned my attention to the obvious bulge in his lounge pants. Before I could move, he shook his head.

"I told you how to make amends. No more guilt or bad feelings. Just tell the truth." He slid a hand onto my hip. "Then you'll feel much, much better. I promise, baby girl." His crooked grin lit up his face as his finger traced the edge of my excruciatingly sore bottom. I flinched, the touch reigniting both the burn of the spanking and the need simmering inside me.

I could do this. No guilt. No empty apology. If a sore bottom and some delayed gratification could ease my heart, I'd take it.

"Now, as much as I love you in my shirt ..." He trailed off for a moment, his eyes holding mine.

"You love me ... in your shirt?" I asked, apprehension forcing my eyes down and my thumb up to my mouth.

He stood up and tugged my hand away, holding it in his. "I love you. The shirt is immaterial."

I stared up into his cashmere eyes, my heart almost bursting.

"But you can't wear it to our meeting," he laughed. "So, I brought you some presents." He pointed to a corner of the deck where several pink boxes with white ribbons sat.

"Presents?" I scurried over to examine them.

The first box had an outfit inside, complete with matching underwear. A buttery soft sweater, circle skirt, tights, and new Converse all in matching shades of green. I loved it.

Upon closer inspection of the underwear, I laughed. "SpongeBob?"

"You said he was your favorite."

The second box was also an outfit.

"Eeyore?" I almost squealed with delight, my mind temporarily off the confusing swirl of sensations in my lower parts. I lifted out a light blue T-shirt with the loveable donkey's dour-sweet face on the front, dark blue shorty coveralls, matching underwear, and gray sneakers with him on them too. And ears! Callie would approve.

The third box was clothes too, but this outfit was different. A gray pencil skirt, silk blouse, stockings, and sharp gray pumps.

I looked at him, questions clear on my face.

"I want you to express yourself, always. No embarrassment." He pointed to the Eeyore outfit. "When you feel Little." He pointed to the dressy skirt. "When you want to feel business-y."

I laughed, my fingers lightly touching the silky top.

"And when you want to be sort of grown-up, but with a reminder that you're my Little girl underneath." He pointed to the green outfit with the cute panties.

Sore bottom aside, happiness radiated out of me like the sun. "They're amazing, Daddy."

The next box had a huge collection of satin ribbons, all the colors of the rainbow and then some.

"I fucking love your hair in ribbons, baby girl," he growled into my ear as I examined them, sending my tummy into somersaults.

One box left.

My smile faltered when I opened it, my eyes going wide.

"A pacifier?"

I thought of the store Callie and I had gone to. The Little accessories had been intriguing, but actually trying them out made me nervous. I still wasn't completely convinced I could be what he wanted me to be.

This one was the right size for my mouth, pink with an image of a heart-shaped lock on the front part.

He took one of my hands in his. "No pressure. I thought you might like it, to help you think. I know you get frustrated when your mouth gets ahead of you or trips you up when you're worried. This can help you slow down till you're ready to talk. You might also find it soothing. And it can help you feel very small and special, when it's only the two of us."

He tipped my chin up and looked down at me, his eyes warm and accepting. "And only if you want to try it. I want you, *and* your Little, however you're happiest."

A cloud lifted in my mind; my mental sky clearing. It wasn't about being something for him. It was about loving and being me.

I wanted this—for me. And so did he. He didn't want me to be a baby for his amusement, he wanted me to feel safe. Comfortable.

I stared at the pacifier in its box. People chewed gum and vaped and bit their nails and did all kinds of things to ease anxiety. Was this so different?

He sat next to me, watching me process. Morning sun dappled the skin across his broad shoulders. His fingers steepled together, patient, waiting for me. Giving me all that I needed.

I stood up and approached him, the edge of his shirt fluttering along my thighs in the light breeze. When he stood too, I pressed myself against him. I lifted my arms around his neck, going on tiptoe to give him a slow, open kiss.

"Thank you, Daddy," I whispered. "For everything."

I CHOSE THE GREEN OUTFIT, deciding I would ease into things and follow my feelings. And knowing that I had an undersea pineapple covering my sore butt beneath my skirt made me happier than I could have imagined. Knowing he knew too only made it better.

We pulled into the parking lot by the main building, and I noticed the sunshine dancing across the hood of his big SUV.

"Daddy," I said, not tired of the little thrill it gave me to call him that.

"Yes, baby?"

"I thought it always rained in Seattle?"

He got out of the car to open my door for me. When he got there, he nuzzled my neck, scratching me with the stubble he hadn't shaved when we were getting ready. "That's our best kept secret."

I giggled and kissed his rough cheek.

His office was at the end of a long hallway on the third floor of the big main building. Like everything here, it had amazing potential, if you squinted past the burgundy carpet and dark wood walls.

"Evie, I didn't mean it that way, I—"

"You never mean anything, Hayden. Just forget it."

We were walking toward the partially open door and right into an argument.

Awkward.

"Hello," Daddy called out as a warning we were coming in.

"Good morning, Ethan." Evie's mask slipped into place when we walked in, her hands smoothing her perfect, tailored black skirt. I tugged at the fabric of mine, almost wishing I'd worn the business-y skirt—almost.

"Hey bro, nice digs," Hayden sounded cool and composed. "Nicer than the station for sure." He nodded toward me, his normally straight face flickering with a faint hint of amusement beneath his beard. "Hello Sophia. He taking good care of you?"

My cheeks flushed, but Daddy put his arm around me, and Hayden's thin mouth turned up into an almost-smile. "And what about Callie? Did she stay put up here like I asked?"

"Helloo?" A loud female voice echoed down the hallway before the door opened.

He smirked. "Ahh, speak of the devil ..."

Callie waltzed in, pulling large, round sunglasses down her nose and taking in the scene. Her blond waves bounced as she walked. Daddy's words echoed in my head.

No more guilt or bad feelings. Just tell the truth.

As daunting as that sounded, his next words teased me too.

Then you'll feel much, much better. I promise, baby girl.

I shivered. He took my hand and kissed it, smiling as if I were broadcasting my thoughts across my face.

"Hey Soap." Callie scooped me into a hug, then nodded her head around the room. "Mister Ethan and Detective Hotness too. Aww. Did you miss me?" Callie cocked her head and winked at Hayden over her glasses.

Evie's eyes snapped and her lips disappeared into a thin, straight line. Callie gave her a wink too. Hayden didn't reply.

"Shall we?" Evie gave one more sharp glance toward Hayden then ushered us down the hall and into a room filled by a dark laminate table surrounded by chairs. A video screen and other various technological equipment sat in disarray along the far wall.

"Why are we here?" Callie asked as we all took seats. She dropped into the chair to my left and gave it a half-spin. "I got a message to show up, but nothing else?"

Hayden took a chair at the far end of the table then pulled the pad and pen from his pocket, lining them up carefully against the table edge.

"I can only assume you want my advice on the atrocious design situation you've got going on here," Callie added, turning her attention back to us.

"Are you a designer?" Daddy gave Callie a considering look. "I thought—"

"That stripping is my only gift?" Callie shoved her sunglasses up onto her head with a hair flip and a grin. "I get that a lot. But no, I went to school for interior design and everything. Dad insisted."

"Her design ideas won't be necessary." Evie looked alarmed. "I'm sure Rook's design team will do just fine."

"The design team that's down to the lead and an intern?" Daddy said thoughtfully.

Evie's lips mashed into a thin line, her olive skin paling. "Hayden," she snapped back to him, and he jerked his head up, looking almost nervous at her attention. "Did you want to get started?"

"Sure," he said. "There've been some developments in the case." He looked directly at me, and I tried not to flinch. "Ethan told me your story, Sophia. I wish you told me sooner."

"What story?" Callie pulled her sunglasses off her head and looked at me. "What's going on?"

I blew out a breath, leaving my mouth open, searching for words. Here was my chance to come clean.

I leaned forward and locked my fingers into a nervous tangle. "I ... saw a murder in the club the night of the raid. That's why I had to leave."

Evie's eyes widened. Callie's jaw dropped.

"Jesus, what murder?" She stared at me, the oversized hoops in her ears swaying into her blond waves.

"Nik Vasili, allegedly." Hayden moved his pen to the other side of his notebook.

"He was killed at the club?" Callie shook her head as she put the pieces together. "Is that why you were attacked? Why didn't you tell me?" Her lips pinched. Hurt and concern battled in her eyes.

"I didn't want to get you involved." I twisted my fingers tighter in my lap. "I panicked and I ... thought ... if you didn't know, you'd be safe."

She opened her mouth then snapped it shut, her teeth clicking together as she gave me a motherly glare. "You think I'd rather be *safe*? With you on the run? Babe, you didn't have to do this alone."

"I didn't want my problems to ruin your life," I whispered.

Callie's eyebrows scrunched, and she pursed her lips for a fraction of a second, as if she were fighting back some emotion unfamiliar to her. Then she flipped her hair back, her face calm again. "So who killed the prick?"

"Mr. Roscoe did."

Callie's mouth fell open again. "Holy fuck."

"Yeah," I agreed, shaking my head at the accuracy of her assessment. Daddy leaned over, touching his lips to my forehead, letting me know he was with me.

"So what's next?" He turned his attention back to Hayden. "Can you take her statement now?"

"Yes," Hayden said, picking up his pen and tapping it against the pad. "But it's not that simple. There's a suspect already in custody."

"You arrested Mr. Roscoe?" I asked, my tummy lurching.

"Not Roscoe," Hayden corrected. "Valerie Vasili. Nik's wife."

Daddy shifted in his chair, sitting up and staring intently at his brother. "Why?"

"We found evidence in her car, the home, and the body was found on the outskirts of their estate," Hayden answered. "It's not looking good for her."

My heart locked up, forgetting to beat. That wasn't right. Nik's wife didn't kill him, so how could the police have evidence that she did?

"She has motive too," Hayden added. "They were seen arguing earlier that night. He's a known cheater and they had a volatile relationship."

"What about what Sophia saw?" Daddy asked, his hand resting on my knee, steadying me.

"Look, what I'm about to say ..." Hayden hesitated, dropping his pen and rubbing his hand against his temple.

"Spit it out." That unfamiliar edge was in Daddy's voice, like when he was negotiating with the shopkeeper for the dolls, cool, strategic, holding back any emotion.

Hayden scratched his chin and looked carefully at me. "Is it true that Tommy Roscoe fired you the night of the raid?"

I shrunk down in my seat, not sure what to say.

"Does that matter?" Daddy frowned, his eyes wary.

Hayden clicked his pen and then set it back down on the pad. "I'm just saying, it doesn't look great. You didn't come forward until after we found the body. There's no motive for Roscoe to kill Vasili, but there is motive for a disgruntled former employee to make an accusation."

I sat with my eyes glued to my lap, letting what Hayden said sink in. He thought I was making it up? Humiliation roared inside my head, dulled only by memories of my father's disgusted voice.

Dolls and nonsense. That's all you care about. It's time to stop being dramatic and join the real world. Get out of the little fantasy running in your head.

Self-doubt slithered in my tummy like a snake. What had I actually seen that night?

"Sophia?" Hayden's voice was kind, placating, which only made things worse. "*Did* he fire you?"

My eyes felt chained to anchors as I forced them up to meet his gaze. "Well, yes but—"

Evie's arched brow stopped me short. I waved my hands in front of me, trying to make myself clear, trying to wave away their disbelief. "It wasn't like that. He did fire me ... but my shoes were full of beer ... so I went back to get them ..."

I sounded insane.

"Then who attacked her?" Callie's indignant voice broke through my embarrassment, and my heart gave a painful thump at her loyalty.

She might be hurt that I didn't tell her, but she believed me. "That's pretty fucking suspicious. Or are you saying she's lying about that too?" Callie glared at Hayden, all silly flirtations drained away. "You saw our apartment. You know this isn't random, or you wouldn't have told me to come here."

Daddy shook his head in agreement.

Hayden pinched the bridge of his nose. He looked tired. "The print we found from the second break-in came back with a match for Brad Talbot. The bartender from the club. I told you, Callie, he's got a fixation on you. And he has a record of assault."

No. That wasn't right. None of this was right.

"I don't know about the second break-in," I said. "But Brad didn't attack me. It was the moon-faced man."

It popped out before I could stop it. Even I heard how crazy it sounded.

Hayden looked at me with blatant pity. Evie pursed her lips and glanced away. I was proving the evidence right. A silly little waitress with a big imagination.

"Why would Brad attack Soap if he's so obsessed with me?" Callie demanded. She also ignored my 'moon-faced man' outburst.

"She's right, Hayden." Daddy put his arm around me, his fingers giving my shoulder a squeeze. "That doesn't make sense."

I couldn't bring myself to look at his face, even though his words were on my side. What could he possibly be thinking of me?

"Brad thought Sophia *was* you." Hayden's face remained calm, neutral, even when Callie snorted.

"Right, because there's such a resemblance." Callie threw a hand back and forth between her platinum blond locks and my own dark brown. "This is bullshit."

My vision darkened and my breathing hitched. I didn't want any of this. I didn't ask to see that jerk shoot that other jerk. I just didn't want to lose the only job I could get. I wanted to stand on my own and not be the disappointment my parents knew I was.

Daddy squeezed my hand under the table. "You have an eyewitness, Hayden," he insisted.

"Yes." Hayden tapped the pen against the pad again like he was trying to regain order. "And I'll take her statement. I just want you to know what you're up against. If Sophia goes through with this, it could be dangerous. And if it goes to trial, these are the things Roscoe's lawyers would say."

"Sophia?" Daddy's voice was strong and firm beside me. "What do you think?"

My mouth was numb like it was full of Novocain, refusing to work. The room went quiet, except for the soft click of Callie's chair as she rocked it back and forth. The weight of their stares sat heavy on me.

"It wasn't her ... and it wasn't Brad ... I don't know how, but ... it wasn't," I whispered, forcing myself not to say anything else about the moon-faced man, or my shoes, or anything else that made me sound crazy.

My tummy roiled with the stress of speaking. Maybe I could finish this awful meeting off by throwing up in front of everybody. It certainly couldn't get much worse.

Hayden slid his open hand across the table toward me, a placating gesture that drew my attention back to the awful pity on his face. "Let's get your statement down and see where you want to go from there."

My eyes burned and my nose stung. What would I even say? Somehow, he had real evidence pointing to another suspect. It was my word against reality.

I wanted to curl up and fade away, shrink into a tiny box tucked under a baseboard of an abandoned house. And then, because coincidence really is a big meanie, a ringtone both dreaded and familiar called out from my purse.

My fingers slid up to clutch at the locket around my throat.

My father.

◉ ◉ ◉

I STEPPED out of the conference room and wandered past boxes and half set-up desks to take the call. I ended up in front of a door with the name *Ethan Abbott* newly etched into the frosted glass. His office.

I leaned against the door, my hand squeezing the life out of my phone at the sound of my father's voice, sharp and unyielding as a blade.

"I've called to tell you to stop being childish and come home." My father skipped over the niceties and got straight to cutting me into pieces. "Your mother has a symposium at the end of the month, and you need to be there."

"She does?" It was all I could squeeze out of my throat as I closed my eyes, imagining my mother lecturing at a podium in a tastefully understated tuxedo suit in shades of cream, giving a keynote speech to subdued but ardent applause.

"You may not care about anything other than your *toys*." I flinched at the acid in his tone, biting my tongue numb as he continued. "But your mother and I have our professional reputations to protect. People know we have a daughter. It's expected that you be there. We can say you're back in school after taking an experiential year. That will explain why you haven't accomplished anything."

An unfamiliar slice of anger cut through the fog of humiliation in my head. "Are you more concerned that I haven't accomplished anything, or that they know about me at all?"

A deadly beat of silence spun across the line between us. I was shocked the words came out of my mouth, but even more shocked to discover the ever-present apology wasn't there.

When I didn't beg forgiveness, his fury flared. "Don't test me, Sophia. You're coming home. Today. I'll not have you ruining the life we've worked so hard to build."

I swallowed hard and lay my cheek against the cool glass of the door. His door. "Dad ... there's a lot going on. I was assaulted. I have to—"

"Assaulted? Were you raped?" His voice was icy.

"No, but he—"

"Honestly, are you surprised?" He interrupted, apparently

relieved about one less scandal. "You surround yourself with trash, you can't be shocked when you're treated like trash." A sigh of annoyance came through the phone. "All the more reason you're coming home. We will not waste the resources bailing you out of whatever self-inflicted situation you find yourself in. We have worked too hard."

My throat closed up, and my breath evaporated. Shame. Misery. Pain. My whole body burned with it. Never good enough.

In desperation, my fingers traced the lines of Daddy's name in the glass, the thick font grounding me.

I'm not your father, Sophie. He sounds like a fucking fool. I am your Daddy. And I'm here to tell you, you will always be enough.

His words turned that burning shame and pain into something else for the first time. The man on the other end of this phone, the man who'd caused me to doubt myself about everything, the man who shriveled me with constant disappointment, *was a fucking fool.*

He was a tenured professor, and I was a stupid girl who played with dolls. But he was never going to make me feel worthless again.

"I'm not coming home." My voice was stronger than I expected. "And I don't care what happens at Mom's symposium. That has nothing to do with me." A giddy whoosh of air swept through me as I let the words come out.

"And ... I don't have to explain myself to you." I stood up straighter, tossing a lifetime of not-good-enough off my shoulders. "I am not the disappointment. You are. I may not have lived up to your expectations. But ... you didn't live up to mine either." I tapped the disconnect button with trembling fingers.

I clenched my eyes shut, waiting for the fear, the shame, the apology to bash its way back into my head, but it didn't. I turned from the door, leaning my back against the wall and marveling at the lightness in my chest, like a boulder pinning me down had finally rolled away.

When I opened my eyes, Daddy was there. Right in front of me, solid, steady, his head tilted slightly, accentuating the crook of his smile, his dimple peeking out from his cheek. He raised a hand up to run through his perfectly tousled sandy hair, sliding down the back of his neck then reaching out to me.

"You okay, baby girl?" he asked, taking my hand and pulling me into him, his chest a haven, a shelter after a storm.

I leaned hard against him, gulping in his clean, comforting scent and counting the steady thumps of his heart before I tipped my head up and searched his handsome face. The amber flecks warmed the clouded gray in his eyes, and what I saw in them gave me peace.

His eyes held no pity or disbelief. No disappointment. No regret.

There was only love.

"Yes, Daddy. I think I am."

26

ETHAN

She trembled in my arms, but there was fierceness in her eyes. I was glad to see it. Hayden's information had hit her hard. I could tell by the way she'd folded in on herself, shrinking into her chair, her sweet pink cheeks going pale.

They'd gone even paler when she got that phone call. Her jaw set like she was going to her own execution when she excused herself. I was burning to know who called, and what they'd said, but I pushed that down. She'd tell me when she was ready. One step at a time.

I laced my fingers through hers. "Come with me."

"I can't go back in there," she whispered, tugging back, her eyes darting toward the conference room.

"Do you trust me?" I asked.

"Yes." She said it fast and sure.

I opened the door to my office, led her in, and closed the door.

She sat in a brown leather chair in front of my desk, her hands in her lap, her knees together, shoulders hunched. "I need to tell you about the phone call. No secrets."

I sat down in the chair next to hers, my elbows resting on my knees near her, keeping my hands open, relaxed. "When you're ready." I reached out to touch her clenched fist. "Whoever it was upset you."

"No," she said, tipping her face up and looking right at me. "I mean ... he did, but ..." That little glint of ferocity sparked in her dark eyes. "It was my father. He demanded that I come home."

I took a breath, forcing myself to be calm, even though I wanted to smash this asshole into the ground for having this much power over her. "You don't—"

"I told him that I'm done feeling bad about disappointing him. That he disappointed me too. That I'm not coming home."

Pride bloomed inside me, watching my fierce little kitten break free of the shackles her father put her in.

Her brow furrowed, and her chin jutted out. "He's a ... fucking fool."

I blinked in surprise at the swear on her lips. At *my* swear. And she didn't flinch or whisper when she said it, though her eyes widened when she looked at me afterward, as if she might be in trouble for the curse.

"Did you tell him that?" I asked with a grin.

"No." She shrugged. "I'm trying to be brave, not crazy."

We both laughed.

"You are brave, my sweet Sophie."

"You gave that to me," she whispered.

"No." I pulled the chair closer to hers and took her hands in mine. "I only gave you permission to see it." I stroked her small wrists with my thumbs. I wanted her to feel her own strength. I wanted to let it harden and become a part of her. I wanted her to know she could stand on her own, so when she chose to crawl up into my lap it was because she wanted to, not because she had no other choice.

"I'm proud of you, baby girl."

A faint smile flitted across her lips. "I'm proud of myself."

In that moment, I couldn't admire her more.

I pointed to the white box on my desk. "Bring that to me."

I didn't take it when she held it out to me. Instead, I patted my lap and held my arms open for her. She came to me hesitantly, perching on my knees. I pulled her in and tucked her up against my chest, loving the weight of her as she relaxed into me. "Open it."

She lifted off the lid, tucked it carefully beneath the box, and pulled back the tissue paper. "Is that ..." She trailed off as she lifted the glass from the packaging.

"Mrs. Helmsley's unicorn," I finished for her, stroking the side of her cheek.

"You fixed her?" She examined the broken unicorn from her nightstand, back in one piece. "How?"

I kissed the top of her head and rested my hand against the curve of her hip. "Called in a favor or two. Do you like it?"

She looked up at me, her eyelashes damp, her fingers tracing the seams where the unicorn had broken.

"She was special to you," I said, not sure why worry was lurking in the shadows of her eyes.

"She was ... is." She bit the correction off as her tongue got away from her. "But I need ... I want to say ..." She huffed out a sigh and tried again. "This skirt has pockets."

Okay.

I wasn't expecting that.

Her gaze locked onto mine as she reached into one of those pockets, pulled out her pacifier and slid it into her mouth.

Understanding me lit up. I held her close to my chest. She relaxed against me as she sucked experimentally, her breath slowing into a steady rhythm. "I'm here when you're ready," I murmured into her hair.

She was still and warm in my arms, and I soaked her in like sunshine. The sweet berry scent of her filled my nose. She was the best thing to happen when I wasn't expecting it, the most wonderful coincidence, the piece of my heart that made me whole.

I thought she drifted off to sleep, but she stirred, sitting up and turning to face me. She put the unicorn carefully back in its box and slid the pacifier out of her mouth.

"I know what I saw." Her voice was quiet but firm. No stutter or hesitation. "I'm not crazy. I'm not a disgruntled employee. I *saw* him kill that man." She shifted, straddling me, her knees against my hips in the chair. "I understand why Hayden doesn't believe me."

"Hayden is—"

She shook her head. "I want to tell the truth ... whether it helps the investigation or not." She paused. "But, at the end of it all, it's you that I care about. I need you to believe me."

She held the pacifier up, considering it. "I didn't discover this part of myself until I met you. It's like a piece of my puzzle has always been missing, and you popped it into place. All of a sudden, I make sense." She tucked the pacifier back into her pocket and leaned toward me. "And I love it, but ... I need you to believe in me too."

I cupped her face in my hands, barely stroking the peach-soft skin of her cheeks. "I do."

Her lip wobbled, but I didn't let her go.

"Do you think that pacifier means I don't take you seriously?" I asked.

She made a tiny whimpering sound, but I held her gaze. "Look at me, baby girl. I saw you the night you were attacked—the night of the murder."

She flinched but didn't look away.

"You trusted me with your secret. I believe in you, no matter what. We'll figure it out with Hayden, but I know you saw what you saw." I nodded my head for emphasis and held back a smile when she nodded her head along with mine. "Dressing up and using a pacifier changes none of that."

She sat frozen for a heartbeat before setting the unicorn box to the side and gripping me in a fierce hug. "Thank you, Daddy," she whispered as she found my lips and offered me a beautiful, soft kiss.

I relished the taste of her strawberry lip gloss. "No thanks needed, baby girl. That's my job."

SOPHIA

"ARE YOU READY?" Hayden fiddled with the recording device, his notepad and pen sitting on the edge of the table next to his elbow.

I stared at the little black machine. I wasn't sure at all about the consequences, but I knew I had to do it. I needed to tell the truth. To stand on my own and speak about what I saw.

"I'm ready." No more being afraid. No more listening to the voice in my head that sounded like my father calling me a foolish child.

Somehow, dressing up Little, playing games, submitting to discipline, and calling Ethan Daddy helped me grow up. I knew what I wanted and, even better, I knew I could have it. I just had to be brave and let the chips fall where they may.

"Okay." Hayden smiled at me, giving a reassuring nod. "Tell me exactly what you saw that night."

I took a breath and began to speak.

27

SOPHIA

"Are you sure going back is a good idea?" I eased the sharp tool into the joint and applied pressure until Caroline's damaged leg released from her hip socket with a tiny popping sound that always made me wince.

It had been a few days since I gave Hayden my statement, and I knew Callie was getting restless, but the idea of going back to L.A. seemed like a big risk.

She squeezed my shoulder. "Now that you told Detective what you saw, Tommy Roscoe would be an idiot to make a move. And what would doing something to me do for him anyway?"

"What about Brad?" I asked, setting the damaged leg down on the coffee table. "It sounds like he wants to hurt you."

"Yeah, I really do think him breaking in was more about me than you." She rolled her eyes and made a gagging face. "He dug through all my shit, my panties ..." She shuddered. "He didn't even mess with your stuff since it was all packed up to come here."

"He sounds dangerous." I looked down at Caroline's body in my hands. Her torso would require a lot of meticulous sanding to fix the melted parts.

"I can handle dumbass Brad." Callie looked out the window and tugged at a lock of her hair with two fingers. "I just ... need to go back. My dad ..."

I nodded. Her dad was in a nursing home. She visited him every Tuesday. She didn't talk about it much, but I knew she was worrying about being away from him. "Maybe you should wait though? See what Da—Ethan says?"

She grinned at me. "Seriously Soap? Call him what he is. I'm happy you have a Daddy."

I did. I had a Daddy and he loved me. I smiled back at her.

"And I can't," she continued. "I don't have time. I just stopped in to say good-bye."

"What about ... Griff?" I asked. "He said you couldn't leave till they had things figured out?"

"Pffft," she stuck out her tongue and blew out the sound. "He's not the boss of me, and he never will be."

She stood up. "I'll be fine, Soap."

I walked her to the door of the cabin and leaned in when she gave me a wonderful, perfume-infused hug. "We're going to be laughing about this at your wedding," she said.

"I don't ... that's ..." I stammered, the idea tying my tongue into a knot.

She just waved, her green eyes twinkling, and blew me a kiss before hopping into the car she'd called to take her to the airport.

I hoped she was right. At least about the laughing part. And maybe the wedding too.

CAROLINE HAD MORE damage than I realized, but I was beginning to see her transformation underneath all the soot. Her skin remained discolored even though I'd cleaned and soaked her thoroughly. Burn marks covered her melted and misshapen back. I doodled on a pad while I looked at the blackened patterns, an idea starting to take shape. She had survived the flames, and now she wanted to show her strength.

Her hair was a complete loss. It was going to take hours to pluck out and replace, but I had the time since Daddy was in meetings most of the day. He promised me a movie night, complete with popcorn and candy, to make up for it, but I didn't really mind. I needed the time with Caroline.

I grabbed Ruthie from her spot on the sofa, so she could keep Caroline company while I worked. My phone was nearby, with two new messages showing. I'd been so focused I must have missed them.

The first was from Daddy, apologizing that his meetings were going even later than expected.

The second was from Callie, probably telling me she made it to the airport. When I clicked on it, I froze.

It was a picture.

Callie – with duct tape over her mouth, green eyes huge, and a man's fist gripping her bright blond hair.

The phone rang.

I jumped, almost dropping it. Callie's number.

I answered the call, my throat frozen, unable to say a word.

"Do I have your attention?" the moon-faced man asked in his cat-torturer voice.

"Where is she?" I gulped out.

"You have a meeting with Mr. Roscoe," he said nonchalantly.

Panic set in. I dropped Ruthie and clutched my stomach to keep from fainting. The moon-faced man had Callie.

"Don't do anything stupid," he warned.

"What do you ..." I couldn't even form a sentence. I couldn't think. The image of Callie flashed in my head, blocking everything else out.

"You have five minutes to gather your shit. Make it look like you took off." He gave me instructions like he was discussing a weather report. "Get down to the turnoff road. A car will be waiting."

"D-Ethan will come looking for me." It was a dumb thing to say, but it was all I had.

"Oh, I hope not, for his sake." He clicked his tongue. "If you tell anyone, if anyone comes after you, they become another loose end for us to cut. Do you understand me?"

I sucked in a breath. "No," I whispered.

"You don't?" He sounded surprised.

"No, I ... yes." Terror made my tongue tangle even worse. "I don't want you to hurt anyone."

"Better hurry up then." Before he hung up, I heard rustling noises and a muffled squeal, like someone in pain, with duct tape over their mouth.

My brain froze, incapable of thought. My body took over, and I ran through the cabin grabbing my things and shoving them into my suitcase. He had Callie. He would kill Daddy if he followed me. Those two facts blared like sirens, blocking anything else out.

With my bag packed, I tore out of the cabin and down a service road through the woods. I wasn't even sure I was going the right way until I spotted a long, black sedan with darkly tinted windows.

When it was clear it was just me, the moon-faced man got out, taking my suitcase and tossing it in the trunk. He waved me toward the open door. "Get in."

"Wh-where's Callie?"

He slammed the trunk closed and pointed to the door again.

A muffled sound like a woman's voice dropped my heart. The moon-faced man opened the door and shoved me in. I fell against Callie in the other seat, mouth still covered with tape, hands zip-tied together. There was another man in the car, sitting across from us, holding a gun aimed directly at Callie's face.

"Brad?" It came out of my throat in a horrified whisper.

"Tough luck, Space Mouse," his mocking voice set my teeth on edge. "I told you Mr. Roscoe did you a favor when he fired you. But you couldn't stay fired, could you?"

The door slammed shut, cutting off any escape. A few seconds later the moon-faced man climbed into the driver's seat and started the car. He pulled out onto the road, and I watched the silent trees roll by as we moved farther away from my new life. After a mile or two, he looked back through the rear-view mirror at me. "Did you tell anyone?"

Brad pointed the gun at Callie again.

"No," I blurted, shaking my head. "No one."

"Leave a note?"

I shook my head again. "Nothing."

His lip turned down and he tilted his head. "Maybe you're not as dumb as you look then."

Callie made a noise behind her duct tape, her green eyes snapping. I noticed a dark bruise forming along her cheekbone where they must have hit her hard.

"Did you bring your phone?" He glared at me through the mirror. "Don't lie, or Brad will have to search you."

My eyes darted to Brad then back to the moon-faced man. "Yes."

Brad held out his hand, the one not holding a gun at Callie's face. I gave her a miserable look then gave my phone over.

"Unlock it," Brad grunted at me. I complied. He started scrolling around.

"I assume your boyfriend is going to try to figure out where you've gone," the moon-faced man said as we sped down the road. "When he tries to contact you, Brad is going to let him know you've had a change of heart."

"Oh man, Space Mouse, wish I'd known you were into this shit." Brad let out an ugly laugh as he scrolled, reading my texts. "He's not just her boyfriend, he's her *Daaa-ddy*." He kicked up his voice in a high falsetto on the last word.

Fury bubbled inside me, alongside my fear.

"Even better," crowed the moon-faced man. "That means you know how to do as you're told." He got onto the highway headed toward the airport. "Let's hope Brad is convincing. If not, Daddy Dearest is dead."

A river of ice poured down my spine. I looked at Callie, my heart slamming in my chest, my eyes wild. She shook her head but all she could do was make muffled huffing sounds behind the tape.

WE FLEW BACK to L.A. on Mr. Roscoe's private jet. It was similar to the one Daddy had brought me to Seattle on, only his was nicer than this one. I sat down in the seat and buckled my belt, because I didn't know what else to do. Brad buckled Callie across from me since her hands were still zip tied together. Her eyes were red, and her cheek looked puffy and swollen.

I stared out the window as we took off, watching the rain drizzle on the window, the life I'd just found fading away into the gloomy gray fog.

When we were up in the air, Callie shifted in her seat and let out a soft grunt. She sounded stuffy, like she wasn't getting enough air.

"Could you take the tape off her mouth?" I asked Brad. "She's having trouble breathing."

Brad reached over and ripped off the tape, causing Callie to let out a shriek of pain.

"You fucking asshole!"

He slapped her, right on top of her bruised cheek. "Don't make me regret being nice."

"Now, now, Brad." The moon-faced man frowned in our direction from his seat on the other side of the plane. "Don't break your new toy."

Callie glowered at Brad and cradled her cheek but didn't say anything else.

"You know," the moon-faced man said to Callie, "your anger is misdirected. We were going to arrange for this one"—he jerked a thumb in my direction— "to have a little accident in a few days, but you wouldn't have been involved. You're the best dancer in the club, and Brad here is very fond of you. He just doesn't know how to show it."

Callie turned a hateful gaze at Brad. He smirked.

"But your little friend had to complicate things by running her mouth."

I squirmed in my seat.

"Valerie Vasili doesn't know who's pulling the strings here, and it's imperative we keep it that way," he continued, turning back to me. "So you're going to do some damage control."

Valerie Vasili? Nik Vasili's wife? The one Hayden said they had in custody?

"I don't know her," I said. Hopelessness threatened to choke off my air. "I'm just a waitress. I can't do damage control."

"You don't have to know anything. You just have to keep being a shitty waitress."

I flinched, remembering how unhappy I'd been at the club even before I saw the murder.

It's simple," he explained. "You are going to call that detective and tell him you lied. You were trying to get even for Tommy firing you. You crawled back, begging for your job, and because Tommy is a stand-up guy, he gave you another chance."

I looked at Callie, and she looked at me. "You're not going to kill us?" My voice sounded surprisingly calm considering we were discussing our deaths, but I was out of ideas, empty of emotions.

He let out a sharp, ugly laugh. "Kill you? I wish. I was kind of looking forward to that." His fingers slipped into a side pocket of his suit and produced a mean-looking switchblade. A tiny click sounded as he popped it open.

Fear flooded in as I watched the light flicker on the blade, making my stomach churn. Guess I wasn't so calm about dying after all.

"But killing you would give your story credibility. We need you alive." He snapped the knife closed and returned it to his pocket. "For now."

"So we're just gonna work at the club?" Callie demanded. "Like nothing happened?"

Like the murder didn't happen. Like the time I'd spent with Daddy never happened. A tear leaked out of my eye.

"Exactly," he agreed. "Under very close supervision, of course." He scratched the sharp edge of his jutting chin.

The awfulness of the plan was seeping into me. We would be prisoners.

"Cheer up girls." Brad leaned over to rub Callie's bruised cheek.

"As long as you behave, you'll be fine." She jerked away and glared at him.

"That's right," the moon-faced man agreed. "As long as your little lie goes away." He smiled, like a great white shark pulling back its lips. "But if Valerie hears a whisper, or if *Daddy* comes looking for you ..." He patted the pocket where the ugly knife lurked. "You're all dead."

ETHAN

THE MEETING DRAGGED ON, and my mind wandered to my sweet girl, tucked away in our cabin, working on her dolls. She was sweet, innocent, brave and loyal. My fierce little kitten. I'd just found her, but already I couldn't imagine life without her. It was crazy, way too soon, but I was thinking about what kind of ring she might like.

My phone buzzed. Hayden. I sent it to voicemail, thinking I'd call when the meeting was over. The phone buzzed a second time. Hayden again. I frowned, a tiny cold feeling in the base of my gut taking shape.

"Excuse me," I interrupted and stepped outside of the conference room.

"Hayden? Everything okay?"

"What the fuck is going on?" he grumbled.

"What are you talking about?" Dread prickled the hairs on the back of my neck.

"With Sophia?" He paused. "She left me a message saying she lied about seeing Roscoe kill Vasili."

I lurched forward. "What?"

"She's gone back to Renaissance."

I broke into a sprint, the hallway blurring past.

She couldn't be gone. Back into the hands of that psycho? "Go get her, Hayden. I'll be there in three hours."

"Ethan," he spoke slowly. "I can't barge in there and drag her out."

I burst out of the Lodge House and ran toward the cabin. "Something's wrong. She wouldn't go back there willingly."

"I know." Hayden sighed. "Get here. Bring Griff. We'll figure it out."

THE CABIN LOOKED like she'd left in a hurry. Her clothes were gone. Her toothbrush gone. Nothing left of her in the bathroom except that tube of red lipstick I never saw her use.

She left her dolls. The ones I had shipped here. The ones I bought for her. The broken ones she'd been working on. Caroline. Ruthie lay on the floor, her little plastic legs sticking up at awkward angles. I picked her up as if holding the doll would bring Sophia back to me. None of it made any sense.

My call was declined.

I started to dial again when a text popped up.

SOPHIE

Leave me alone

> What's going on? Where are you?

I said fuck off

> Answer my call. Let's talk about this

Then nothing.

The cabin door crashed open. Griff stalked in, shoulders brushing the threshold, talking to someone on the phone. "I'm here. We're heading to the airport now."

"She's gone," I said miserably. He must have been talking to Hayden.

"Callie's gone too." He clicked his phone off and stuffed it in a pocket, his scowl dark.

It still didn't make sense four hours later, sitting in Hayden's apartment.

"Listen to me," Hayden said earnestly. "She's okay."

I glared at him from the same spot on his couch I'd been sitting on the night we got her call for help. "She is *not* okay. She's in there with that bastard."

He held up his hands in a calming gesture. "I mean they haven't hurt her. I saw her. Confirmed her phone call before Roscoe's lawyers started threatening to sue the department for harassment if I didn't leave." He sighed. Griff scowled from where he was leaning against the back of the couch.

"Callie's there too. I thought I saw some bruising on her face, but neither of them want to talk to me," Hayden said.

Griff's eyes darkened, but he said nothing.

"Officially, there's not a lot I can do," Hayden added. "They went there by choice."

"That's bullshit and you know it," I snapped, dropping my head in my hands.

"I do," Hayden agreed. "Doing this the legal way is going to require paperwork and warrants and probable cause. I just don't have enough. It'll take time."

"We don't have time," Griff said.

Hayden nodded, looking at him warily.

"I can make a call," Griff said.

I hesitated. The need to get her back was like a tornado inside me, but what Griff was offering could have a steep cost.

Griff and Vincent were half-brothers, like Hayden and me. But unlike us, they weren't orphans. None of us talked about the time before we came to live with Aunt Carol and Uncle Joe. We all understood somethings were best left in the past.

Right after high school, they both left home and all but vanished for years before showing back up when Uncle Joe got sick. We didn't talk about that either. Wherever they'd been, it was a dark place. We had suspicions, but, because Hayden was a cop, it was all best left unsaid.

Hayden's phone rang. "Fuck, it's my captain. I have to take this." He slid his finger across the screen before bringing it up to his ear. "Detective Valero."

He grimaced and waved to us to continue without him.

"Are you sure that's a call you want to make?" I asked Griff.

He shrugged. "Valerie isn't going to take a murder rap without a fight. I'm just offering information for a favor. It doesn't have to go farther than that."

"You know Valerie Vasili?" I tried not to think of the implications.

"Don't ask stupid questions," he grunted.

Whatever this was, Griff was on a dangerous, slippery slope. I knew it, and he knew I knew.

"I love you, brother," I said simply. He looked uncomfortable, like I knew he would, then he looked away.

Hayden was shaking his head and starting sentences without finishing them, his phone pressed hard against his ear.

Griff watched him pace in the tiny kitchen a few steps away. "Hayden can't be involved."

I nodded.

Griff pushed off from the couch. "She's a good girl. She makes you happy. I'm gonna go make that call."

28

SOPHIA

I was back. Back at the club. Back to serving drinks. Back to wearing the stupid toga uniform and those awful gold platform gladiator sandals. Callie was dancing on the stage, her eyes blank, her face covered in thick makeup that almost covered the bruises on her cheek. Almost.

The only difference was that we were in Mr. Roscoe's VIP room, where he could keep a close eye on us while he conducted business. The same VIP room he killed Nik Vasili in. The same VIP room that had changed my life forever.

Club regulars sat around, drinking and lounging while the blue neon flashed and the music pounded. Blank-eyed Roman statues lurked in every corner, every alcove. Before Mr. Roscoe told us they housed hidden cameras, their empty stares had made me sad. Now they lurked like scary reminders. He was always watching. No hope of escape.

He stood at the floor-to-ceiling one-way window, overlooking the club's main floor like a petty lord surveying his lands, a self-satisfied smirk on his face. Brad lingered next to him, like the kid that desperately wanted to sit at the cool kids' table in the cafeteria. I almost felt sorry for him until I saw Callie touch her swollen cheek and tug a strand of her hair as she danced.

I loaded champagne flutes onto my tray from the bar, staring at the bubbles rising in pale fluid, not quite able to believe I'd held the hand of the man I loved in another state less than twenty-four hours ago.

Mr. Roscoe snapped his fingers at me, waving me over. I sniffled and forced myself to walk over to him.

The moon-faced man joined the group from where he'd been lurking in the shadows, and each of the men took a glass. I tried to slip away, but Mr. Roscoe slid his free arm roughly around my waist, pulling me in tight. His cloying scent of bergamot and tobacco filled my nose, and I tried not to gag.

"A toast?" He raised his glass, his arm like a steel band around me as I tried to pull away. "To our little maid, finally coming home and getting her story straight." He gave me a dangerous smile.

"To my little accomplice," the moon-faced man added with an ugly laugh.

"What?" The word popped out of my mouth.

"The timing of that police raid was a bitch of a coincidence," he continued with a smirk. "My plan was to clean things up here, then take poor old Nikki and the gun back to his house for the cops to find later. Then come find you." He leered at me, and I shivered. "I almost walked right out into them prepping for the raid. But then, you pop out the back and distract the cops." He laughed his cat-torturer laugh, enjoying my confusion. "Like we planned it together. And then you didn't even have the guts to tell them."

The irony of it turned my stomach. I had blundered out the back door before the cops did their raid. The perfect distraction for the moon-faced man to sneak the body out and plant it and the evidence someplace else, after giving him time to clean up. No wonder they hadn't found anything that night. Horror wrapped around me like a layer of suffocating gray slime oozing down my throat.

"I had plenty of time to put the body and the gun where they needed to be for Valerie to become the only suspect." The moon-faced man took a slug of champagne and tipped the glass to me again.

"Another good reason for you to put all this behind you and never mention it again, isn't it, little maid?" Mr. Roscoe licked his lips, still clutching me.

Another nail hammered into the suffocating coffin closing in all around us.

Callie and I met eyes across the room. She was barely dancing, eyes glued on me, her face pale. Her hand reached up to tug at a strand of her hair, wrapping it around her index finger and brushing the edge against her cheek. We were helpless. Trapped.

"You're sure Valerie doesn't know about your change in loyalty?" Mr. Roscoe asked, his grip on me relaxing. To me he said, "go serve my guests, little maid."

The moon-faced man scoffed. "She's so focused on the accusations, she's not paying attention to anything else. She trusts me completely."

I scurried away, thankful to be away from them. I hated all of it. Their schemes and double-crossing and whatever else they were doing. I didn't want any part of it. I didn't want to be involved. I wished I'd never taken this stupid job.

You wouldn't have Daddy if you hadn't.

The little voice in my head made a point. But I'd lost him too. Maybe he still loved me, but I couldn't risk ever seeing him again.

The weak part of me pleaded with the universe to let me wake up from this nightmare curled up in the safety of his arms. But that wasn't going to happen, and begging wouldn't make it so.

The song booming out from the speakers changed and Callie waved me over. "You okay?" she asked, stepping down from the small stage.

I shrugged, my shoulders heavy with misery. "Yeah. I mean, not really. But they were just toasting how I helped distract the cops, and that the Valerie lady—"

"Nik Vasili's wife?"

"Yeah." I tossed a nervous glance but none of them were watching us. "I guess she doesn't know that the moon-faced man betrayed her."

Callie snickered and looked over toward the men. "I get it now. He *does* look like the man in the moon."

I smiled at her, but then it faded off my face. "I'm so sorry you are in this. I don't think we're gonna—"

"Don't." She shook her head, a finger twirling a strand of blond hair. "We are getting out of here somehow. We're not gonna let these assholes win. We just have to be ready when the opportunity hits."

I bit my lip, wishing I could believe her.

Brad stalked over, and we stepped apart. Callie kept her face blank like I'd seen her do with a thousand guys in the club. He leered at her barely-covered breasts. "Did I tell you to stop dancing?"

Callie took a deep, cleavage-swelling breath. "No, but I was bored with you not watching."

His leer turned into a full smirk. "Oh, I'll watch, Babe."

She crawled back up onto the stage and started dancing again. Brad completely missed it when her eyes flicked to mine, eyebrow raised. I could almost read her thoughts on that eyebrow – watch for the opportunity.

But if it came, would I be able to take it?

I was still wondering when John the bouncer came into the room and whispered something in Mr. Roscoe's ear. Whatever he said, it brought a frown to Mr. Roscoe's face. His black eyes turned directly onto me, filling my tummy with ice.

"Clear the room and show him up," he snapped. "Check him for weapons too," he added. John nodded and began ushering the regulars out of the VIP room.

Mr. Roscoe stormed toward me. "Your boyfriend doesn't know how to take no for an answer," he growled, grabbing my hand and pressing it against his side so I could feel the lump beneath his perfect Armani suit. A gun-shaped lump. He tipped his chin toward a corner, where the moon-faced man faded into the shadows, barely more noticeable than the empty-eyed statues. He saw me and smiled one of his hideous smiles, his chin jutting out even further in the awful blue light before he dragged one finger across his neck in a slicing motion.

My mouth went paper dry, and my skin itched like a million ants crawling on me. My heart ripped in two, one half leaping up, hoping Daddy had come for me, the other half horrified at what would happen if he did.

The room emptied out, but the music kept thumping, almost as loud as my heart. Callie kept dancing, but her eyes darted around and her movements were stiff. Too soon, John returned, leading a man in and then standing, stoic as stone, at the door.

I didn't want to look at the man. Didn't want to know. And I was helpless to resist.

It was Daddy.

Alone. No police for back up. Not even his scary brother Griff?

I froze, staring at him. Even across the room, I knew those cashmere eyes, the perfectly tousled, wet sand hair, that crooked smile. My blood stopped flowing. My heart stopped beating. I blinked back the burn in my eyes. He was there. Right in front of me.

Which meant he was in danger.

"Good evening Mr. Abbott." Mr. Roscoe led me over to the blue velvet couches, holding the hand that wasn't clenched around my forearm out in a magnanimous welcome gesture. "John said you were here to see about Sophia. Can I have her get you a glass of champagne?" He shoved me forward and sat down, waving Daddy over to join him.

I stumbled on my stupid shoes, catching myself on the edge of the couch, still unable to believe he was really here, cool and composed in his navy suit, his hair barely ruffled, his face shadowed in the lurid, blue-glowing lights. "Daddy?" I whispered before I could stop myself, my eyes glued onto his handsome face. "You came for me?"

"I always will, baby girl," he said, his smile as handsome and sure as the evening I met him in the police station.

I shifted from one foot to the other, my tray dangling in my hand. What should I do? Was this the opportunity Callie was talking about?

The feel of the gun under Mr. Roscoe's suit jacket still tingled on my fingertips. My heart hammered sickeningly in my chest as I watched Daddy walk over and sit in the same place Nik Vasili had the night Mr. Roscoe had shot him.

Brad headed for one of the blue velvet chairs. Before he could sit, Daddy looked at him coolly.

"Actually, I'd love a glass of a good Pinot Noir if you have it." His voice was smooth, silky. Like the day with the mean shopkeeper who tried to overcharge us for the dolls. His eyes barely twitched in my direction. Brad gaped at him, his chest puffing up and his face turning red.

Mr. Roscoe laughed and waved Brad off. "Bring me a whiskey sour while you're at it." He turned his gaze back to Daddy when Brad slunk away. "You have balls, I'll give you that." He leaned back, stretching his arms across the back of the couch. "Now, why are you here?"

"You have something of mine, and I'd like it back."

"Something of yours?" Mr. Roscoe raised an eyebrow. "Do you mean her?" He looked over at me, still frozen, unable to move or do anything. He sighed. "How regressive. I assure you, she's here of her own free will. I don't 'have' her. Go ahead. Ask her."

I squeezed my eyes closed. I was going to pass out. Throw up. Fall down. All three. I needed to leave. Exit my body. I couldn't do this. The moon-faced man cleared his throat softly from his spot in the corner. Just to remind me he was there. To remind me what was at stake when I answered.

Daddy stared at me, his face calm, other than a slight tick in his jaw. His eyes swept over me, taking in the uniform, the platform sandals. I was dressed exactly like I had been the night we met. I suddenly wondered if he had a lollipop in his pocket. I almost let out a hysterical laugh. I had to keep it together.

I tossed my hair, a move I'd watched Callie perform hundreds of times, hoping it looked confident. "I ... I'm sorry ... Ethan." It felt so wrong to call him that. Everything was so very wrong. Crying over that would have to wait till later.

"Sophie?" The pet name almost broke me.

The air leaked out of my lungs like a slowly deflating balloon. I wanted to run to him, throw myself into his arms and beg him to take me home. But I couldn't do that. Not if I wanted us to live.

I shook my head. "It's Sophia." The words were cold, metallic in my mouth. "You shouldn't have come."

I bit the inside of my cheek and reminded myself to breathe. I needed him to leave and never come back, but I also needed to crawl into his lap and hide my face against his chest until this awful nightmare was over.

You need him to live.

I took in a shuddering breath.

Callie came to my side, gingerly touching the bruise on her cheek with one hand, the other slipping into mine. "We're here by choice."

Daddy frowned, his stare moving from my face to her still-puffy cheek, his eyes sharp, the ember flecks almost glowing. Was Callie sending him a message? Letting him know we needed help?

Maybe we could let him know he needed to get the police, to get Hayden and all the other officers. My mind raced. What could I do? What message could I send?

And then, as if on cue, an Amber Jade-inspired idea opened up like a slow-blooming flower in my mind. Something so crazy, only a plucky heroine could pull it off. Was I expendable cocktail waitress number two? Or could I be the lead in my own story?

Be bold. Be brave.

It was all I had. It *had* to work.

"Is that true, Sophie?" His stern voice sent shivers through me.

My mouth opened, and my eyelashes fluttered, fighting back tears for the words I was about to say. He was my Daddy, in my heart and forever, but for this moment I had to be strong. Callie tensed next to me.

"Remember when we played Would You Rather?" I asked, trying to make my voice into a sneer.

Mr. Roscoe snickered.

I ignored him. I had a message to deliver. "I told you that I wanted filet mignon, and all you could offer me was a *sandwich*. Why would I ever stick around for that?" I gave myself exactly three seconds to stare directly into Daddy's eyes, sending my sheer force of will at him like a psychic punch, hoping it would be enough.

I caught the briefest flicker of recognition in his beautiful eyes, the tiniest nod. A spark of hope flickered in my heart. Had he understood? Would he go and get the police? Could they really rescue us?

"Well," Mr. Roscoe plucked at the creases of his pants and rolled his eyes. "Not sure what that's all about, but I think it's clear." He glanced at his watch as if the conversation bored him. "No one is here against their will."

"I suppose," Daddy said. I waited for him to stand. To leave. But he didn't. He tilted his head, considering Mr. Roscoe. "Still, I hate to leave a deal unfinished. And I sense a deal here."

I blinked, twice. What was he doing? I wanted him to get my message, but not try rescuing us alone. It was too dangerous.

Mr. Roscoe snapped his attention back to Daddy. "What kind of deal? Apparently, I have something you want," he looked at where I hovered by the couch, still clutching Callie's hand and my server's tray. "Though I can't see what it is about that one that's got you so hooked."

"Exactly," Daddy said, though his lips turned down. His eyes, cool and subdued, stayed riveted on Mr. Roscoe. "She's nothing but a problem for you. She's already discredited her statement. Let me take her off your hands."

My mouth gaped open, but Mr. Roscoe shook his head. "I still don't see the benefit for me," he said in that mock-regretful tone I hated. "You don't have anything I want. She's still a liability. And I already have a problem-solver."

The moon-faced man stepped out of the shadows. I flinched, terrified of what he might do.

"Have you considered expansion?" Daddy asked calmly. He scanned the room, his eyes lingering on the busy club through the wall of one-way mirrors.

Mr. Roscoe paused, steepling his fingers together. After a moment, he said, "I'm listening."

"Twelve thousand square feet of premium night club space. Westside. Eighteenth floor of the recently renovated Hotel Hedon. And access to some foreign investors with exceptionally deep pockets."

"You're involved with Hotel Hedon?" Mr. Roscoe sat forward, suddenly laser-focused.

"I am Hotel Hedon."

Somehow the room was quiet, despite the booming club music.

Mr. Roscoe leaned back again and tapped his forefinger on the arched back of the couch. "Tell me more."

Daddy ran his fingers through his perfectly tousled hair. "High end, recently remodeled, catering to very exclusive clientele."

My tummy churned at the idea of Mr. Roscoe getting his creepy hands on Daddy's beautiful hotel. It was too big a sacrifice. We would never be free of him, even if he let Callie and me go, which I doubted he would do.

"Investors?" There was a hungry tone in Mr. Roscoe's voice.

"They have a lot of money and ask very few questions." Daddy pulled out his phone, glanced at it then tucked it away again.

Mr. Roscoe chuckled. "They sound perfect."

"Sir?"

We all looked over to John the bouncer, who was still standing by the door.

"What is it?" Mr. Roscoe sounded annoyed at the interruption.

"There's some trouble on the floor." John pressed his finger to his ear and cocked his head, listening.

"Fine, take care of it." Mr. Roscoe frowned but kept his attention on Daddy. "And find out where Brad went. How long does it take to fetch drinks for Christ's sake?"

John nodded and left.

"I thought you'd understand the opportunity," Daddy said, returning to the business at hand.

"I'm still not sure I understand why you'd hand over such a lucrative option," Mr. Roscoe said, his eyes sliding up and down my body, "for such an unexceptional creature."

Daddy's jaw tightened, the muscles of his neck flexing past the crisp white collar of his shirt.

"And there is still the problem of leverage," Mr. Roscoe added, his eyes narrowing. "If you have the little maid, then you have too much." The regret on his face looked almost sincere. "I'm afraid I can't have that."

The moon-faced man took a step toward Callie and me, his eyes slithering up her long legs and lingering on her cleavage. She let go of my hand to flip him her middle finger, but he just laughed. "We could keep the feisty one," he said. "She'll be more fun to break anyway." He tossed a glance at me. "This one would fold too quickly."

An awful pounding started in my head. We weren't getting out of this alive. The cold reality of it smashed into me like a concrete wall. There was no deal Mr. Roscoe would honor. No matter what, they were going to kill us all.

Deep inside me, something snapped. My fists tightened around my stupid server's tray until my knuckles were white.

I was the main character of my story. Maybe it wouldn't have a happy ending, but plucky heroines don't go down without a fight.

I sidestepped to the right, away from Callie and toward the moon-faced man, who was still looking at me with an amused smirk, like I was so easily broken he wouldn't even enjoy it. I took another half-spinning step for momentum and slammed the hard edge of the tray into the side of his head with all the anger and pent-up frustration of a lifetime.

For all the forced apologies, pleading forgiveness for my existence, for all the people I cared about who he threatened, for each time in my life someone told me I was small and pathetic and insignificant. I channeled every bit of it into that swing and let him have it all.

He gave out a little whoof sound that mingled with a sickening crack. It might have been bone breaking.

I didn't care.

I watched him fall to his knees, slowly, like an old man with arthritis easing down to the ground. His eyes stared up at me in bewilderment through two thick rivers of blood before he collapsed onto the floor.

"Holy shit!" Callie screamed, lunging for me as I lost my balance from the swing and the impact. The tray crashed to the ground next to his limp body. Callie threw her arms around me, and we clutched at each other like two women drowning.

Panic rose from deep in my guts. What had I done?

We both spun our heads in time to see Mr. Roscoe jump up and pull his gun from its holster. Callie stifled a scream. Horror and fear washed through my moment of bravado.

"No need for that," Daddy's voice cut through my hysteria. I turned toward him, my jaw dropping when I saw him standing, a gun in his hands too. Pointed at Mr. Roscoe.

"I think there is," Mr. Roscoe snarled, his voice low and menacing. His eyes darted around the room, as if he were just realizing his only back-up was unconscious on the floor.

"I'll kill her," he threatened, aiming the gun at me.

I stared at the dark hole of the barrel. My brain replayed the wisp of smoke that came from it the night it killed Nik Vasili.

"And I'll make you regret it for the rest of your short life," Daddy answered, his aim steady at Mr. Roscoe's chest.

Mr. Roscoe glared at him, his eyes shrewd and calculating. He licked his lips, the arm holding his gun pulled back a bit but stayed aimed at me. "Then we're at an impasse."

Daddy cocked his head. "How so? The way I see it, you are vastly outnumbered."

Before Mr. Roscoe could answer, the door opened. His eyes widened. He jerked the gun reflexively toward the group of people coming in.

Daddy took that moment to get to us in two fast steps, tucking us behind him and keeping his gun leveled at Mr. Roscoe.

John the bouncer walked in front of the group with his own gun also pointed at Mr. Roscoe's chest. Several people I didn't recognize followed him.

"What the fuck, John?" Mr. Roscoe yelled, his eyes darting from John's gun to the tall, razor-thin woman with sable brown hair and a red pantsuit standing next to him. "Valerie?"

His gun arm dropped.

"I'll take that." Daddy stalked up to him and slid the gun from his hands. Then he kicked him down hard onto his knees and bent close to his head. "And she's more exceptional than you could ever comprehend."

My heart swelled at his words.

Mr. Roscoe's shoulders slumped, and he swiveled his head to blink stupidly at me as if he still couldn't understand how his circumstances changed so quickly.

John, the woman, and her entourage of six burly men in dark suits walked further into the room.

"B-but, Valerie? You're supposed to be in jail," Mr. Roscoe stammered out.

"Oh, Tommy," she said, pulling out a small, silver box from her pocket and retrieving a cigarette. One of her men held a lighter up before she even had it pressed to her lips. She took a long drag and walked closer to Mr. Roscoe. "You're not the only one with good attorneys."

Another of her men pulled the barely conscious moon-faced man up from the ground and onto his knees too. "It's Lewis," he said grimly.

She blew out a plume of smoke and glared at Moon-Face-Lewis.

His face was still bloody from my tray, but the utter horror in his eyes was crystal clear.

"This isn't what it looks like, Mrs. Vasili," he said, his voice quivering. "I was only here for recon. I swear I didn't—"

"Shut him up," Valerie Vasili snapped. Wife of Nik Vasili, woman that Mr. Roscoe had framed for murder. I sucked in a deep breath at the realization. Her man stuffed a thick handkerchief into Lewis's mouth, so his pleas became garbled.

Daddy left Mr. Roscoe kneeling in the blue shag carpet and held his arm out to me. I pressed in tight to his side. He pulled me close, his mouth resting against my temple now that the danger was past. "You okay, baby girl?" he whispered. "That was a hell of a swing you have there."

"I thought he was gonna kill you," I gasped out, barely able to speak my fears into words.

"Not a chance," he murmured into my ear.

Valerie turned her attention back to Mr. Roscoe. "You're also not the only one with an inside man, Tommy." She drew a fingernail down John's bulging biceps. "I knew about Lewis, but I didn't know what else you'd been up to." She turned a steely gaze to Daddy and me. "Until I got an interesting phone call from a long lost relative." She took a drag and exhaled, sending smoke in a wave up to the ceiling. "This is the witness?"

Daddy nodded, his arm tight and protective around me. I trembled, but Daddy brushed his lips against my cheek, whispering, "I got you, baby girl. You can do this."

"Tell me," she commanded. "What did you see and hear the night Nikki was killed?"

I swallowed hard. "He was here. In this room. And they were ..." I hesitated. Daddy gave me a reassuring squeeze.

"They were fighting over you – I guess – that you owed him something."

Valerie snorted and waved for me to continue.

"And ... Nik said ..." I bit my lip. This woman looked like she wouldn't take an insult well. I took a deep breath and continued. "He said you just thought you called the shots?"

Her eyebrow shot up and her eyes glittered dangerously.

I squeaked out the next part fast, anxious to be done. "Mr. Roscoe said Nik could help solve that problem. Then, I left, but ... when I came back to get my shoes ..." I hesitated again, but no one seemed to think I was foolish this time. "I saw Mr. Roscoe, holding the gun, and Nik was ... dead." I stared at the chair in the space where Nik had died. Where Daddy had sat just a few minutes ago.

"She's lying Valerie," Mr. Roscoe yelled from his place on the floor. "She's a stupid little waitress trying to get revenge for me firing her."

Daddy bristled but stayed with me.

"How the hell would a waitress know about any of that?" Valerie flicked the ash of her cigarette at Mr. Roscoe's face. "John? Did you find it?"

He nodded and pulled a jump drive out of his pocket. "Once Griff told me what I was looking for, it was easy enough to find."

Mr. Roscoe's face paled. "Valerie, you don't—"

"Shut up," she hissed. To John she asked, "It's all there?"

He nodded. "The murder by Tommy and the clean-up by Lewis."

I blinked, trying to understand. Griff knew John? Had he told him to check the security footage from the night of the murder? Of course. Mr. Roscoe had told us the statues were cameras, and they were everywhere. They would have captured everything.

"But you could give that to Hayden," I blurted out before I could stop myself. "That's the evidence he needs to arrest Mr. Roscoe."

Valerie Vasili eyed me with cold, dispassionate eyes. "Detective Valero will get the evidence he needs to clear my name in due time. Mr. Roscoe, however, will not be going to jail. I have other plans for him."

"Valerie, wait, we can talk about—"

Whatever Mr. Roscoe might have wanted to talk about ended when one of her men shoved a handkerchief into his mouth too. I pictured him and Lewis, tied to chairs in an empty warehouse somewhere before I forced myself to lock the thought away. I buried my face in Daddy's chest as her men dragged those monsters out the door.

Valerie tilted her head like a bird of prey, her piercing gaze boring into me. I lifted my head and looked at her.

After a moment, she dropped her cigarette onto the floor and ground it out into the carpet with the toe of her stiletto. "Thank you." She said it like the words tasted unfamiliar. "You've saved me a lot of trouble."

She looked at Daddy, staring at him hard and unblinking for an endless moment before she shrugged and added, "Griff's still downstairs, dealing with some bartender. Tell my little brother that Father would love to see him." She waved a dismissive hand as she turned and walked through the door, her entourage following in her wake.

I jerked my head up and swiveled to look at Callie. She mouthed the word *brother* to me and widened her eyes in disbelief. I widened mine right back.

The three of us stood there in silence for what seemed like an hour, but might have only been a few seconds. "We should go," Daddy said finally.

Callie came over and squeezed me tight, in a beautiful perfume-infused hug. "You were amazing Soap," she whispered.

"I wouldn't have done any of it without you," I whispered back.

She let me go and looked around, tugging at a strand of her hair before walking toward the door. "I'm gonna go ... downstairs. You take care of her, Mister Ethan."

Daddy nodded and pulled me back into his arms. I pressed my face against his chest then realized there was something lumpy in his pocket. He grinned down at me and pulled out a bright pink-and-white lollipop.

"Cotton candy?" I asked, not quite believing it.

"You said it was your favorite." He dropped it into my amazed hands.

I tore it open and popped it into my mouth, the sweet flavor flooding my senses. Suddenly, it was all too much. The stress of the last twenty-four hours surged over me. I couldn't draw another breath. My body sagged against him. He picked me up, holding me like I was tiny and there was no trouble in the world that could get to me through him. I wrapped my arms and legs around him, curling into his embrace.

"I didn't mean it," I sobbed into his shoulder. "The things I said. I ... had to—"

"I know, baby girl," he whispered into my hair, holding me safe in his arms, rocking me gently. "I know." His chest hitched. "I know your heart. What you did was so smart, so brave. I'm so proud of you."

"I love you, Daddy," I whispered against his neck.

"I love you too, baby girl." He cupped my face in his hand and took my lips in a slow-burning kiss that absolved me, consumed me, vanquished the haunted parts of me. In his love, I was free. In his love, I was safe.

29

SOPHIA

"Are we going to the waterfall after Aunt Carol's, Daddy?" I asked a few weeks later, trying to sound casual. I had a plan for the next time we went there, and thinking about that would calm my nerves.

"Yes baby," he said with a teasing grin.

"Oh good," I clapped my hands and ran to the back room to grab a small black bag.

He noticed the bag but didn't ask. Instead, he said, "I thought it might be the only place we wouldn't be interrupted."

"But what about the elk?" I whispered, my mouth turning upward.

"I gave them the night off," he whispered back.

I giggled. He gave me a wink and led me out to the SUV.

We pulled into Aunt Carol's driveway, and my nerves flared up again. Maybe this wasn't such a good idea after all. I looked at Daddy, so handsome in profile in the driver's seat. A sense of peace washed over me. I had a Daddy and he loved me. He rescued me from the monsters, helped me find my strength, and loved every silly, tongue-tied part of me. I trusted him, and he thought this was a good idea. My nerves would just have to accept that.

He helped me out of the car just as Aunt Carol came bustling out through the screen door.

"To what do I owe this pleasure?" she asked, a huge, welcoming grin on her face. "I wasn't expecting you?"

She pulled me into a wonderful hug while Daddy grabbed the box from the back.

"We have a gift for you, Aunt Carol," he called out. "Kind of a belated Mother's Day present."

"You're getting married?" she squealed, clapping her hands together with glee.

My cheeks turned bright pink, but Daddy just laughed. "Not today."

She gave a tisking sound and led us inside. Daddy set the box on her kitchen table.

"A baby?" she asked with hope in her eyes. "I'm progressive, I can handle it if the baby comes first." She winked at me when I squirmed.

Daddy pulled me in and kissed me on the head, laughing even more. "Would we have a baby in a box?" He pointed to the big white box.

"Fine," she scoffed, her eyes sparkling. "But you didn't need to get me anything."

"This isn't something we got," he said, watching as her brows raised in question. "Sophia was able to rescue something ... someone special to you."

Her mischievous grin faltered, just a fraction, and my nerves revved up again. What if she hated what I'd done? She was so different from before.

I bit my lip and twisted the toe of my converse against the bright yellow tiles of the kitchen floor. "It's not ... it's okay if you don't ..."

"Just open the box, Aunt Carol," Daddy encouraged softly.

She reached out her hands, fingers tracing the edges of the box as if she were almost afraid to see what was inside. She pulled off the lid carefully and set it aside. She folded back one layer of silver tissue paper, and then the next, until the box lay fully open before her.

The dress fanned out, the shades of yellow, gold, orange, red and black in strips of silk shimmered against the tissue, showing glimpses of her legs. The original burn marks now wrapped in intricate swirling tattoos from her ankles to her thighs. Her hair sparkled in a blend of shocking scarlet, vibrant orange, glittering gold and a small percentage of iridescent tinsel that gave the illusion of a flame's flickering light.

Aunt Carol picked her up and held her reverently, revealing the gossamer wings I'd fashioned to work with the damage to her torso and back. They arched triumphantly up on either side of her body, just short of touching over her head, morphing from glowing red and lightening to a soft pink at the very tips of the feathered edges.

"Caroline," she whispered, staring at the doll and then at me. "You did this?"

I bit my lip nervously. "She's a Phoenix," I said. "The fire ... hurt her, but she wanted you to know she survived it. That she is stronger than the flames that tried to take her."

I tried to gauge her response. Did she think I was crazy? Did I ruin her doll? I looked to Daddy, but he was watching Aunt Carol too, his eyes soft and full of love.

"You knew about this?" Aunt Carol looked at him, and I realized she was crying. He nodded and handed her a tissue.

"I don't know what to say," she said after dabbing at her eyes.

"I know she's different," I said. "The damage was too much to simply restore her."

"She told you she wanted to look like this?"

I looked at the floor. "I mean, that's kind of ... how I do it ..." It sounded so crazy out loud.

Aunt Carol gently laid her back in the box and took my hands in hers. "That sounds exactly like something she would say." She beamed at me and pulled me in for a warm motherly hug I'd been waiting for my whole life. "She's perfect. And so are you."

A box of Kleenex or two later, we walked down Aunt Carol's driveway to the SUV. She stood at the door, waving to us and still dabbing at her eyes. Just before Daddy put me in and buckled me tight, I heard her whistle, low and clear. I recognized it but couldn't place it. I was never going to win this game. Daddy paused, tilting his head for a moment before he broke into a grin.

"OneRepublic. Good Life." He turned back and touched his chest, pulling his hand from his heart toward her in a little wave. "I agree, Aunt Carol. I agree."

THE DRIVE WASN'T long and soon we were heading up the path to our spot by the waterfall. I clung to his hand in the fading daylight. The roaring water sound started far away, building as we approached. We rounded the bend and there it was, in all its wild and rushing glory, the larger lake behind spreading out in its wake. It was exquisite. But that's not what stopped me in my tracks.

Fairy lights hung from posts creating a warmly lit space around a thick pad of fluffy blankets and pillows. A fire pit with fresh logs waited to be lit. A wooden tray with an ice bucket, champagne bottle, and two glasses rested nearby.

"Oh Daddy, it's magical," I breathed.

He led me to the blankets and sat down, patting his lap. I lay down beside him, my head resting on his thigh.

"You did all this for me?" I looked up at him as he adjusted the pillows and poured us each a glass of bubbly champagne.

"No way." He tapped my nose. "I did it for purely selfish reasons. I figured this was the only way we could finish *A Ruthless Choice*. I've been dying to find out if Captain Harlow escapes in time to rescue Ruthie from the evil Lord Borthwick."

"Do you think the captain will understand the deal she made with her father was in exchange for his life?" I asked, biting my lip.

"Harlow knows Ruthie's heart." He rubbed his chin. "And he'd never let her go, no matter what the risk." He stroked my cheek and leaned down to kiss me, then pulled back, his smile turning into an evil grin. "He'll probably still use it as an excuse to give her a good paddling, but after that she'll be fine."

I giggled, amazed for the millionth time by this man who was so happy playing with me, caring for me, loving me.

He reached into his coat pocket and pulled out my Kindle. A sweet sense of contentment enveloped me as he started to read.

Captain Harlow dashed through the dark tunnels of the dungeon, keeping to the shadows and making no sound. He came upon the main corridor's end, and just as the guard had said, two passages loomed. He cast a glance down the right hall. At the end was a service entry where his loyal first mate was waiting with a cart and horse to take him back to his ship. Open sea by nightfall. Two days to Isla Del Diablo. He had the last piece of the map, he had the Devil's Key, nothing stood between him and Edward Swindler's gold.

Nothing but a lass with eyes like the sunset after a storm at sea and honey-sweetened lips.

He eyed the left hallway. It led to the officers' quarters, where Ruthie was held captive, awaiting the escort that would take her away on Lord Borthwick's manor.

Her words had been daggers in his heart, but her reasons had been fire to his soul. His little wench had bargained for his life with the only coin she had. If he had to fight every man in the entire British Navy, risk a prison cell or the hangman's noose, then so be it. He wasn't leaving without her by his side.

His feet turned left as he muttered to himself, "I'll need to find my sword."

"He chose her," I sighed happily.

"I had a feeling he would," Daddy chuckled, running his fingers through my hair.

When the story ended, and the moonlight sparkled on the water, I decided the time was right.

"Daddy," I whispered.

"Yes, baby?"

"Is this lake really ... bottomless? Is that true?"

He sat up, rubbing his chin and looking out at the water.

"That's what they say. My brothers and I used to dare each other to dive down. We never saw a bottom." He put his arm around me. "Why?"

"I need to do something."

I grabbed the bag I brought and pulled out the awful gold gladiator sandals from the night we escaped. Ethan raised a questioning brow but waited, giving me time to collect my thoughts.

"These were always ... wrong for me. Even before I almost died in them ... twice." I looked down to my feet at the Eeyore sneakers he had given me on his brother's boat, the morning after he told me he loved me. "And these are my Cinderellas."

"Cinderellas?"

"The shoes that changed my life."

He reached out to trace my calf with a finger.

I buckled the sandals' straps together, connecting them in a tangle of leather while he watched me. Then I reached up to my locket, rubbing the engraving that used to fill me with longing. Words my father never noticed.

I undid the clasp and took the necklace off for the first time since middle school.

He inhaled sharply but kept silent.

"This isn't right for me either. And I don't have to carry it anymore." I wove the chain around the shoe buckles and locked the clasp, then stood up.

He followed me silently to the water's edge.

I pulled back my arm and threw it all, the wrong shoes, the wrong thoughts, the wrong choices into the depths and watched them sink, their ripples stretching out until they met the roiling waterfall and disappeared.

He kissed my forehead and held me loosely for a moment. "I'll say one thing, you *do* have one hell of a swing, baby girl." He chuckled, then put an arm around me. "I'm proud of you."

We stood together, quiet, watching the dark water swirl in the moonlight, lost in our own thoughts. Then he swooped his arm around my waist and hoisted me over his shoulder, like Captain Harlow when he carried Ruthie onto his ship in the closing scene.

I screamed out a hysterical giggle and kicked my feet. He rewarded me with three solid smacks to my backside. The sweet sting sent heat roaring through me.

He strode over to our makeshift captain's quarters, dropped me gently onto the blankets and pillows and towered over me, slowly removing his belt. I stared up at his cashmere eyes, warm with amber flecks. My insides melted with need.

"Know this," he growled. "I'll always come for you, even if it leads me straight to the gallows, little pet."

I whimpered as he lowered himself down, thrusting my knees apart and tapping my chest with the tip of his belt.

"But it's a pirate's life you'll get," he warned, dropping the belt and grabbing my hair, tugging my head back to expose my neck. His tongue traced my bare throat till I arched my back, begging for him with my body. "No fancy balls, or gentlemen kissing your hand and begging your pardon."

I squirmed beneath him and almost forgot my line. I wanted him so badly.

"I don't care for gentlemen," I finally panted out as his hand slid up my thigh. "I prefer a rogue ... a scoundrel."

"Sweet talk, little pet." He squeezed my bottom. "I'll not go easy on you." He flipped me over and tossed up my skirt, exposing me to the cool night air.

"I'd be disappointed if you did, Sir." I tried to sound sultry.

"I'll keep your bottom bare and heated with my belt," he threatened. "And you will beg for more."

I had one word left to deliver before the book ended with Captain Harlow giving Ruthie the spanking of her dreams. Only one little addition would make this story perfectly ours.

I looked over my shoulder at him and grinned.

"Please ... Daddy."

Saving Sophia

THE END

THANK YOU FOR READING

I hope you loved Sophia and Ethan's love story as much as I loved writing it! I am honored that you chose to spend some time in their little world, and I would be thrilled if you left a review on Amazon.

And stay tuned for Callie's story, where she gives a certain bald grump a run for his money!

www.ingramcontent.com/pod-product-compliance
Lightning Source LLC
Chambersburg PA
CBHW022027240626
47154CB00007B/2296